Barbt
Sara !

Andra Watkins (signature)

I AM NUMBER

13

NEW YORK TIMES BEST SELLING AUTHOR

ANDRA WATKINS

WORD HERMIT PRESS LLC • USA

WORD HERMIT PRESS LLC • USA

Copyright © 2018 by Andra Watkins. All rights reserved.

For all inquiries, Word Hermit Press LLC, P.O. Box 20431, Charleston, SC 29413-0431

Printed in the United States of America.

Front cover image: Word Hermit Press LLC

No part of this book/ebook may be reproduced in any format without the express written consent of the author.

I Am Number 13 is a work of historical fantasy. Apart from the well-known actual people, events, and places that figure into the story, all names, characters, places and incidents are products of the author's imagination or are used fictitiously. Any resemblance to current events or locales, or to living persons, is entirely coincidental.

ISBN-13 978-0-9982794-8-0

Library of Congress Catalog Number Applied For

FOR ALICE AND CAYLEIGH

BOOKS BY ANDRA WATKINS

Fiction:

To Live Forever: An Afterlife Journey of Meriwether Lewis
Hard to Die: An Afterlife Journey of Theodosia Burr Alston
I Am Number 13

Nonfiction:

Not Without My Father: One Woman's 444-Mile Walk of the Natchez Trace

Photography:

Natchez Trace: Tracks in Time

PRAISE FOR **HARD TO DIE**

"A knock-out. Top-notch, white-knuckle reading." —*The Huffington Post*

"Tender, fierce, and well done." —*Portland Book Review*

"*Hard to Die* takes readers on a pretty amazing journey." —*The Good Men Project*

"Filled with deceit, double agents, unanswered questions, and passionate romance. Readers remain rapt at each turn of the page." —*Charleston Magazine*

"Read the book the cast and crew of Hamilton: An American Musical can't put down!" —*LA Splash Magazine*

"Hard to Die is hard to put down." —*Charleston Currents*

"One of the most imaginative books I've ever read." —Jen Mann, NYT best selling author of *People I Want to Punch in the Throat*

"I loved this book!" —Nicole Knepper, author of *Moms Who Drink and Swear: True Tales of Loving my Kids While Losing my Mind*

PRAISE FOR **TO LIVE FOREVER**

"A thoroughly enjoyable reading adventure unlike any other. Give it a try...I DARE YOU!" —Cassandra King, NY Times best selling author of *The Sunday Wife*

"A compelling read. Pages turn of their own volition. Courageous and wonderfully told." —*Portland Book Review*

"So amazing. It's such fun to find a book that's truly original." —Hank Phillippi Ryan, award-winning author

PRAISE FOR **NOT WITHOUT MY FATHER: ONE WOMAN'S 444-MILE WALK OF THE NATCHEZ TRACE**

"One literary ride you do not want to miss!" —*The Huffington Post*

"Definitely adds to the literature of the family dynamic." --Portland Book Review

"The opportunity to share epiphanies, hardships, and revelatory change. A really good read." —*We Proceeded On, Journal of the Lewis and Clark Heritage Foundation*

"One ordinary Rotarian doing extraordinary things." —*The Rotarian Magazine*

Remember me when I am gone away,
Gone far away into the silent land;
When you can no more hold me by the hand,
Nor I half turn to go yet turning stay.
Remember me when no more day by day
You tell me of our future that you plann'd:
Only remember me; you understand
It will be late to counsel then or pray.
Yet if you should forget me for a while
And afterwards remember, do not grieve:
For if the darkness and corruption leave
A vestige of the thoughts that once I had,
Better by far you should forget and smile
Than that you should remember and be sad.

–Christina Rossetti

I Am Number 13

EMMALINE
September 28, 1986

"Emmaline!" Sisa was my immediate superior in the Honduran Mosquitia, one of the densest jungles on earth. Viscous muck sucked at her boots as she marched up to me, her short-cropped head stopping at my chin. "Hurricane Paine's twelve hours from landfall! The refugees are all safe in the bunker. Except for Maria."

A blonde curl blew free of my tangled ponytail. I hauled it back into my hair elastic and eyed the sliver of bruised sky peeking through the tree canopy. "I can't leave a nine-year-old refugee child out here during a hurricane."

"She survived the hell between here and Nicaragua and the death of her parents. Not to mention the horrors of the Sandinista regime. She'll manage."

Sisa had been working in these Honduran backwaters for several years, since she graduated from an American college she refused to name. Do-gooding, she called it. Without her, I wouldn't have survived these few short months of refugee work I undertook upon graduating from high school. Why go to college right away when I could enroll in the school of life?

And what an education. Sisa showed me how to slash a path through impossible terrain, which slithering reptiles might kill me, and what things Nicaraguan refugees needed most. Gunfire popped around our camp almost daily, and I learned how to defend our position with a pistol—and a machine gun! I was still shocked every time I hoisted its heft to my shoulder, peered through the scope, and chewed through targets. The Sandinistas were going to lose Nicaragua, because everyone deserves the right to breathe free of the Communist fist.

Leaves thwacked together overhead, a preview of the approaching storm. I turned my attention to Sisa. "Give me thirty more minutes and I'll come inside."

"Fine, but if you get stranded out here, you're on your own."

"I guess we'll see how well you taught me," I muttered to her back, but if she heard me, she didn't indicate it before the bushes swallowed her.

"Maria! Where are you?"

"Emmaline," a New Orleans drawl drifted through air and leaves. I shuddered at its familiar cadence and swiped my forehead with my sleeve. "No, it can't be," I whispered and raised my machete to attack another stand of green.

"Maria!" I yelled again.

When the knot of leaves fell, I stared into a bloated face I never thought I'd see again: Judge James Wilkinson. Raising my machete, my only weapon, I screamed, "Wilkinson!"

"Emmaline Cagney, it's been a while."

That voice. How was it possible? The man standing a few feet from me was dead. I saw him die. Well, I didn't exactly witness him draw his last cursed breath, but I was sure Merry killed James Wilkinson the day we found my father.

But when I charged through the opening to run him through with my knife, I encountered more swirling plants, more saturated soil. With a shout, I tore into the wet foliage and shredded everything in my path, but after several frenzied minutes without another sighting, I fell back. My arms and shoulders burned from exertion. Glancing at the overhead tree cover, I murmured, "Is this place causing me to see ghosts now?"

I sheathed my machete and slapped relentless sand flies as they vampired around an exposed sliver of neck. Wilkinson wasn't here. Maybe I imagined him.

Besides, the only ghost I wanted to see was my father's. He died the day I graduated from high school.

I didn't want to believe Dad's body vaulted over the dashboard and smashed through the windshield of his red pick-up, a single-vehicle accident on the Natchez Trace about seventy miles south of Nashville. What was he doing on that desolate stretch of highway? Did he misjudge a turn? Or did he swerve to avoid an animal? Could it have been something more nefarious, like another driver running him off the road and leaving him to die?

Six months of life without Dad pummeled me in the gut, doubled me over. Muck leaked through my fingers and splashed my cheeks as my hands hit the ground, choked and breathless. I didn't have time to cry.

Tragedy made most people adults before their time.

A banana leaf slapped my face and left a stinging trail of dampness along my right cheek. When I touched it, my fingers were sticky with blood. Pulling out my machete, I sawed the limb to bits and shouted, "Maria? Where are you? Maria! I can't leave you out here during the storm!"

An audience of wet leaves smacked together.

Volunteering with Nicaraguans was supposed to shift the backstory of my own grief. I tried to escape the void by building camps or feeding the hungry or organizing supplies or helping save lives in the medical tent. Anything to forget that I was a refugee too. My father was dead and my mother—well, I tried not to think about her.

I scraped soupy filth from my palms onto my thick canvas pants and stood. Wilkinson was a a distraction, an illusion. I couldn't stop looking until I found Maria, because she was just like me. Parentless. Alone in the world. Her mother died during their flight from Nicaragua to Honduras, and her dad perished fighting for the Contras.

I blinked against burning pressure behind my eyelids and hacked through another knotted barrier of limbs and leaves. Milky sap seeped between my fingers and stuck my palms to the handle of my machete. "Maria! Come out now!" I hollered in Spanish.

I'd find Maria, just like I found my father when I was nine years old. But I didn't have time to dwell on that now.

Another leafy knot thudded to the ground and revealed more basket-woven walls of growth behind it. "Maria!" I called, but the flora suffocated my sound like a pillow pressed over my face. Hurricane-force wind turned the overhead foliage into a relentless boxing match of slugging fury. I tore into the thorny vines and branches, oblivious to the fiery welts cutting across my skin. The lost child had no one to protect her. I was her savior, her only hope for redemption. I threw my head back and bellowed, "Maria! Answer me!"

A mewl sounded over the gale, ahead of me and to my left. I thrashed toward it, oblivious to the overgrowth sawing into my arms and snagging my pant legs. "Maria?"

Five brown fingers shot up from the foliage and wiggled my way. "A *fer-de-lance*, Emmaline. Please help me. It's slithering this way."

Dear God. I froze, panting and helpless. A *fer-de-lance* was the deadliest land snake on earth. A gruesome execution by two poisonous fangs. Victims sometimes broke their own spines and necks in the violent seizures that preceded death.

If the *fer-de-lance* struck, I'd never get her back to the compound in time to give her antivenom. The snake's poison raced through the bloodstream like a nuclear explosion of necrosis. In two quick bites, it could kill both Maria and me.

I picked up a pronged stick, stripped it of leaves, and inched my way toward Maria's cries. "Don't move, Maria. Stay right there. I'm coming for you."

"It's almost here. Please hurry, Emmaline. It's going to strike me. It's—"

A shriek stabbed through air. My voice mingled with hers as I leapt toward a brief flash of movement and speared it to the soil with my stick. In one swift slice with my machete, I beheaded the beast and impaled its head on a tree, its fangs spewing a radioactive cocktail that shriveled everything on contact.

Maria clawed her way toward me, her tan skin speckled with guck. She opened her black eyes wide and flung herself into my bloody arms. I buried my face in her stringy black mane. "It's okay. I've got you."

I shouldered a sobbing Maria and hurried along the sodden path to the shelter, a cinder block and metal-roofed structure built for emergencies. Otherwise, nobody would spend time in that hotbox.

I slipped and grabbed a clump of banana leaves to steady us. Maria dug her fingers into my shoulder blades and wrapped her legs around my waist. "I've got you, honey. Almost there."

The words were mine, but the voice was my father's.

Thickets blurred around us as I ran. My eyes ached from holding back tears. Grief always blasted in like a hurricane, crushing me at the most unexpected, inconvenient times. I couldn't predict it. In fact, I tried to hide it, because nobody empathized with its onslaught. Instead, they tried to solve. "Be glad you're alive." They dismissed my need to sob. "I don't need anyone. Why do you?" Or they made it about their experience. "Yeah, I remember how I felt when I lost my grandmother. It'll get easier. Eventually."

Nothing helped, not when I needed everyone to listen, to let me cry, to baptize my father's memory with tears. Dad was the engine of my life. Now, I wished I could tell him how much he mattered. I'd give anything to turn around and see him following me toward our shelter.

But when I swirled to thank him for getting Maria and me through the final stretch, the claustrophobic mass closed in on me. It obstructed the sky and entombed me in a living tangle of greenery. Rain fell like static overhead. If my father's voice was out there, I'd never hear it in the crush of water against leaves.

"Let some remnant of him be here," I whispered. Salt stung my cracked lips. "Please, please let him linger long enough to tell me what happened the day he died."

Maria tugged on my collar. "Did you see the man out there?"

I cut my eyes her way, skin tingling. "What man?"

"The one along the path where you found me. He was trying to help me escape the snake, but he went away right before you came and saved me."

"What did he look like?"

She closed her eyes and said, "He was big and muscley and white, like you. And he was trying to help me. He was really nice."

Was it Dad? No. Wilkinson? I convinced myself he wasn't real, but now I wasn't so sure. Aiding a child was the last thing he'd do. I squeezed Maria closer and convinced myself she saw a U.S. soldier or CIA operative. Maybe I did, too. With America's effort to topple the Sandinistas in full press, I was accustomed to seeing a spook or a sergeant from time to time in Honduras, where the Contras often amassed. Abroad Together sent volunteers into danger zones like Honduras to help prepare the Nicaraguans for a new life in the United States. I was proud of how many lives my work transformed. And the U.S. government promised to protect us.

So much for empty pledges.

I rushed the last hundred yards toward our refuge. Rain sprayed sideways with the power of a fire hose. I leaned into it and waved to Sisa holding the door. Idiot. I was an idiot. Dad was gone. Life was a blistering course in pain management. The magical thinking of childhood no longer offered relief.

Loose leaves and small branches bulleted past my head. Sisa's calloused hand beckoned from the open doorway. "Emmaline, I'm glad you found her. You're the last ones out in this madness. Hurry."

I hobbled up the steps and released Maria, who was shepherded deeper into the oppressive space. I heard her beginning to tell the story of our scrape with the *fer-de-lance*. As her voice trailed off, Sisa and I leaned our bodies into the reinforced door to bolt it against the wind. With storm shutters blocking the windows and no electricity, the room was a hellacious tomb.

A strong hand gripped my arm and breath tickled my ear. "Good job finding Maria." Trece's husky baritone resonated in my head and caused my muscles to clench. One of the first Nicaraguan refugees, he now guided his fellow countrymen through the wilderness and brought them into our camps alive.

One glimpse of his sturdy shoulders or a random smile always quickened my heart a little. Even better? He was only a couple of years older than I was. I turned toward him in the oppressive blackness.

"How can you see anything in here?"

"Like this." His muscular arm went around my waist and guided my hand along a wall. His touch set goose bumps pricking the skin along my arm, even in the overheated space. "Sit here until your eyes adjust. Our ten refugees are camped out in the other room. I settled Maria in there. She's already asleep."

"Good." I melted into his side and closed my eyes.

His lips moved near my hairline. "Did you really behead a *fer-de-lance?*"

"Yeah. Everyone's okay in there?"

"*Sí.* Thanks to your organizational skills. You've really come a long way in six months, Cagney. Bossy ladies are sexy." His chuckle pinged through my stomach. I was glad he couldn't see my face redden.

Wind shrieked against the building, and I got up and felt my way into the adjoining room. For a few hours, I sat with them and muttered comforting words of Spanish to each person under my care. They shared stories of surviving bigger storms than Hurricane Paine. Since they made it out of Nicaragua alive, they ran the gauntlet of the biggest disaster of all, but their fight wasn't over until they were given the chance at a better life. Many dreamed of finding that life in America, and I wanted them to get there.

I volunteered in Honduras because I thought it'd help me grow up. Every day, I met refugees who personified strength. They left everything in Nicaragua: possessions, loved ones, careers. I didn't blame them. Who'd want to live under the communist Sandinista regime anyway? Only the tortuous hell of the Mosquitia kept everybody in Nicaragua from streaming across the Honduran border to get away from persecution. I spent my high school years hearing about the horrors of the Soviet Union in the classroom, from the pulpit, and on the evening news. I didn't want it in my back yard.

Maria snuggled next to me. Her matted hair snagged between my fingers, but her breathing was childlike peace. I'd stand up to something bigger than Hurricane Paine if it meant keeping these people safe. When most of them drifted to sleep, I got up, my thoughts too busy to rest.

The man in the woods gnawed at me. Would anybody in camp know who was out there? I felt my way to the spotlit place where Trece and Sisa worked to cover our most sensitive supplies with plastic tarps. A faint camp light glimmered on weapons and ammunition piled along the concrete floor of the gloomy room. Taking a breath was like opening a heated oven and sticking my face in the updraft. Shaking out the coverings only fanned torrid air. I fell in beside them and grabbed a plastic corner, determined to play my role in securing our sole means of defense.

"Do either of you know which CIA unit's operating in the Mosquitia these days?"

Sisa shrugged, pulled a tarp taut, and secured the edge with loose cinder blocks. "They're called spooks for a reason, Emmaline. They don't ever tell me anything extraneous. We're *need to know* around here."

"But when was the last time they came around?"

"A guy stopped a couple of days ago, to warn me of the approaching storm."

Trece sealed a final opening with tape. "From what I hear, the Contras are close to defeating the Sandinistas in the Nicaraguan capital. They've transferred their manpower to bases near the border."

I leaned against the jutting edges of our weapons cache, folded my arms, and unfolded them as soon as my slick skin touched together. Fanning my face with both hands, I said, "Maria claims she saw a man out there. That's why she ran into the thickets." I decided to keep quiet about my own sighting, because saying it aloud made it real.

Sisa snorted. "This landscape has been throwing out mirages for thousands of years. Maria has a hyperactive imagination."

Another term for *overly-dramatic*, something my mother used to accuse me of. Only this time, I wanted her to be right. Biting my lip, I pushed her back into the memory vault and sealed the lid.

Sisa's scorn didn't make Maria's disappearing man any less real. I believed the scrappy little girl.

Picking up my machete, I said, "I think we should do a patrol."

"Negative, Emmaline." Sisa rubbed the back of her head. "If anybody's out in this, they won't survive." A crash rattled the whole structure, like the whole jungle might fall. Hunkering down on the concrete floor in the room's center, she hugged her knees to her chest. "I'm not sure we'll outlast this hurricane, either."

EMMALINE

Howling wind and rain ricocheted like gunfire along the metal roof and shutters of our shelter. I whistled. "Sounds like somebody's throwing a tantrum."

Sisa laughed. "Yeah. Hurricanes suck, especially in poor countries like this. We're the infrastructure for these folks."

Some protection we'd be. The building trembled with every fresh gust. Metal rattled against concrete as the gale tried to tear our shutters from their underpinnings and fling them into oblivion. We huddled together near the weak lamplight.

Trece gulped moist air. "It's been several hours. Probably going to see the eye soon." His arm flexed when he ran his fingers through his dark locks. I swallowed hard and looked away while he continued. "You know, from everything I've been hearing, the Sandinistas are getting desperate enough to attack outposts on the Honduran side of the border."

I grimaced through another thud of a tree falling somewhere close by. "So, you think it's possible they might organize a coordinated attack during a hurricane, when we're likely to be scrambling?"

Trece nodded and got up to scrounge through the plastic-encased pile, cutting into one area of film with his machete. Keys flashed between his nimble fingers, and with a couple of lock-clicks, he brandished military-issue pistols.

To volunteer in an unstable zone, my first spate of training centered on self-defense. I learned basic hand-to-hand combat techniques and tropical survival skills, but I was also schooled in the safe, effective use of guns. At first, I was surprised, because I thought volunteering for Abroad Together made me a humanitarian, not a soldier. But defending myself and my charges required discipline and practice with various weapons, a reality I grudgingly accepted.

Not that I ever wanted to point a gun at another living thing and pull the trigger. I couldn't imagine choosing to snuff out a human life. Wilkinson's face fluttered through my mind. I might make an exception for him, but he was gone.

Trece passed pistols to Sisa and me and gripped his in a steady left hand. Cool steel weighed against my palm.

Sisa clipped her ammunition into place. "You and I can handle a patrol. Right, Trece?"

He loaded his weapon and grinned at me. "Sounds like the eye's passing overhead. Hear it?"

After hours of deafening noise, the quiet was like someone vacuumed all sound from the face of the planet. The world beyond our shutters and walls stilled.

I stepped forward. "Perfect. Then I can go, too."

Sisa inserted herself between us. "No. Somebody needs to stay here. You may've found Maria out there. And you mutilated a *fer-de-lance*. I'll give you those victories. But you don't know this landscape well enough to crawl around in a storm like this."

"But it's calm right now."

Trece nodded. "Yeah, that's the eye for you. The wind will whip around the other way soon, and the jungle will buck like a churned-up sea. You'll never find any paths. Hell, you could get lost a yard from this clearing and never chart your way back. Happens all the time out here, even in good weather."

I stood taller and clenched my weapon between right palm and fingers. "I'll stay close to one of you. Come on. We've got a small window in the weather. We need more eyes out there."

Sisa stomped into the other room with the refugees while Trece moved to block the door leading outside. His arms tensed in the flickering light, and he leaned in close enough for me to see individual beads of sweat on his cheeks. When he spoke, his voice was intimate and raw, almost carnal. "You're not up for this, Cagney. You understand that, right?"

An image flitted across my brain: Trece's lips claiming mine, tracing the curve of my neck, telling me he wanted me.

To banish the thought, I pushed past him and sprinted into the eerie silence outside. A few feet beyond the door, I stopped and surveyed the wind-lashed world. Several trees splintered into our clearing, and more leafy debris littered what was once open space, like a rain forest sprouting from nothing. Trece was right. I couldn't make out any of our paths. Every vista was a tumult of shredded, watery green.

I clung to my gun and fought my way to what I thought was the edge of the clearing. Guck grabbed at my boots and slopped to my knees, but I stayed upright, focused on the one break where I knew a path to be.

Gunfire strobed to my right. Trece came up behind me and steered me toward the building with an arm slung over my shoulder. In a few quick steps, we were beyond range, hugging the concrete block wall along the side of our shelter.

"Somebody's out there," Trece's sultry breath tickled my ear and sent fire shooting along my extremities.

"We'll never get backup in this storm." And we wouldn't. Catacamas, the closest town, didn't have enough bodies to defend our position, even if they could find a way to move personnel during the hurricane.

Gunfire whizzed past my head and chewed up the wall behind us. Disembodied concrete nicked our exposed hands and littered the sodden ground. Trece and I fired blindly into the shuddering trees. Once we both emptied our clips, we ducked through a door and locked ourselves inside the structure to regroup.

Sisa met us near the entrance. "You're shooting out there?"

I gulped. "Somebody fired on us. Right, Trece?"

"Yes. Gotta be Sandinista assholes."

Sisa gripped her pistol and motioned to the other room. "Dammit. I was just getting ready to follow you. I handed out weapons to the refugees and sent Maria to the secure bunker. Organize them into teams to patrol the perimeter. They have enough training. Plus, with extra bodies, we'll cover more ground."

I bit my lip. "No. We don't need to put them at risk, not when they've given up so much already. The passage through the bunker's still open, right?"

Trece nodded. "Last time I checked, but given the storm, who knows what we'll find if we go out that way. A tree might've fallen and caved it in. Or it might've collapsed with the weight of wind and water."

Stepping around him, I scrabbled through our cache of weapons and shouldered a machine gun. Bullets draped around my torso like perverse metal jewelry. I didn't volunteer to work with refugees to play a female Rambo, but as I scraped blonde locks from my forehead, I understood why the mercenary always wore a headband. I snapped, "Let's go, Trece. Sisa, you stay here with the others. We'll be right back."

"Since when are you giving the orders?" she barked, but I ignored her and pressed toward a trap door in the room's back corner, lifted the latch, and entered a grave-like underground. Acrid earth stung my nostrils.

"Emmaline?"

Maria's sing-song rung out to my right.

"Stay there. Trece and I are checking on something outside. We'll be back in no time. Don't worry."

Without waiting for her reply, I felt my way along the soggy walls. Ancient peoples built mounded cities throughout the Mosquitia. We had tunneled through a forgotten remnant and shored it up with wooden beams to create a hidden escape should one ever be needed. The claustrophobic work was my first assignment when I arrived in Honduras.

Images of my father's decaying corpse rocked me more than once as I dug. How could I leave him in a neglected strip of Nashville ground? Every time my pickaxe clanged on a root or a bit of hardened dirt, I expected to uncover empty eye sockets or human finger bones pointing, accusing, whispering, "Remember me."

I shuddered and crept along the tunnel, trying not to think about lingering ghosts. Substantial populations never lived in this wildness, did they? Not for long anyway. The place lashed itself to the ankles, burrowed into membranes, and rotted a mortal from the inside-out.

The eye's tranquility teased through the cracks as I approached the door. I worked the handle and tried to quiet my father's voice. Trece grabbed my arm and turned me toward him. With one finger, he caressed the line of my cheek before we stepped into a gash of foliage about a hundred yards behind the bunker. While I wanted to dwell on his touch, the weather had other plans. Torrents of tropical fury could streak my face at any time, because the eye only provided a short window of calm. I held my breath and crouched in the twig-and-leaf-strewn ooze. Trece followed close behind me as we inched along with our elbows and knees.

Downed leaves whiplashed our faces and spanked our shoulders. After going about twenty feet—though it could've been two—I stuck my head above a screen of severed greenery and scanned the clearing. A unit of soldiers, three of them in view, stormed through the overgrown landscape, using thick tree trunks and our abandoned jeep as cover. In less than ten seconds, they took up attack positions outside our shelter.

Concentrated gunfire rocked the concrete walls and crumpled the metal roof. With a shout, Sisa ordered the refugees to open fire from inside the building, while Trece and I bedded down behind a fallen log to avoid the spray.

A few invaders were no match for thirteen focused guns. Sisa and her team wounded two enemy combatants, pitiful creatures who writhed on the squishy ground. I diverted my eyes at the sight of one bleeding from an artery in his leg. Blood still made me squeamish, especially when it came as an unstoppable torrent. He couldn't last long.

Another soldier streaked into view and pulled his gun on the fallen. He moved his hefty frame with a luxurious, athletic ease.

"It can't be," I murmured. The storm whipped my imagination into untenable territory. I put my gun sight to my right eye and trained it on his ghost-like frame.

"Turn around." I shouted. "Let me see your face before I shoot you, you bastard."

The last remaining attacker stepped between us, disrupting my aim. He faced away from me and leveled a pistol at the other man's head. "Drop it, asshole. Drop it right now. I'm going to end this. Finally."

An underwater world muted replies. I held my position and squinted through my gun sight. "Move. Let me see this guy," I whispered and crawled through flowing dirt to get closer. I needed to see his face to convince myself he was real. A few more feet, and I'd be sure enough to either stand down or pull the trigger.

"You always were over-confident, Dickie boy."

Wilkinson. No mistake. He was alive and standing mere feet from me. I swallowed to stifle the rollicking gallop in my chest. A cocktail of wind and rain couldn't resurrect anyone from the dead, especially not when I had the means to kill him. I rocked to my knees, gripped my weapon, and prepared to fire.

The accursed man with the pistol stepped between us, once again blocking my shot. Who was this guy?

With the upright carriage and assured stance of a seasoned soldier, he snapped his jaws and snarled, "All I have to do is kill you, and I'm through with this damned place. Getting rid of you is my mission, and I will accomplish it." He leveled his gun at Wilkinson's head. "Right. Now."

I braced myself for the sound of his bullet leaving the muzzle. He had a clean shot, but if I rolled to my left, so did I. I ducked and squeezed my trigger a second before he did. Our projectiles streaked across the sky like deadly pyrotechnics. Intense light whitewashed everything. Lightning plowed a bloody stripe through the shooter's almost hairless skull.

Or was it my bullet?

We were on the other side of the eye. Water poured from every direction, like somebody threw the Gulf of Mexico up in the air and let gravity take over. Trees rippled and whipped, merged and breathed in one continuous frenzy. Disembodied leaves stuck to my cheeks, my arms, my sodden clothing. I opened one eye and blinked to force darker lines and shadows into focus. Another bolt of lightning stripped my eyes of color and depth. I groped toward the crumpled pile at the edge of the clearing.

When I parted the scrim of branches, I screamed.

The lightning man, the intruder with the pistol, the guy Wilkinson called *Dickie-boy*, was vanishing, like the atmosphere ate him. I mean, his body levitated horizontal above the ground. His shattered head was swallowed by the air around him, followed by the rest of his quivering body, a torturous, frame-by-frame repast. His feet disappeared last.

Did lightning strikes cause people to evaporate from head-to-foot? What just happened?

I rubbed my eyes and peered at the shimmering air. Where the victim once stood, James Wilkinson, my childhood foe, took his place.

I wanted to wail, to tear my scalp, to fall to my knees. My bullet was meant for Wilkinson. The worthless, craven villain who destroyed my childhood.

"Judge Wilkinson!" I shouted over the maelstrom and leveled my gun at his bulldog head. "I'm glad you survived, so I can kill you myself."

I Am Number 13

WILKINSON

Emmaline Cagney was predictable, standing there with her shaky-handed firing posture, ready to revile me as ever. And for what? Did she think this soggy entrance, upstaged by a reprobate from my past, was really the first time I made myself known in this here-and-now?

I reentered this tale six months ago. April, 1986. I did what lost characters like me always do. My mysterious death in 1825 by opium poisoning landed me in Nowhere, an in-between purgatory where I was charged with completing a do-gooder assignment to move on.

Imagine. Me? A do-gooder? What the hell was anyone thinking when they sent a general/spy/traitor/assassin/ambassador to this skewed dimension, a place where we were supposed to influence the living to create a better world? I chucked all that nonsense as soon as my boots landed on the ground, because if anybody could flout the rules of a place, it was I, General James Wilkinson. Nowhere was easy when a guy knew how to work the system.

Or so I thought until this time.

I always made grand promises to myself as I hurled through the Nowhere void. Instead of dwelling on my most recent flop, I bucked up, set goals, and planned for my next venture. I was one of the few who grasped Nowhere. We all got thirteen Nowhere lives. I'd only burned three.

Failure had a way of robbing a guy of misplaced bravado. Well, that and the bullet that chewed through my chest on my last sojourn through this Nowhere world. My sworn enemy from my real life shot me mere steps from dear Miss Emmaline and ended my quest to make her mine. Vanquished, I rocketed through the void trying on old ruses like unfashionable sets of clothes. I left each gambit in another tired clump of fabric, clueless as to what might work for me.

I slithered into a cemetery during night's darkest hour. Yeah, I was the *clichéd* Nowhere man who came back via a cemetery portal. Other occupants got bartenders and train conductors, but who was my Nowhere gatekeeper? A gravedigger.

Up ahead, moonlight sparkled on marble-and-granite monuments to forgotten lives. The Mexican National Cemetery was cursed more than most. What did my countrymen expect when they threw a bunch of American bones in mass graves, including mine? Because I suffered my unresolved death and entered Nowhere from Mexico City, my dusty remnants were strewn here, places even I couldn't find. Leave it to the United States government to build the most haunted place on the planet and saddle Mexico with its identity.

But living in the past was wasting time, and I didn't have much to start with. A virgin sunrise already teased the horizon. My Gravedigger needed light to work. He wouldn't show up until daybreak, giving me just enough time to do what I needed to do.

I propped my hand against the wall of a baroque crypt. Most of its gaudy flourishes were broken or smashed, but I thought the jagged curlicues matched the mood. At a glance, the building resembled a gaping mouth waiting to chomp down on random passersby. Death has a ravenous appetite.

And I contributed to the destruction. For over fifty years, I used one Nowhere life to sell my country's secrets to the Russians. With the money they paid me, I bought myself a law degree and greased enough New Orleans palms to buy a judgeship. I used my seat on the bench to build my own lucrative empire of corruption and greed. In the process, I killed the bitch who ruined my life and almost conquered her darling daughter. That darling daughter was Emmaline Cagney.

She gripped me to my very core. Oh, she didn't hold the spirit of my dead wife Ann, as I once thought. I saw that clearly from this side of the divide. But she was electric, compelling, different from any human being I'd ever known. What was it about that girl?

I slipped my fingers through the metal bars guarding the door. A quick rattle, and the gate squeaked open. The altar was bedecked with moldy flowers and faded ribbon, but it didn't interest me. My prize was hidden in an alcove just behind the urn. I reached into the limestone crack and pulled out my lifeline: a rusted metal box.

God, I hated crypts. I scrambled outside with my precious container. The lid squawked as I opened it. I joined its screams seconds later. The box was empty.

Where was my journal with its words and symbols, the record of my other Nowhere lives? I always brought it back to its hiding place once I committed it to memory. Unlike every other Nowhere soul, I always knew everything I'd done in each Nowhere outing. I took advantage of their scrubbed memories, their blind groping, because I kept a record of everything I did. My journal was the key, my decrypter. It ensured I'd never be like them.

Only my journal was gone. As soon as my Gravedigger said my name, my memory of my most recent Nowhere life would be erased before I could record what happened. I'd enter my next Nowhere life without knowing anything I'd done in my previous three outings.

I tore into the crypt, toppling a crucifix choked with rosaries. Beads of glass and plastic scattered over the cold stone floor. I fought to stay upright as I wobbled on marbles. "Where's my journal?" I demanded of the silent corpse. Ridiculous for a guy who's been in that position to think she'd answer, but desperation robbed me of my usual finesse. Her skull detached and thunked across the floor as I shook her lace-shrouded shoulders and spat, "What have you done with it?"

A pink arc stained the lip between sky and land. I probably had two minutes before my Gravedigger showed up and said my name. His *hiya Jimmy* would scrub my brain of every detail from my other Nowhere lives. Without my notebook, I wouldn't recall who I met, what schemes I devised, or where my enemies lurked. I'd navigate Nowhere like all the other clueless schmucks. How would I ever gain the upper hand?

I flopped onto the ground outside the crypt, mopped my sweaty face with a hankie, and looked skyward. Five minutes before, I soared into this place thinking maybe I needed to change, to be a better man. Without my notebook, I wouldn't have a choice.

My Gravedigger's flashlight cast shadows over the rise. He clanged along the pavement and threw his pickaxe in the dirt beside me. The thing stood like morning wood against the sunrise, a bit of bawdiness I would've relished in less frantic circumstances. I squinted up at him while he placed hands on hips. Unfamiliar eyes stared down at me.

I swallowed. "You're not my Gravedigger."

"Am now. Started this god-awful assignment last week."

His shoulders rounded as he picked up his pickaxe. I watched him hew into the dirt a few feet from where I sat. "You digging a fresh grave?"

"Yeah. For you, asshole."

I scooted backwards and scrabbled to stand. "But I've only used three Nowhere lives. I've got ten more coming to me. You can't put me in the ground."

He moved closer. His breath reeked of stale chewing tobacco, and his broken teeth were the color of Mississippi mud, the same stuff that swallowed my wife Ann's tuberculosis-ravaged body. I stumbled backward, but he followed until my back hit the side of the crypt. I was cornered.

He lowered his voice. "I have some news for you. I don't like you. Not one iota. I've learned everything about you in anticipation of your visit. Your arrogance and duplicity. The way you flout every rule of Nowhere and make yourself richer and richer without any consequences." He whipped out a leather-bound book and tapped my chest with it. "Illuminating read, this. You disgust me."

"My journal. How'd you know about it?"

"Doesn't matter. But I'm not giving it back. I've a good mind to kill you right now. Bastard like you deserves to be taught a lesson. I can't think of an ass wipe who ought to be forgotten more than you."

I swallowed a lump of mounting fear. "You can't do that. Gatekeepers can't kill their charges to cancel out Nowhere lives. The rules don't work that way."

"Who says?"

He released his grip and whirled on me. His pickaxe cut open the flesh between my ribs. Howling laughter punctuated each dull thud and tearing of muscle and bone. He was raking out my psyche like glistening entrails. I threw up my arms and tried to deflect his blows, but he rendered one a bloody stump with his sharpened steel. Pain screamed from every gaping wound. I fell forward and landed on my face in the shallow hole he prepared for me. Light sputtered, and my world was dark.

I don't know how long I lay in that Nowhere grave, but when I tumbled through the void like I always did after someone ended my Nowhere life, I knew he'd taken out number four. Nine more, and I'd be doomed to fall from life's timeline, forgotten for eternity. Just like my Gravedigger.

I came to in front of my usual crypt. He was already there, swinging a pickaxe sticky with my blood. A cigarette burned between his upturned lips as he drove the point into the top of my skull and kicked me into the waiting grave. Sonic booms of agony ripped into me with every new appearance. In less than fifteen minutes, the bastard robbed me of lives four through twelve. I staggered into the clearing one more time. My thirteenth and final Nowhere life dangled from the pickaxe's murderous tip.

The Gravedigger leaned on his ruthless weapon. "I hope taking nine of your miserable lives proved my point. When you're on my turf, I make whatever rules I want."

"I'm sure we can come to some kind of arrangement here, yes?"

He spat rancid tobacco juice onto my cheek. My skin sizzled, and hot agony radiated along my jaw. "You don't warrant any deals. You've made a mockery of this place for almost two hundred years, and I'm here to put a stop to it."

"By killing me again and again?"

"I'll leave you this last life if you agree to focus on your mission."

"My mission?" I squeaked.

Nowhere lives had a productive point: I was supposed to help a living individual make the world a better place. In my zeal to accumulate wealth and power, I didn't care what my mission was, never bothered to figure it out.

And where did my duplicity land me? I was teetering on the precipice of a nameless existence. The Gravedigger was about to turn me into his unwilling twin.

I landed in this graveyard with fleeting questions about prior unsavory motives, but I was still Wilkinson. I never had any intention of changing. During my Nowhere lives, I amassed too much power and money from mob connections, child pornography, drug cartels, bribes for my judicial favors, prostitution, and spying. I might've fucked up living, but I knew how to milk the afterlife. Because above all, I mastered the art of slipping into a cloak and becoming the man the other person wanted to see.

Marshaling every shred of theatrical sincerity, I fell to my knees next to his mucky boots. "I swear, Gravedigger. If you let me have this final Nowhere life, I'll do whatever you say to the letter. No diversions. No selfishness. No tricks."

"It's not like you have much choice, given I'm holding you over the yawning jaws of hell."

"I'm not paying lip service to get some kind of fire escape." I fell back on my ass and looked up at him, the picture of penitence, a broken man begging on his knees. And I chanted the same shit I always said to the priests in those confessional boxes at New Orleans' St. Louis Cathedral when I was alive. "You're right about me. I wrecked too many good lives. And what for? I was thinking about what a waste I've been on my way here. I can do better. I know it. Just give me this single chance to make things right."

God, I almost believed myself. But just like confession, once my

Gravedigger absolved me and let me go, I could do whatever I wanted.

He tilted his head to one side and studied me while I held my breath for an eternity. "All right. I'll allow you to experience your final life. But if you stray from your mission, I'm finishing you. No more chances. You do the right thing, or you're done. Understand?"

I slow-motion nodded, all the while wondering whether I just made a deal with Lucifer himself.

He reached into the chest pocket of his dirt-stained overalls. "We don't usually give charges explicit Nowhere instructions regarding mission, but we're making an exception this time. Certain world events require your unique skill set, or the whole thing may blow apart. I don't know if even Nowhere types survive something like World War III."

"A military mission? Another ambassadorship?"

"Guerrilla warfare, the scrappy kind of fighting you led during the American Revolution, only with better guns and killing materiel."

Hell yes. A legitimate mission I might actually enjoy. I helped George Washington rout the British in the Hudson Valley and rose through the ranks to lead the United States Army when he became President. I rocked to my feet and dusted off my knees, done with playing sorry. "Can you tell me the situation? Or is that classified?"

"Like I said, you're getting specific instructions because of a crisis. A top-secret group of CIA operatives have been working to topple Nicaragua's communist government, because the United States President doesn't want the Soviets to gain a stronger foothold there. If they establish another presence in our hemisphere, they'll have more options for missiles and military bases within striking distance. And by fomenting instability in Central America, they will work to spread Communism until it reaches our southern border. The President's using surreptitious channels to support the Contra resistance, something he deems vital to the survival of democracy. A man with your skills could tip the balance in America's favor. You can help the Contras win."

"So the President knows about me?"

"The rest of your mission's spelled out in the envelope."

Turning my back to him, I ripped open the flap and scanned the typewritten page. Clandestine government work was always my forte. Who else could serve the first five United States presidents, all the while selling our secrets to the Spanish for millions of dollars and never getting caught?

When I was done reading, I spun on him, pocketed my instructions, and offered my hand. His grip was limp and womanish, which surprised me given his strength with the pickaxe.

I stepped back, fished a Cuban cigar from my breast pocket, and flicked open my lighter. Fresh smoke twisted through my airways, a burn that always let me know I was still in the game. Misty rings floated around his head as I smiled. "A simple operation. The Contras will continue to get their arms. Communism in Central America will fail. Whoever gave me this assignment was right. I'm your Nowhere man."

"And now you're on life number 13."

Another flashlight cast a shadow along the walkway behind me. He grabbed my elbow. "Hurry. We don't have more time."

I lost him as we ran through the gravestones. They whipped by faster and faster until my world was a blur of motion-on-white. I wouldn't realize the Gravedigger's mistake until later. He forgot to say my name. I recalled everything about my most recent life.

Especially Emmaline Cagney. And here she was, getting in the way of my mission. Again.

WILKINSON

"Don't shoot. I'm CIA." I took out my leather wallet, flicked it open, and waved an official-looking medallion above my balding head. CIA operatives never carried badges, but most civilians didn't know that. Owning my status as a spook was worth a try.

She ignored my fake badge and keened, "What happened to that man? The one who was just here? What did you do to him, Wilkinson?"

Trece motioned toward the shelter, his gun also drawn. For an instant, we locked eyes, and I knew how he wanted me to play it. Given my responsibility for the success of the Contra operation, he and I worked together sometimes. We found our best recruits among those desperate enough to flee the Sandinistas. Like Trece. We were good at reading one another. "We're not going to resolve what we think we saw if we let the hurricane pummel us to death. Let's move under the eaves out of the wind. Now," he ordered.

"But you admit you saw it, too?" Emmaline jogged alongside Trece, while I kept my hands overhead and dashed toward the structure in front of them.

"What I think I saw was too bizarre. It had to be a trick of the storm. Or something." Trece's high-pitched inflections indicated he was as bewildered as I was.

My shoulder hit cinder block about the time Emmaline and Trece got there. She planted herself between him and me, raised her gun to my face, and spat through clenched teeth. "What did you do to make that man disappear?"

"You fired the only shot."

Her voice carried the pinched undertones of panic mixed with the bansheeing wind. "No, no, no, he shot at you the same moment I squeezed my trigger. I know he did. I couldn't have killed an innocent person with a bullet that was meant for the disgusting likes of you."

My hands started to pulse from keeping them above my head, but I didn't dare move them. "How do you know he was innocent? My CIA cohorts and I have been tracking him for weeks. You did us a favor by whacking him."

"But I didn't kill him! Did you see what happened? It was like an invisible monster swallowed him one vicious bite at a time."

In the moment, I was more concerned about convincing her not to doom me to the same fate. But I would definitely need to explore the impact of a bullet from Emmaline Cagney's gun on Nowhere souls. Because the guy she shot was stuck in Nowhere like I was. I was sure of it, because I killed him on a previous Nowhere jaunt.

Trece panted over her left shoulder, black eyes giving life to his thoughts. He gave me another pointed look and said, "Despite what we saw out there and how creepy it was, we can't kill a federal agent."

She scraped a curtain of blonde tresses from her forehead. Her gun's blowhole didn't quiver, not anymore. In place of momentary uncertainty, her posture bore the determination of the girl I remembered, the child on a quest to find her father. That gritty young lady would pull the trigger and send a bullet into my face at point-blank range.

The hurricane shredded the trees overhead. Another one the circumference of a tank splintered and crashed into the clearing where I'd been standing a few seconds earlier.

Emmaline didn't notice. Instead, she huffed, "He's not CIA. He's a perverted judge from New Orleans. I met him when I was little. He tried to ruin my childhood."

I inched closer. "I'm sorry, Emmaline." Saying her name coated my tongue like high-shelf scotch. Burned through my chest, too.

Surprised, Trece looked at me wide-eyed and murmured, "How do you know her name, Wilkinson?"

Emmaline gasped. "You know each other?"

Damn Trece. He broke character. Before he confirmed anything, I crooned, "Leave him out of this. I admit it. I was a monster the last time you saw me, but I'm not the same man I was."

Metal snapped when she flicked off the gun's safety, cementing my feet to the sticky ground. Bits of torn greenery hummed along my jawline and stuck to my flesh, but I couldn't afford to swat them away, not when Emmaline Cagney stood on the other side of a weapon. I deserved her bullet, even several, but I'd never tell her that.

Instead, I kept my hands in full view and locked onto her arctic stare. "You wouldn't believe the roles I've been forced to play in the spy business, but your case was me at my worst. I know I abused you."

She sniffed. "Merry made sure you never got the chance. Without him, I would've been your child bride. I thought he killed you the day he reunited me with my father."

I swallowed. Emmaline still reminded me of my dead wife, my adored Ann. Same coloring and identical tangle of golden corkscrews. Sometimes when Emmaline looked at me, I swore my Ann called through those innocent eyes. Grief untethered me from all sense of propriety, but could anyone who's truly loved condemn me? We convince ourselves we hear our departed calling to us from beyond the scrim. In the dark, we sense them breathing, and by day, we replay memories over and over again trying to capture a scent, a note, a sensation. I'd never apologize for loving my wife. Her absence was my life's earthquake. It tore a chasm in my heart.

But Emmaline was right. She wasn't my Ann. Not now. Not when she was a kid. I whispered, "Please. You saved my life. Don't shoot until you hear me out."

She closed one eye and stared down the barrel of her gun. Petite fingers caressed the trigger. "You tried to buy me from my prostitute mother when I was a child in New Orleans. And when I escaped, you chased me across three states to stop me from finding my dad. I was nine years old. Nine, you disgusting predator."

I took another step in her direction, my hangdog face painted with strokes of conciliation. "Look. I'm not proud of some of the things I've done in my role as a spy, but we're ordered to break rules, to do illegal things. Whatever I did, in the end it kept the American people safe, and I'm damn proud of that. Chasing you across the south was cover for busting up your mother's prostitution ring. You were too young to know, but she managed illegal brothels all over Louisiana, Mississippi, Alabama, and Tennessee."

"That's a lie. She could barely keep up with her place in the French Quarter."

"Oh, your mother was smarter than you ever imagined. You'd be gobsmacked by the things I could tell you about her."

"I don't care about her. I didn't when she was alive, and I don't now."

For the first time, I was afraid to breathe. Her eyes flashed with pure hatred. I thought girls always had some mystical thing with their mothers but bringing up hers was a misstep in my game of manipulation.

"Fair enough. Fuck her. I can still show you how I earned government credentials, you know, prove I am the man I claim to be."

A tanned little girl burst from the building and ran up beside Emmaline. Tugging her pants, she cried, "That's the man! The one who tried to save me from the *fer-de-lance* before you came along. He was nice to me."

Emmaline kept her finger on the trigger, but the metal tip shivered. Slight, no overt admissions of weakness from that one. So much her mother's daughter. I noticed the ghostly outline of her pluck in the set of her jaw, the spark fueling her gaze.

Could she burn through me like she just incinerated Richard Cox, my rebellious charge from another Nowhere life? I rewarded his refusal to spy for the Soviets with an unresolved death, shot point-blank on the frozen Hudson River near West Point. I carried his still-warm body to a New

Jersey warehouse, slashed it apart, and threw it in an incinerator. We spies couldn't leave tracks.

My mistake. I should've discarded a remnant, anything for someone to discover and close the case on his disappearance. Because nobody ever found a shred of Richard Cox, he wound up in Nowhere. With me. Only not.

I never thought he'd spend Nowhere trying to kill me, but the kid – what was his name? – well, he was always too square for his own good. Undetected, I scrolled through my previous thoughts about the man Emmaline shot. Not five seconds ago, his name flitted across my brain. Now, nothing. Who was he again? How did I know him? I ratcheted my head from side-to-side, trying to clear it.

Or did Emmaline already shoot me, and I missed it in my slog through incomplete Nowhere memories?

I squished up my face and ran one hand along my rain-slicked scalp. Everything was intact. A scan of my front revealed no gush of blood, no shredded cloth. My mud-spattered uniform was otherwise whole.

Why couldn't I recall who Emmaline killed? Who was he to me?

Focus on what's in front of you, Wilkinson. Washington thundered those orders in my direction more than once during my tenure in his Army. One of many reasons the man was suited to be our first President. He stripped everything down to simple.

I rocked my head to-and-fro to banish confusion and slid another foot toward her. The ground slurped like walking across a lake full to the brim with muck. "Listen to the child, Emmaline. I'm your destiny. You know I'm not making it up. Your mother was a scheming bitch."

The muscles in her neck tensed when she swallowed. Her weak reply couldn't stir a leaf. "I still don't believe you."

"She was gone a lot, right? Leaving the place in the hands of that African-American. What was her name?"

"Bertie," she whispered through parched lips. "Aunt Bertie."

"She helped me take your mother's operation down from the inside."

A tear sketched a boggy path down her right cheek. "That's not true."

"In your gut, you know it is. Why do you think she helped you get away that night? You hid under her robe and ran when she gave you the signal. I told her we were raiding the house, and I followed you to make sure you found your dad."

She bit her lip and wobbled a bit. The muzzle of the gun fell an inch. Almost where I wanted her. Sometimes, I longed to applaud the intricacy of my own bullshit.

Trece gripped her shoulder and squeezed, almost proprietary. He didn't look my way. "The storm's still got hours to go. Since we can't do anything else, we can keep him here until the weather clears, and we can reestablish communications with our satellite. It'll only take a few pings around the area to verify his story."

I nodded. "Listen to him, Emmaline. If I'm not who I claim to be, if what I've told you doesn't check out, you'd be right to execute me."

Her right arm remained rigid, the gun its morbid extension. "You were supplying my mother with women. How many times did I see you visit them yourself? At least twenty."

"Of course, agents are often required to compromise themselves to protect our covers. It lends credibility to the role we're playing."

"Like you're doing now."

"Clearly, your mother was more devious than you realized. A gifted criminal mind and an abominable nurturer. I made sure you found the parent you wanted, the father who longed for you."

Her hand shook. "That's not true."

"It is. I swear it."

Trece finally stepped between us. His musical accent wafted my way. "He's really CIA, Cagney. Look, I know he is because I've been coordinating with him to move Contras and materiel closer to the border for several weeks." He glanced my way. "I wasn't sure I was supposed to say anything."

"I'm glad you did. Better for her to know the truth."

"He's your contact with U.S. forces?" She shook free of his grip and rubbed her forehead with the back of her free hand. "That pig of a man? You've been working with him?"

In one fleet movement, Trece kicked her pistol into the trees and pinned her arms behind her back while the little girl watched, open-mouthed. His breath fluttered stray ringlets around Emmaline's ear. Though she elbowed him in the stomach, head-butted him, and stomped on his toes, he didn't lose his hold on her. "I can't let you make a mistake. Killing a U.S. government agent will ruin your life. You don't want to be saddled with that baggage, especially when you're here to help these refugees. They need you, Cagney. We all do."

She stopped struggling and swallowed. "You do?"

"Yes. You belong here. You're part of our pathway to a better existence on this planet. Think about your work, not some misguided memories from a long time ago."

Her eyes almost shot fire. I expected poor Trece to combust from her glare. "My recollections are not misguided. I know who Wilkinson was. Reprobates like him don't change. Ever."

I threw my gun into the lashing trees, but I didn't hear it land. "At least wait until you confirm what I've told you with people in Catacamas or DC or wherever. You've got a secure satellite connection someplace in this camp, don't you? I know the technology is recent, but it works pretty well in these remote backwaters."

She bit her lip. "It looks like I don't have a choice."

"You don't," I replied. "Because whether you like it or not, it's my job to get these refugees ready to go back to Nicaragua and fight for their country."

She rounded on me, eyes aflame. "What? I'm here to help them get to the U.S. They fled because they didn't want to fight."

"Well, somebody has to replace the Contras who fall, and it may as well be people we don't need in the States anyway."

Emmaline broke free of Trece and charged me, teeth bared and fists punching the air. "I won't let you do that to these poor people."

Before she made contact, Trece tackled her and pinned her to the ground. "Cagney, no. Let's wait out the storm and check his story. All right?"

Without looking my way, she let him help her stand. With an arm flung across her shoulders, Trece steered her toward the bunker and through the open door, and the little girl and I followed.

I helped Trece close and bar the door against the gale. Leaning my back against the door, I sniffed the stink of kerosene and imagined the swirling clouds beyond our shelter, a temper tantrum on high. Why did Nowhere gift-wrap a delectable temptation like Emmaline Cagney and deliver her to my feet, just when I was on track to fulfill my legitimate mission and exit this in-between world?

But this time, Nowhere presented even more maddening conundrums. Disappearing men and magic lightning. Or was it bullets? I could barely reconstruct what happened a few short minutes ago. Why? Was hurricane-force wind scrambling my brain?

Realization almost made me shout. Perhaps Emmaline had something to do with my amnesia and deserved closer scrutiny in her own right, not from the fringes of my heartsick mind. Last time, I was too busy looking for my lost love to really see Emmaline Cagney. I wouldn't make that error this time.

I glanced around the empty bunker. "What happened to the other soldiers out there?"

Trece motioned toward the clearing. "Both were wounded. Maybe they crawled into the thickets. Once the storm's over, I'll canvass the area, make sure they're not hanging around."

I nodded. "I'll go with you since I need to report this blackguard unit to central ops in Catacamas. Besides, I'm sure Emmaline'll shoot me if she comes out and finds me here, especially since she knows I'm sending her precious charges back into harm's way."

But hours later, as we chopped through sopping vines and green, my thoughts thundered louder than Hurricane Paine had been.

Emmaline's bullet might've erased a person—their whole identity—from history's timeline, and that was why I couldn't recall anything about that person now. I saw the gunshot and witnessed the gruesome exit, but that's all I could recall. And if she possessed that kind of power, how could I get her to use it for me?

EMMALINE

Wilkinson? He was really in Honduras? I looked up at the cloud-clotted sky and shuddered. How did he find me? Could I stop him from ruining the lives of the refugees in my care?

His lumbering presence shredded my confidence like Hurricane Paine macerated the jungle. I eyed bloated piles of fallen limbs and vines, my core a shriveled husk, a hollow void. It took us almost a week of non-stop work to set the refugee camp aright, but it would never be safe with Wilkinson in the picture. Not to me.

And Trece was working with him, sending his fellow countrymen across the border to be slaughtered. Why did that news sit between my shoulder blades like a lumpy knot of betrayal? Hormones and practicality frothed me into a cocktail of confusion. I liked Trece. I mean, really liked him. I didn't want him to be working for Wilkinson in any capacity.

But if Wilkinson really was a United States government agent, which I doubted, refugees like Trece wouldn't have a choice but to fall in line. He probably took U.S. government dollars from the military to use his talents. And they decided whose orders he'd follow. Right? Maybe Trece was doing the best he could en route to a better life in America and hated Wilkinson as much as I did.

Regardless, knowledge of their connection untethered a knot of emotions next to my heart. How could I nurture a crush on somebody who collaborated with James Wilkinson? All those stolen kisses of fantasy, his very real fingers brushing along my cheek, his ripped arms pulling me to safety. My shoulders slumped a little to squelch the renewed fire in my abdomen, because the act of recalling a few bits of longing made me burn anew. I'd lost someone I never really had.

Rank sweat clotted my pores and ran down the back of my neck. In the Mosquitia, I was always, always wet. I heaved limp strands of my mane into a messy knot on top of my head and shouldered my cot. Aloud, I promised myself, "One more refugee to get settled, Emmaline, and you can zip yourself into your tent and rest."

What an empty pledge. I'd never sleep, not as long as Wilkinson lurked along the settlement's overgrown margins. Clearing the camp of hurricane debris, pitching our tents, and restocking our humanitarian supplies couldn't dispel thoughts of him. Every time a vine snapped, a cougar snarled, or a monkey caterwauled, my neck craned in its direction, convinced I'd find Wilkinson's greedy eyes watching me.

And I refused to let him send my people to their deaths. I'd die first.

Sisa sloshed past and held up a free hand. "High five. Everything's back in order."

"Not until I find my soap," I shouted over my shoulder and pushed through the opening into the last tent. My sanctuary. The only place I could cry and question. Nobody allowed me any weakness. I was expected to be strong for everyone else.

"Maria!" I jumped at the realization of two eyes meeting mine. "How long have you been here?"

Her black tresses were shiny and clean, secured in two high pigtails above her pierced ears. Someone already let her bathe and gave her a fresh jungle green coverall. She sat on the plastic floor beneath the spot where I suspended my cot from hooks at the tent's ceiling. The ground was too sponge-like to sleep on anything anchored to it. Most of our number slept in hammocks, but my citified body wouldn't comply. Besides, after everything I'd lost, I pretended the gentle rock of my cot was my father's ghost moving the frame. Magical thinking still worked sometimes.

I stepped toward Maria. Her nervous fingers picked apart a banana leaf and threw its bits like confetti. She wouldn't look at me, but her tentative voice wafted my way. "Is it okay if I sleep here tonight? With you?"

I shooed her across the tent, heaved the cot over my head, dropped it on the plastic floor, and prepared to connect it to the hooks I'd drilled into a sturdy tree branch above my tent's roof. I was proud of how I threaded them through a notch and still kept everything reasonably watertight. I couldn't do anything about the floor, though. Even with layers of plastic, the ooze slithered into our living spaces like it was alive. And some of it was.

Recalling our close call with the *fer-de-lance*, I pulled Maria to me and smoothed a few stray frizzes from her forehead. "Are you still thinking about that snake? Because it's gone. It can't hurt you."

"No. I know if anybody comes after me, you'll kill them."

"I hope I can protect you for as long as you're here, but I'm not a killer."

She wrapped her skinny arms around my neck and put her dark forehead against mine. "Sure you are. I saw what you did to that snake. You saved me."

Plastic slurped at my boots when I got up to pace. The scene in the clearing was scrambled in my mind. Did I really shoot the mystery invader, the one Wilkinson claimed threatened us? I closed my eyes, but beyond a flash of surreal gore, I couldn't replay the tape of what happened after I fired. No matter how much I concentrated, it was erased. Wilkinson was the only person in view.

I turned to Maria. "You need to promise me something."

"What?"

"Never be alone with Wilkinson. You don't know him like I do. Whatever he told you out there, he's vicious. He preys on little girls. Steer clear of him. Do you hear me?"

She bounded across the space to stand in front of me. I kneeled to put us on eye level, just like Merry once did with me. His deference always made me feel like a grown-up.

Maria spread her fragile arms wide and nodded. "I hear you. Now please, can I sleep here tonight?"

My mind lit up like every stage light on Broadway had illuminated it. I winced at the blaze. Even though Maria and I were from totally different backgrounds, we had the same story. Maybe that was why I cared about these refugees so much. I knew what it was like to be lost in the world at nine and maybe never see the only parent I loved again. Who else would be their Merry if I didn't?

I wasn't going to find out. Wilkinson could recruit fighters someplace else.

In less than a minute, I hung my cot and left it rocking gently to retrieve Maria. Picking her up, I carried her, my arms a basket, and settled her onto my cot. "Promise me you'll stay here until I get back."

She snuggled under my thin coverlet and yawned, her tongue bright-pink in her bronze face. "Where're you going?"

"To talk to Sisa. I won't be long."

Her eyes were already closed by the time I zipped the tent flap. I sighed. I missed the witchery of being able to sleep through anything.

Dazed, I staggered through the clearing. Darkness settled into the jungle's crevices and unleashed a thunderous riot of noise. I was convinced the Mosquitia at night was louder than Times Square at its busiest. Thousands of alien, primal cries from unidentified creatures hammered my eardrums and almost banished every thought.

I halted my sludgy boots in front of a ten-by-ten sheath of plastic and netting, just like mine. "Sisa?" I shouted over the melee. "Can I come in?"

She unzipped the flap and motioned for me to enter. "Sure, but be quick." She was already pulling me through by the arm. In one deft move, she zipped us into her sanctuary, a stark space decorated by a lone hammock and a battery-powered lamp. She thrust her bare hands into the pockets of her canvas cargo pants, leaving her shaved head the only skin exposed. "Sorry to hurry you, but the sand flies are always stirred up and famished after a storm."

I swatted one away from my clammy neck. "Did we have enough extra netting for everyone in camp?"

"Yeah." She moved toward her hammock and pulled a bundle from its depths. Throwing it my way, she said, "I saved some net for you."

I caught it and tucked its scratchy bulk under one arm. Trying to doze off while shrouded in the stuff was like sleeping under sandpaper, but it was better than my blood being sucked dry. "Thanks for taking care of me."

She closed the couple of feet that separated us and put her palms on my shoulders. Sisa could erect three tents in the time it took me to raise one. Whenever anyone in camp needed something done fast, they turned to her. Her hands bore the brunt of her body's machinery. I felt her calluses through my shirt when she pressed. "It's my job, but besides that, you're my friend. I always try to take care of you. So, tell me. What's the matter?"

I shrugged away and turned to avoid her questioning stare. The rippling walls of the tent closed in on me. I came to Sisa to talk through Wilkinson's admission about the fate of our refugees, but I wasn't sure where she stood.

Sisa stepped in front of me. "Emmaline, I know you. You can trust me. We haven't had time to talk about it, but I've been watching you this week. You're freaked out about what happened during Hurricane Paine."

My spine pressed against the inside of my skin like a metal rod. "What do you mean?"

"You know, with Wilkinson."

The overheated space tilted. I staggered backward, my steps sloshing across the floor. "You know him, too?"

"Of course. As a senior leader of Abroad Together, I have to meet every new person the U.S. government sends down here."

I clutched my throat and swallowed a choking knot of confusion and fear. "How long has he been here?"

Sisa covered her pert mouth with one hand. "You're acting like a paranoid freak. He arrived a few weeks ago, but I haven't seen him much."

"And you like him?"

"He's in the chain of uniforms who decide what happens to us, so I try to play nice, but no, I don't really like him. I'm really pissed about all the good people he's sending across the border to fight. They braved the Mosquitia to escape that life. Most of them don't want to go back."

My legs buckled. Sisa grabbed my arm and stopped me from becoming a puddle on the tarp floor. I leaned into her, grateful to have made at least one friend in this wilderness. Because I wasn't sure I could count on Trece, not with Wilkinson in the scene.

"So you're fighting him, too?"

"As much as I can. Don't worry, Emmaline. I'm on your side."

"Thank you," I whispered and let myself out.

Back in my tent, Maria's soprano snore posed stiff competition for the jungle chorus. All three feet of her were stretched sideways across my cot. I didn't have the heart to move her. Plus, I was too wired to rest.

I trudged across my tented cage, trying not to wake her with my splashy tread, and knelt in front of my foot locker. Being metal, it kept my things mostly dry.

Rummaging through t-shirts and stiff cargo pants, I found the book rolled up in some socks in the back corner. Wiping off the dusty leather, I stuck it to my nose. "Merry. Your journal still smells like you."

God, how I missed his haunting blue eyes and his steady view of the world. Losing him hurt almost as much as losing my father.

I still looked for him. Every day. A few times, I thought I sensed him behind my dad's unwavering scrutiny, but that was so much stupid childishness. They were both gone, leaving me with a grief like the ocean. It pummeled me in unpredictable waves. Every time I thought I'd licked it, dark madness drowned me again and again.

I undid the leather ties and opened Merry's book. Blank pages were marbled like parchment. They crackled a little when I turned them, in spite of the dampness. Merry wrote in it all the time when we were together on the Natchez Trace. I never understood why it was blank when I found it, but by then he wasn't around to ask.

Droplets splotched paper. And just like that, I was crying again.

For years I kept the blank journal in my nightstand drawer. I'd pull it out and thumb through it with a flashlight, imagining all our Trace adventures written there. To me, his journal was never empty. Whenever I studied its pages, I saw the story of Merry and me.

I grabbed a blue Bic pen from the spine and pressed the book open at its blank first page. A hopeless sob choked through my cracked lips, but when I pressed pen against paper, I couldn't make it follow the arc of my thoughts. Besides, to whom was I even writing? Merry was as gone as my dad. I couldn't summon either of them by writing in a stupid book.

The pen cracked, and ink bloomed across the page. Defeated, I dropped the pen and whispered through clenched teeth. "I wish somebody could tell me what to do about Wilkinson and his treatment of human beings."

EMMALINE

Trece stuck his head through my tent flap a few minutes after midnight. His vivid eyes burned into mine. I shifted Maria's sweaty weight from my chest and crept across the floor. Imagining my hands full of rocks kept them heavy enough to avoid slapping him. Still, my elevated whisper conveyed my pique. "You've been gone all week. Did you and Wilkinson send a gaggle of innocent humans to their deaths?"

He pushed into the stifling space, zipped the flap closed, and switched on a small flashlight. Ghost-like shadows danced along the walls of our waterproof shroud. His mouth pumped like my pet goldfish. Open. Shut. Repeat. Only I couldn't flush him down the toilet like he was dead to me.

His fingertips trembled near my cheek. I wanted to lean into it, to let him touch me, but it was like Wilkinson physically stood between us. A few loud heartbeats pounded in my ears, nervousness I hoped Trece couldn't detect. Finally, he sighed and dropped his hand to his side. He ran nimble digits through his thick hair, and I imagined what they'd feel like clutching me. Reddening, I turned skyward and studied the ghostly ripples on the tent ceiling.

His voice extinguished my fire. "I—I should've told you about Wilkinson and the refugees, Cagney, but he ordered me not to."

"Of course he did. All the better to figure out how to turn me into what he craves."

"Look, I don't know what went down between you two when you were a kid, but he's in charge here now. Defy him, and I promise, he'll send you home. Think of all the refugees you're still helping reach America."

"I want them all to make it."

Trece took a couple of steps back. "You're too idealistic. Maybe some of them want to fight for the Contra cause. Why can't you settle for helping the ones you can, and let the rest of them make up their own minds?"

I stalked to the tent flap and tugged at the zipper. "Get out."

"Wait, Cagney. I didn't mean—"

"Look, I didn't defer college and give a year of my life to lie to everyone who staggers into our camp. I meet every single person who makes it this far, and nobody wants to go back. It's like they fled one kind of slavery only to be forced into another untenable situation. That's not what we promise, and Wilkinson can go to hell."

"Stop it. You're going to wake Maria."

Maria stretched and spun sideways on my cot. Its frame creaked, but she didn't wake. Her sleep-clogged voice muttered dreamy gibberish until she stilled. I wheeled on Trece. "You need to go. We can talk about this in the morning."

"No." He took one step toward me, his breath heated and fast, desire a living thing between us in the box-like space. How could I know he worked with Wilkinson, yet still want him? And even though he just said I was being hysterical, I could tell he wanted me, too. When he licked his lips, his pupils dilated, and I longed to smother them with mine. Teenagers are seriously screwed up sometimes.

He broke eye contact and took a step backward, and I was certain a frigid wind blew through the space. My wanting shriveled when he said, "You've got some decisions to make come sunup. Look at this." With a snap of his wrist, he pulled a rolled-up tube of papers from the back pocket of his cargo pants and waved it toward me. Gold glimmered from a seal near the bottom corner of the first page. *Property of the United States*

Government, it read.

I grabbed the whole stack and moved closer to the flashlight in his other hand. He ground his teeth when I brushed his fingers, but I was too transfixed by the ordered words to be dragged off-kilter again.

"I finally got through to somebody on the sat-phone and requested this dossier. Roads are open enough now. It came earlier today. Wilkinson's the read deal, Cagney. You've got to do what he says whether you like it or not. It's all in there."

I thumbed through the pages, certified details of Wilkinson's mission in Central America. Black redactions littered whole paragraphs in places, but I could read enough to get the gist. On the next sheet, his hangdog face crowned the neck of his uniform. The following page contained a letter of introduction in both English and Spanish signed by President Reagan. The story unfolded like a spy novel, outlining Wilkinson's charge to overthrow the Sandinistas and help an American-trained Contra force set up a new government in Nicaragua.

When I was finished with every salacious sentence, I fanned his face with the traitorous heap. "Anybody can forge this stuff. These papers prove nothing. Wilkinson's the villain, whether you believe me or not."

Trece snatched the pages from me, flipped through them, and pointed to a string of numbers under the President's signature. "See that? Those numbers right there?"

I squinted. "So?"

"That's the authentication code for these documents. CIA can verify them. Let's fire up the sat-phone and call the CIA base in Catacamas. They can tell you these orders are real."

He grabbed my arm and tugged me toward the exit, but I hit him with my other hand and wrenched myself free. "It's almost two o'clock in the morning, Trece. I'm not calling anyone now."

"Not even if it means protecting these refugees?" He waved toward Maria. "Even her, from a man you claim is a monster?"

I folded my arms across my chest and dug in. "Where'd you get that file?"

"I requested it from the CIA base in Catacamas."

"So, he didn't give this stuff to you?"

Trece shook his head. "No. I got it directly from the person I trust most over there, and I spent part of this afternoon triple-checking everything myself. You may not like Wilkinson, but he's legit. I promise he's on our side. He was stalking that trio of thugs through the Mosquitia when they ambushed us. They've been raiding refugee camps and sending people back to certain death in Nicaragua." He ran a torn fingernail over the authentication code. "Call them in the morning. Relay this number. Somebody in Catacamas will verify all this."

I shrank into myself and cleared my throat. "What about —what about the stuff he did to me when I was little?"

Trece rested a hand on my right shoulder and squeezed. "Cagney, look. I'm really sorry those things happened to you. I can't imagine how afraid you must've been. But you heard his explanation. Now that you have the whole story, does your past look a bit different to you?"

His palm burned through my thin t-shirt. When I raised my eyes to his, I wanted to believe him, to accept his explanation, to fold myself into the refuge of his embrace and rest.

But I couldn't, not as long as I was in charge of a camp filled with human beings Wilkinson would flippantly send to their deaths. I survived what he did to me as a child, but they might not make it through the life he forced on them.

"No. I lived every bit of the torment Wilkinson caused, and I refuse to let him ruin anyone else."

I shrugged away from him and leaned over the cot to adjust Maria's coverlet and smooth locks from a damp cheek.

Turning back to Trece, I murmured, "Did you find the other soldiers who ambushed us during the hurricane? They were wounded."

His eyes stayed locked on mine. "Yeah. Took a couple of days, but when we found them, they were dead. Wilkinson and I stripped them of any identifying markers and buried them. He took their gear to Catacamas to see if we can use it to ID them."

"Show me."

He blinked. "Huh?"

"In the morning. Show me where you buried them."

"Come on, Cagney. We buried them several days ago. I mean, you know these parts. Five yards in, it all looks the same. I'm not sure I can find the graves, and besides, the ground's so saturated. We slopped out what we could and covered the rest over with storm debris. Given how much of that there is at the moment, I couldn't begin to locate them now." He took a step toward me, his eyes teasing. "I can think of plenty of other things I'd rather do."

I shifted Maria on the cot, sat on the edge, and crawled in underneath her. Pulling up the coverlet, I closed my eyes to blot out his advances and spoke through gritted teeth. "Sunup, Trece. Meet me here and lead me to their graves. I want to see them. I don't care if it takes all day and we have to carve up half the Mosquitia to find them."

When I heard the zipper snick open and closed, I allowed myself to breathe. Sure, I could verify some of his story via the CIA agents in Catacamas, but seeing the graves would answer my biggest question. Did Trece really comb the jungles for those other two invaders? Did he and Wilkinson bury them? Or did they spend almost twelve hours on some other quest? Making an official-looking cache of papers testifying to Wilkinson's legitimacy, perhaps? Coaching the person who answered my call with all the right stories?

Maria's stringy mop tickled my chin. I reached a hand under my pillow and pulled out Merry's journal. The leather was cool and smooth beneath my fingertips. "I'm being paranoid. Right, Merry?" I opened the book to the first page and ran my thumb over the dried blotch of blue ink. "I wish you could tell me what you'd do. Maybe give me a sign." I thwacked the pages shut and put the journal back under my pillow. Settling in next to Maria, I scolded myself in a slight whisper. "Idiot. Nobody can hear you."

Vegetation throbbed beyond the wall of my tent. I fell into a weary, restless sleep, one where Wilkinson leered behind a vanishing body cleaved in two by lightning—or a bullet from my gun.

WILKINSON

"You can't tell me you don't remember where you buried those soldiers, Trece." Emmaline crashed through living walls of green and stomped into camp, her blonde tresses a frizzy aurora in the wet heat. She rounded on Trece as soon as he emerged from the overgrowth behind her, meaning she didn't see me standing in the mess tent and sipping hot cinnamon tea.

I've always enjoyed a good show. My fingers twitched to light a cigar, but the smoke would be a scent beacon for someone like Emmaline.

Trece glanced in my direction, snapped his spine taller, and rained righteous indignation her way. "Look. I told you the ground was more water than sludge. We dug out what we could and covered the rest with branches and leaves. For all I know, animals dragged them off as soon as we walked away. It's not like there aren't plenty of them out there."

"But you didn't even point out a general spot." Anger burned from the tips of her fingers. I expected her to shape it into a flaming ball of fury and hurl it at the poor guy. The air sizzled and sparked between them.

Interesting.

A couple of male refugees sauntered in their direction, their government-issue fatigues still pristine. The one on the right rolled up a sleeve and flashed a stained dressing. His Spanish was refined. "Does the medical clinic still open after lunch?"

Emmaline's face morphed from the planes and angles of rage to soft concern. She took the man's arm and studied the bandages. "That must itch. Head over there now. I'll be there in a minute or two."

With a stubborn tilt to her head, she watched both men shamble across the clearing to the tent with a red cross on the flap, unzip the opening, and vanish inside. As she pivoted on her heel to resume her argument with Trece, her eye snared mine. Abandoning Trece, she wasted no time closing the space between us.

Her grime-soaked arms fanned like ungovernable propellers. "I want you to leave, Wilkinson. Now."

A couple of female refugees picked up their lunch sacks and fled the mess tent. Emmaline sported a toughness that commanded respect. Oh, I saw glimpses of her power when she was a child, but her charges knew not to cross her. She'd matured into an assured leader, charismatic and captivating.

Trece stepped between her and me, holding back our reckoning with a firm hand on her shoulder. "We called Catacamas this morning. What did they tell us, Cagney? About Wilkinson?"

"He's a real government agent, but I'm not stupid. I've read plenty of spy novels. Anybody can plant a decoy at the other end of a fake number." The high-flying kite of her fury wobbled a little, though. Her arms slowed their whirring, and she no longer threatened to lunge at me. Instead, she turned her energy inward. She ticked like an unexploded land mine.

I stepped around Trece but kept my distance. No need to loom over her, right? "Look, Emmaline. I know seeing me here is a shock. I never expected to run into you again, you know. But I was reassigned. Another continent. A new mission. That's the CIA life."

Trece whistled. "Is her story true?"

She took a step backward and rolled her eyes. "Of course it's true. Only I wish you'd believed it when I told you."

I pushed Trece out of the mess tent. "Leave us be." He nodded and raced in the other direction while I stepped back inside, unholstered my pistol, and handed it to her. I spread my arms wide and threw my head back. "Go ahead. Shoot me. If you're determined to stop me from carrying out the directives of the United States government regarding these refugees, then pull the damn trigger and rid the world of me for good. In your mind, I'm sure I deserve it."

Water dripped from the trees and plonked on the canvas roof. Beyond the camp, jaguars and toucans and tapirs vied for screeching supremacy. I tried to record it all at once, every animal sound, every sticky sensation, every living scent. If I branded them into my brain, maybe something would be familiar when she blasted my last Nowhere life away and rendered me nameless, without a past, digging graves in a haunted cemetery in some rank patch of globe.

But how else could I get her to trust me?

Metal thunked onto the tarp-covered floor. Emmaline stood, hands on hips, her mouth agape. "Wouldn't it be convenient if I shot you? Easy way to get rid of the person who will give her life to make sure you don't send another person back to Nicaragua against their will."

Ignoring my pistol, I put one hand over my heart. "Look, I wish I could save all of them, but I have my orders. Cross me, and I'll make sure you're assigned someplace where you can't interfere."

Emmaline's eyes went wide. "I can't abandon the refugees here. They're—they're my only family now."

"What about your father?"

Her chin trembled. "He's dead."

I hung back and waited for her to enlighten me about her father's demise, because I wasn't the most empathetic character.

When she offered nothing else, I waited a breath and whispered, "I'm sorry."

She gave a slight nod, her chin a notch more defiant. "I give to these refugees because my father invested so much in me. Whenever I find myself stewing in self-pity, even if I've earned the right to some depression, even when men like you plunge me into my darkest hours, depriving me of more time I could have had with Dad, all I have to do is think about them. These people left persecution and agony behind in Nicaragua, just like I left you at the Parthenon. We're all refugees here. The leavings bind us together. It's what makes us family, and you'll never take that away from us." She turned on her heel and started toward the medical tent. After a couple of steps, she stopped and rotated to face me. "I don't expect somebody like you to get it, because you don't have a soul. Clearly, given what you're willing to do here. Now, excuse me while I go and do my job."

"To take care of the guy with the busted arm?"

"Yeah. He's been dealt more hell than you put me through. You're part of the evil these refugees face."

"The world is packed with folks who are worse than I am."

She bit her lip and stuttered. "Who—who knows what you might've done to me? But it doesn't matter. I got away from you. Nine years with my dad was my reward for surviving you." She waved her right hand in the direction of the medical tent. "But that man? Life didn't give him a medal. His arm was slashed from elbow to hand in a Sandinista raid. The Sandinistas murdered his baby daughter. They held him at gunpoint, and he watched them pick her up by her feet and smash her downy skull into a wall. They killed his wife, his other children. Thinking they hit an artery when they sliced his arm open, they left him to bleed out. He escaped, but I don't think he's relieved to be alive, because he lost every human being he adored. They were slaughtered right in front of him. I can't believe you'd send him back."

She fired with the idealistic gasoline of most teens, but I didn't make the mistake of pointing that out. Besides, she was right about Sandinista brutality. I'd witnessed it myself in my brief sojourn. Pyres made of bodies. The stench of burned flesh filling the nostrils for miles. Torture victims with leg bones splintered like wet spaghetti. Sure, I'd inflicted suffering in my time, but even I was doubled over by some of the sights I encountered in Central America. The Sandinistas were depraved fuckers, and I knew a thing or several about depravity.

God, I longed for a stogie.

Not wanting to spook her, I stood my ground and cleared my throat.

"That's why we're fighting the Communists. We can't let their brutality spread across this hemisphere. How'd he escape?"

"Somehow, he hung on until the Contras overran the place and ferried the survivors to the border."

I held open my empty palms. "Look. I can't make you forget my contribution to screwing up your childhood. Hell, in your shoes, I don't think I could set it aside. But we both have jobs to do in these jungles, and I fully intend to do mine."

"Fine. And I fully intend to stop you."

With that, she turned and hurried toward the medical tent. The steamy sunshine outlined her form like a full-body halo. I held my breath until she was out of sight.

On my way to my jeep, I bumped into Trece. He clicked his heels and mock-saluted. "She didn't murder you, I see."

"Not yet, anyway." I took a few steps and motioned for him to follow. He fell in behind me as I picked my way along the sloppy path to the gravel road. More than a week after the hurricane, I knew it'd still be an obstacle course all the way to Catacamas.

I took a cigar from my front pocket and snapped off its curved tip. "Listen, I've got an errand to run. It'll take me away from here for a couple of days. In the meantime, I've got an assignment for you."

Trece's charcoal eyes didn't flinch. "Sir?"

"If you notice any other unusual teams creeping around this part of the Mosquitia, use the satellite phone to alert Catacamas immediately. Tell them to find me wherever I am."

"Who do you think they are, sir? Because the last ones weren't Nicaraguan."

Flame licked the end of my cigar, and I swallowed a comforting puff of burnt tobacco. Blowing smoke through my nose, I said, "I think I know who they are. And if I'm right, this whole operation is fucked."

WILKINSON

"The President will be with you shortly, General Wilkinson."

One of the privileges of the CIA credential is hopping a flight back to the States at a moment's notice. Recent developments in Central America required a face-to-face with the man at the top. After the storm, I play-acted rooting around the herbage for a few hours with Trece, but we never found the other nameless soldiers, let alone buried their bodies, because Nowhere souls don't leave behind vessels to find. Our bodies vanish as we die.

I was certain the unit that attacked during the hurricane was part of Nowhere.

The one Emmaline shot suffered the most unusual Nowhere death I'd ever witnessed. The others probably disappeared into the void and went back to wherever they started. But Emmaline's bullet erased every pencil-drawn line of her victim.

What was with Emmaline's bullets?

Could I use her to eliminate these Nowhere enemies? Because they were prowling to stop me from sending those damn refugees to their deaths. I was sure of it, and I didn't understand why anyone cared about a bunch of indigent brown people from a shit hole country like Nicaragua. If they died, so what?

It was just the sort of logic a bleeding-heart woman would apply to a situation, and not only Emmaline Cagney. If I was correct, I faced an even greater Nowhere foe. Theodosia Burr was a hellcat when I was alive, yes, but she also found me here. I'd never forget how she ruined the one dream of my life.

I didn't tell Trece, but she was with the Nowhere team we slaughtered. I was tracking her right before her unit attacked, but she melted into the bramble before I could corner her. She'd probably torment me on the other side if I failed this mission. She was the picture of vengeance, her lava-like eyes lit with volcanic fury.

I could finally be rid of her. Emmaline and her toxic ammunition could give me an edge. I had to figure out how to win the girl over, which meant tolerating her do-gooding for a bit.

I sighed and tapped my boot on the parquet outside another President's office. Not the famed Oval Office, where discussions were always on the record. The President never met secret operatives there. No, he excused himself to take a leak, the only place he ever found some privacy. His holy of holies existed on the other side of his urinal, a windowless closet he accessed with a second flush.

Where every other space crawled with secretaries and interns and suits brokering their pathways to power, this room housed one person: a geriatric receptionist. He scanned my fingerprints through a machine on his desk. When it beeped, he pointed to a chair. "Have a seat. You're clear."

I settled into the plush upholstery, so different from my other White House outings. Meeting presidents was a big part of my life when I was living, but by 1986, I found myself a few notches up the grandeur chain. The White House was nothing like the humble building of my day. And before that, I met George Washington in makeshift tents and hovels. I avoided stick-up-his-ass Adams as much as I could.

Jefferson and I understood each other. We usually held our Monticello confabs over a few bottles of French wine he brought up from his exquisite cellar. I always marveled at the dumbwaiter he designed. And his cigars were a veritable orgy of sensation.

Madison, on the other hand, he was a pedant, always pushing me to color in every box when a couple of shades should have given him the total picture. God, I lost weeks of hours helping him understand military machinations and native relations on the old southwestern frontier without spelling out anything that might incriminate me.

And Monroe. I probably loved Monroe best.

He sent me to Mexico. I posed as a representative of the American Bible Society. Me, a man of the cloth. What a load of bullshit. It's the reason I don't believe in God; he would've struck me dead for that ruse. Besides, I was really there to carry out Monroe's wishes. He charged me to protect the interests of the United States and influence the burgeoning Mexican government to be favorable to us. The Mexicans wanted to break with Spain, and I fed them every piece of useful intel I had. Even made up a few tales to stoke the flame.

This life, crawling around insect-ridden, silt-clogged backwaters, well, it paled in comparison. Since my Gravedigger robbed me of so many Nowhere chances, I'd stuck to my somewhat vanilla mission. Sure, helping the Contras was illegal. Congress stood up to Reagan and passed laws forbidding it. He had the balls to cross a few lines, make a few deals, and someday show the world who was most powerful.

I hoped to be gone by then. Maybe this meeting with the President would release me from Nowhere. But could I stand to move on before I unlocked the mystery of Emmaline's gunfire and forced her to take aim at Theo? After toeing my Gravedigger's line for a couple of months, I'd earned a little extracurricular adventure. If I could convince her to use her bullets for me, Emmaline might make my time in Nowhere more, let's say, colorful.

The receptionist's sandpaper voice rousted me from my reverie. "Wilkinson, the President will see you now. Door's a little tricky. When you open it, don't be alarmed at how fast it sucks you through."

"Thanks for the warning, but I've been here before."

I stood and stepped forward. The door unsealed with a familiar whoosh.

It shut behind me before I had time to knock, and I was entombed in total darkness, the last place somebody who's been in an actual grave wants to be. After a few suffocating moments, I was greeted by the President's Hollywood smile and helmet of unnaturally brown mane.

"Jimmy. Always a pleasure." He indicated a wing-backed chair covered in federal blue velvet. "Have a seat. Would you like some coffee? A little tea?"

"Coffee please, sir." Even as I said it, I longed for the days when every national decision was made over madeira, whiskey, and cases of wine. When did Americans become so uptight and decide every pleasure was bad for them? I took my shitty coffee in its cream-and-red cup and saucer flecked with gold leaf.

Pretending to drink, I eyed the President over the rim of my cup. He had the gift of giving people his undivided attention and making humble gestures to put them at ease. Like making me coffee even if it was undrinkable. His thoughtfulness mattered. Everyone left his presence walking a little taller, drunk on their own importance. Garbage like that never used to work on me, but I appreciated it now.

He settled into a matching wing-backed chair across from me and took a handful of jellybeans from a cut crystal dish on the table beside him. As he put a yellow one in his mouth, he said, "Well, Jimmy. I didn't expect to see you so soon. Things swell with your southerly assignment?"

"Yes, sir. The Contras are gaining ground in every fight. We're systematically training more refugees from our bases in Honduras thanks to a capable Nicaraguan named Trece who joined us early. We've got another two thousand Contra soldiers coming online over the next two weeks, hard-fighting, capable men."

"I would've thought they'd be lazy or ill-equipped, given where they come from."

I leaned forward. I fought side-by-side with immigrants of many nationalities during the American Revolution. They were some of the ballsiest soldiers I ever had, willing to risk all for the dream of America. Of course, most of them were white. But I couldn't tell this President that.

Instead, I said, "No, sir. It takes guts to stand up to those who want to kill you."

"All down to you, Jimmy. All down to you."

I swallowed. Coffee nuked my esophagus and sat like acid in my stomach. My whole life, I played the good soldier when what I really wanted was a throne, a chance to rule my own dominion. Was it a trick of Nowhere to force me back into that stifling *good boy* box as my only means to succeed?

The President leaned forward. "Well, I'm sure you've been following the feeding frenzy in the press regarding the arms-for-hostages situation."

"You mean, selling weapons to Iran in exchange for the release of American hostages in Lebanon?"

"Yes."

I waved my hand like I was smashing a buzzing gnat. "Annoying reporters always need to have something to talk about, don't they? Even if they're fabricating their own dots to connect."

The President flashed his camera-loving grin. "One of the biggest burdens of a free press, Jimmy. As much as I'd like to muzzle them, I can't tell them what to say. Oh, but don't think I don't dream about wielding that kind of power. Every president does. Maybe someday, one will cross that line."

He paused and looked me in the eye for a long moment. I'd worked with enough men of his ilk to know he communicated a lot more with that look than he ever would with words. He was telling me he already pushed the boundaries of presidential power, and he wanted me to dig myself even deeper in something illegal.

I didn't flinch. Decent men and women sacrificed themselves for their countries all the time. Carnage isn't restricted to the battlefield. Nameless, faceless people like me carried out all sorts of risky covert operations to keep our country free. Sure, it meant assassination and adultery, theft and duplicity, but someone had to do wrong for the greater good. Hell, it was more satisfying than doing good for the greater good, at least to me.

I nodded slightly. "What's the money we're using to supply the

Contras?"

"Well, here's the thing. Until recently, liberal Democrats in Congress blocked all Contra funding. No matter how much proof we gave them about Soviet activity in Central America, the bleeding hearts wouldn't budge. They actually made it a crime for anyone in our government to help them. So, a small army of patriots got creative."

"Creative?"

"The Boland Amendment doesn't restrict what private citizens do for the Contras."

"Are you saying—"

"Strong, reliable men and women have been fundraising for the Contras for some time. I don't want to get into the details, because I'm not privy to them." He chuckled. "Well, I'm not supposed to be. But the Contras have their firepower. And interested parties are finding more weapons for them every day. But this arms-for-hostages thing is a smoking gun. The damn press and the liberals won't stop until they uncover the deeper players, and once they do, we're done in Nicaragua."

"What do you need me to do, sir?"

He opened his jacket, removed a cassette tape from his interior pocket, and placed it on the table between us. "I'm sure you know what that is."

"It's a tape containing instructions for what's left of my mission."

"Take good notes. You can only listen to it once before it self-destructs." He laughed. "Pardon an old Hollywood actor his ridiculous celluloid *cliché*."

I picked up the tape and flicked it between my fingers. "I didn't hear anything ridiculous, sir."

"I've got faith in you. America needs to rid itself of the Soviet threat in our hemisphere. Our friends across the aisle aren't privy to our classified communiques, and, well, they always think I'm overreacting when it comes to the Russians. Believe me, Jimmy. I'm not. The American people deserve to go to sleep at night in a shining city on a hill. And I intend to guarantee them that safety and security for as long as I can. We've got to finish this Nicaragua thing. I need you to marshal all the firepower we've got down there and make it happen."

"How long do I have?"

"A month. Forty-five days at most."

He stood and offered me his steady hand. The man had a warm handshake: perfect pressure on the palm with a hand on my other elbow. Were I prone to idolizing world leaders, I would've worshipped him a little.

Back in the limousine, I settled in behind the blacked-out, bulletproof windows, breathed in the decadent scents of cedar and leather, and poured myself a real drink from the bar. As I swirled scotch and ice in my lowball glass, I contemplated the cassette tape on the seat beside me. Plastic teeth would spit out an abbreviated spool of words and phrases. The President handed me a roadmap for my ultimate redemption. I was a short-timer in Nowhere. All I had to do was follow directions, amass the biggest Contra army I could.

But Emmaline's hidden talents dogged me. She might be the key to stopping anyone who stood in my way or threatened my mission. If I couldn't win her to my side, I could always order her to fire a shot, right?

EMMALINE

Sisa nudged my leg just before the sun sent a few pathetic rays through gaps in the impenetrable rain forest foliage. Though I was usually up and moving before sunrise, on that morning I was still on my cot. I rolled onto my back and squinted up at her. She beamed a little when she spoke. "I'm going on another clean-up run through the jungle. Want to come?"

After several restless nights wondering how to stop Wilkinson from sending innocent people to die, worrying whether I was safe with him in close proximity, and rehashing how lightning or my gunfire caused a weird death I couldn't much recall, I wasn't in the mood for exercise. An hour of unconsciousness sounded better. I nestled under my paper-thin blanket. "Why bother clearing trails, Sisa? The jungle grows faster than we can bat it back."

She kicked the foot of my cot. "It's been over two weeks since Hurricane Paine. Somebody's got to get this area fully functional again. Trece's checking out another trail we use to ferry refugees from the border, but you and I need to clean up a couple of others. We've got to have every option open for some refugee movement later this week. Come on. Let's go."

I sat upright and shrugged into a sweltering long-sleeved shirt. It had to be made of the same fabric as those shiny foil suits I saw on television, contraptions designed to cook the fat from overweight frames. I couldn't fathom anyone buying them, let alone spending weeks in the Mosquitia sheathed in an equivalent.

But we had to keep our skin covered if we wanted to avoid being one walking, talking insect bite. The sand flies were especially menacing. One nick of their fangs could insert a flesh-eating parasite into my blood. Once it spread, parasites could gnaw my face off from the inside. Nobody had a cure. Hence, suffocating in too-warm clothes was a better option.

"I can go for an hour or two, but I've got to file a full aid order by the end of the day. We're running low on some key medical supplies. Catacamas headquarters is expecting it."

"You can do that later. Meet me outside in three minutes. I'm not asking, Emmaline."

She ducked through the flap while I forced my sleep-addled locks into a ponytail, pulled on pants and boots, and trooped into watery sunshine.

The camp was already abuzz with life. Lights burned in the mess tent, and a couple of burly refugees exercised on a raised platform near the perimeter. I wobbled a little, still groggy from a confusing sleep, but Sisa tugged my sleeve and steered me into the rain forest.

"We're checking a trail, remember? This way."

She ducked under a low-hanging vine and held it up for me to pass underneath. With her lean limbs, she hacked at leaves and branches that clogged our way, kicking the cuttings toward the sides of the waterlogged path. Overhead, the foliage was a living roof too thick for a shaft of sunlight to penetrate. In the murk, I unsheathed my machete and attacked another clump of wreckage. The soft ground sucked at my boots, but I stayed upright. Sisa's breathing was effortless, even when the air held enough overheated water to boil us alive. She never complained. Somehow, she made it okay to be silent together, a quality I valued.

Unlike Sisa, I tended to fill every void with chatter. Merry taught me the importance of being still, assessing a situation, and waiting to share my opinion, but I always grappled with impatience.

Like almost writing him a message in his journal the other night. I broke the pen and now I've ruined the one thing I have of his. I really wish he could help me. I miss him so much.

Within thirty minutes, soaked with perspiration, we cut our way into a small clearing. My eyes burned against the harsh light. Limbs and dead debris littered the sloppy ground. Overhead, the sky was a yawning strip of blue. With the humidity, it resembled an inverted lap pool hovering above us.

Sisa pulled up and touched my upper arm. "I've been doing some poking around."

I leaned over and gripped my knees, panting. "When are you not being nosy? Seriously, why do you think I talk to you? You've got the goods on everybody within striking distance of this camp."

"And you couldn't do your job without my insights." She scratched her buzzed scalp and beamed. "Admit it. I'm not just your supervisor. I'm also your indispensable friend."

"All right. You are." I rubbed my side. "So why did you haul me away from camp?"

She studied her mire-caked boots. "Because obviously, we couldn't have this conversation around eavesdroppers. I don't trust everybody there, not given what happened the other day. You know, during the hurricane."

"You mean when Wilkinson appeared?"

Sisa stepped closer to me, put her mouth close to my ear, and shielded it with her hand, like she thought the surrounding flora teemed with lip-reading witnesses. When she spoke, her voice was almost swallowed by competing bird twitters and monkey calls. I moved my head closer to her mouth. Her breath tickled my ear. "Whatever proof he gave you, don't believe Trece. This Wilkinson guy? He's dirty."

I staggered backward and chewed my lip. "You think I don't know that? He's treating these defenseless refugees like animals."

"Hey, I don't know about that. Many of them want to go back."

"Nobody I process tells me that."

"Well, maybe this information'll fire you up. The proof Trece gave you, the phone call and dossier and stuff, it's all fake."

"How do you know that?" I squeezed her arm. "Tell me."

"Ow! You don't have to be rough, Emmaline."

"This matters! If you have something that can get Wilkinson out of our lives, hand it over. Now."

"Let go of me, and I'll tell you what I know. Only once it's out there, I won't be able to take it back. And you're going to have to figure out how to use it without incriminating me. Okay?"

"Agreed. Spill."

Her breath mingled with mine for a bit before I released her. She sloshed sideways through soupy mini-lakes of sludge and stopped. Hands on narrow hips, she glanced heavenward. "The team leaders of Abroad Together get different briefings. I'm not saying you're not informed about what's happening between here and the Nicaraguan border. Not at all."

I rolled my eyes. "Because clearly I haven't been in the loop. I mean, seriously? Sending these people back there is a death sentence. We might as well line them up and shoot them by firing squad."

"You think I don't know that? I'm in charge of the units who ferry refugees through these overgrown mazes. I've got a more complete picture of Sandinista capabilities. Who the players are. Where guerrilla bands are most likely to pop up. Their estimated firepower. Bottom line: a lot more is happening here than you realize."

"You mean, you think it's okay to send them back to fight against their will."

"I never said that, Emmaline. But you don't have the full picture. You only know what's necessary to keep the refugees who want to go to America safe. That's your job. You were given very basic training in whatever military tactics you might need to protect your charges. Nobody briefed you on the entire Honduran operation because you only deal with the needs of your specific camp. You're small picture. I'm big. See?"

I took a step toward her. "So, if you're privy to the big picture, tell me. What's Wilkinson's larger role in this tragic little play?"

"I'm not sure. I did some digging, tried to find out where he came from, but he was assigned to Central America from who-knows-where."

66

"How long has he been here?"

"All total? A few months maybe. The Contras are making real inroads in Nicaragua, and the Americans are determined to see them succeed. Hence, the recruiting and training of refugees. They've been sending more military types this way for a while. Wilkinson is near the top. I heard he reports directly to the U.S. President."

"But Congress forbade the President from authorizing or supporting military action down here. I mean, during my training, I was told to ignore covert operations, keep my questions to myself, you know, focus on the refugees. I wasn't prepared to occupy a war zone. I thought that was all happening across the border in Nicaragua."

Sisa shrugged. "The Contras train in the Mosquitia, on our side of the line. They're outfitted with every military toy imaginable, even some I honestly never imagined, weapons bought from a short list of countries and funded by American money."

"I still don't understand how this makes Wilkinson a phony."

"I didn't say his role wasn't real. But the information Trece gave you to legitimize him is fiction. All agents like Wilkinson get an official-looking file, always fabricated, when they land in a new place, in case anyone questions or threatens them. Someone like you, perhaps."

I thought about the way Trece's eyes devoured me sometimes. As much as I wanted our heat to be real, he could be using attraction to mess with my head.

Lost in my interior world, I stepped away from Sisa and took a couple of steps along the clearing's perimeter. My gut told me the whole sheaf of Wilkinson's documents was convenient. Sisa wasn't telling me anything I didn't already suspect. And little Maria insisted Wilkinson was okay, but what could a child know about him?

She was right about one thing, though. Something shifted in me when Wilkinson dared me to shoot him. But I couldn't risk killing a government agent. I'd be sent home, and nobody would be here to stand up for the imperiled. No matter how much I wanted to be rid of him, I couldn't strike until I could prove he was lying.

I turned back to Sisa. "He's not on our team, Sisa. You know that." Water tumbled from broad leaves and joined the pool at my feet. The stench of wet decomposition made me lightheaded. A rain forest stank like no other place on this planet. More stuff to die. Harder to kill.

She shrugged. "Most likely, he's in this for himself."

"A mercenary?"

"Maybe. I can't give you anything to prove he's not with the CIA, but I know the stuff Trece gave you is fake. That's all I'm saying." She closed the space between us and hooked an arm through one of mine. "I'm your friend, Emmaline. Do you want me to try to find out who Wilkinson really is?"

"I've already told you who he really is: first, he almost ruined my life. And now he's ravaging countless others."

Sisa stepped back like I slugged her. Her dark eyes flared. "This again? We can't exactly go to his superiors with that, Emmaline."

My cheeks flamed. "Why not?"

"I'm not saying I don't believe you. I mean, I don't know what happened when you were a kid. You have your story, and Wilkinson has his."

I stood toe-to-toe with her, my nose inches from hers. "And my story is the truth. I lived it. But I don't even matter. What he's making these helpless humans do is wrong."

She ran her hands across her scalp and sighed.

"Look, Emmaline, I'm sorry, but if they're willing to fight, it isn't wrong."

"You keep telling me you're my friend, but you don't know anything about me or my motivations. Wilkinson is the reason I care about the people here so much. Because of him, I know what it's like to flee my home, live on the run, wonder where my next meal will come from. I know why so many of these people want to get to America: because they don't want to die. They at least want a shot at a decent life for themselves and their children."

My voice cracked. I took a step back and blinked at the sky to keep from crying.

Sisa's breath caught. "I'm a jerk, okay? I didn't handle this well." She turned me to face her and held my upper arms while she talked. "I don't doubt anything you tell me about Wilkinson. If you say he did those things to you, he did them. Period. But if sending Nicaraguans back into a war zone is his job, then what are we actually accusing him of? We have to come up with actual evidence of something damning to show anyone in his chain of command. It'll be easier to dig into who he really is and find a fact or two we can use to destroy him, leaving you in peace to continue your ministry here. And that's the most important thing, okay? These refugees will make it to a better life because you're willing to fight for them."

I breathed. As my ribcage expanded, my ire fled. Sisa was right. It wasn't enough to watch the endless stream of horror on the nightly news, only to beam thoughts or prayers to those in need, not when I could feed them or hug them or give them back a little of what life stole. Actions spoke to one's intentions more than words or feelings ever could. I wanted others to see what I meant by what I did.

Sisa sighed and wiped her heart-shaped face with her sleeve. "I'm risking a lot to poke around this Wilkinson thing, but that's what friends do, right? I don't like how he showed up out of nowhere and started changing everything."

"What do you mean?"

"He made new rules for how we meet refugees at the border and how we ferry them to Honduran camps. He sped up the timetables for training them to the point that they're hopelessly unprepared. It's like he knows the endgame, a stepped-up deadline, but he won't fill the rest of us in." She hugged me to her again, threading her arm through mine once more.

I'd only known Sisa a few months, but she was so much more solid and real than my friends from high school. I never followed trends or invested in what was popular. Sometimes, I went through the motions of caring about clothes and makeup and stupid stuff like that, but I couldn't wait to get out of high school and do something substantial. Sisa never wasted effort on anything superficial. In a short time, she had already taught me more about how to make a difference than any friends from my former life.

She nudged me. "And the whole raid during the storm? You should've seen Wilkinson's face when he glommed onto you. It was like he was watching the one true God unveiled three feet from him."

I leaned into her warm side and started guiding us back toward camp. "I'm still weirded out by that. I don't like him. Not one bit."

"But that whole spectacle means something in the bigger picture, Emmaline. If I were you, the next time you have a chance to shoot Wilkinson, you point your gun at him and deal with the consequences later."

"Yeah, and if he's a government agent I'm screwed."

She glanced skyward. "We'll have the truth soon. I promise."

Back at my tent, I was unsettled by Sisa's observations. I had the chance to get rid of Wilkinson in the mess tent, something I didn't tell her. And I passed. Why? Fear of punishment? A misplaced sense of patriotism? How many times did we Americans keep scumbags in positions of power because of fear? Fear of the unknown. Fear stoked by propaganda. Fear of change. Fear of truth.

I couldn't be afraid. Not when so many lives depended on me. I crawled onto my cot—trashed clothes, soiled boots, and all—and felt under my pillow. The worn leather of Merry's journal was a familiar friend. Having it with me was almost like sleeping a few feet from him on the Natchez Trace.

I rested the journal on my knees, grabbed a pen from a pouch in my trunk, and flipped to a fresh, unstained page. After chewing on the end of my pen, I touched its tip to blank parchment.

> *Dear Merry:*
>
> *I don't know where you are. I used to talk to you all the time, but you never answered. Don't get me wrong. I'm sure you're there. Somewhere.*
>
> *I need your help. Writing in your journal won't be like talking to you, but maybe it'll help me sort out my feelings.*
>
> *Wilkinson is here. He claims we're on the same side, but I'll never forget how much you hated him or how he threatened me. That's why, in the deepest part of me, I can't believe him*

when he says he's a patriot. But if I challenge him, I don't know what'll happen to me or to these people who depend on me. They're the ones who matter.

I wish you could tell me how to be more like you.

I've always been mad at you for leaving me. I dreamed you'd move in with my father and me and we'd be a family. I was a stupid nine-year-old then, but you could've kept in touch, maybe sent me a letter every once in a while. I don't know whether you're alive or dead. I need a sign from you. Anything. Give me anything to tell me I can do this.

Please.

I've always loved you, Merry.

Your Em

EMMALINE

A few days later, Maria stepped into my tent, her cheeks wet with tears. "You have to help him. Hurry."

"Help whom?" God, who was Wilkinson harassing now?

She tugged my hand and dragged me through the flap and toward the medical tent. When I stopped at the doorway, I doubled over and almost wretched. Trece was digging into his shredded side with a bloody pair of metal tongs. Perspiration dotted his upper lip and pasted his hair to his agonized forehead. Every time he probed deeper into himself, dark blood dribbled down one pant leg while he clenched his jaw in agony.

I pushed past Maria and felt my way into the space. "Go to the mess tent. Get Manuel to boil some water and bring it to me."

Maria hovered, still crying. "Will he be okay? You have to make him okay."

"No time. Go. Now."

I pushed her toward the door. With one pensive step backward, she was gone. Too many gruesome sights. I couldn't imagine the long-term impact on a nine-year-old.

The incessant clamor of the rain forest was no match for Trece's groaning. His eyes started to roll back in his head when I touched his blood-soaked side. All around him, the once-white sheets were slimy with gore.

He couldn't die. I wouldn't lose him.

Taking the tongs from his fingers, I cradled his neck and eased him onto his side. Just below his left ribs, the wound was tattered and meaty, like hamburger. I wasn't a doctor. While I was trained to handle basic scrapes and strains as part of volunteering, surgery was above my ability. If someone was seriously wounded, we radioed Catacamas for transport to the base infirmary.

But since the hurricane, helicopters and pilots were in short supply. With the cleanup still in progress, it might be days before one could peel off and head our way. Sensitive sites were given top priority. The roads to our camp were still clogged with debris. Refugee teams were almost finished with the main artery, a gravel-filled mud hole thirty miles long. I pitched with such backbreaking work where I could, because I was willing to do everything they did to keep them safe. Because of my work on the front lines, I knew I'd never get Trece to Catacamas overland before he bled to death.

Maria hurried into the tent with Manuel behind her. At only five feet, his boniness hid wiry strength. He'd only been in camp a week or so, but he'd already reorganized the mess tent and cooked regional dishes that filled the camp with the scent of memory, the flavor of home. While I didn't recognize much of what he prepared, roots and banana-like plantains and such, my charges lined up with plates as soon as the aroma snaked through camp.

Manuel set a pot of steaming water on the ground with a light thunk. "I boiled it as long as I dared. I can stay and try to keep him still while you work, but that's all I've got. I was a lawyer before the madness started."

"Then why do you want to go back and be a soldier?" I asked him.

He avoided my eyes. "I never said I did. Now, how are you going to work on Trece?"

I took in all the blood and knew I couldn't question Manuel further. Trece's life was in danger. Sighing, I barked, "I know as much about surgery as you do, meaning squat."

Maria tapped my leg. "What does that mean? Squat?"

Trece groaned and shifted on the blood-soaked table. "One bullet. So close. Almost—"

His head lolled back and his eyes closed. His body went limp when he fainted. Without overthinking, I plunged my hands in the scalding water and soaped them until I was satisfied. Maybe they weren't sterile, but they were bright pink and as clean as I could make them. Picking up the metal tongs, I plunged them into the pot, too, to kill as many germs as possible. Which probably wasn't many, but at least the tongs weren't gross with blood when I stood over Trece's wound.

"Manuel, hand me a pile of those sterilizing wipes and hold him in place. Since he's unconscious, he probably won't feel anything but he might roll off the table." I pointed to a metal bin filled with shrink-wrapped packs. One by one, Manuel tore them open and fed them to me. I mopped around the pulpy rim of Trece's wound until I made a filthy pile of used cloths. Manuel whistled and scraped the mess into a plastic waste bin. "Once you take care of the blood, it doesn't look so bad."

I surveyed what remained. The bullet taunted us from just beyond the meaty opening, silver and solid. When I inserted the tongs and prodded, it popped out in another shower of blood. Both Manuel and Maria stepped back to avoid the spray, but I didn't move fast enough. The front of my outfit resembled a Jackson Pollack painting, only fashioned with soil and blood instead of oils and acrylics.

With no time to think about what I was doing, I cleaned the wound with more wipes, sewed up the gash, and covered everything over with a sterile dressing. Thanking whatever providence kept Trece unconscious, I switched into command mode. "Manuel, move that cot over here and help me transfer him to a clean surface."

Glancing heavenward, I picked up a pair of scissors and cut through what remained of Trece's clothes. I tugged them to one side and blushed. I looked up, caught Manuel watching me, and reddened again, because of course, this wasn't the naked scenario I ever imagined for Trece and me.

Stepping aside, I said, "Manuel, can you, um, clean up what's left?"

He chuckled. "I'm sure this isn't your first *pene*." But he made quick work of wiping Trece's skin and covering his nether regions with a square of cloth to protect my innocence. Like I wouldn't have wet dreams about what he might do to me when he was whole, especially now that I knew the extent of it. I swallowed. He might not ever make it that far.

Between the two of us, we maneuvered Trece from table to cot with relative ease. I unfurled a clean sheet and covered him while Manuel sealed the bloody things in a trash bag and set to work scrubbing the table.

Trece's eyes fluttered open, and he fought to sit up. "Argh. My side."

I crouched beside him and brushed my lips along his temple. "Shh. I got the bullet out and sewed you up, but I think we'll need to radio Catacamas to have a real doctor look at that wound. Wouldn't want it to get infected."

His teeth chattered. "No time. Need to talk to Wilkinson. They're closing in on us."

"Who's closing in? The Sandinistas?" Was he hallucinating? I took his face in my hands to steady his gaze. His pupils were normal-sized.

His head lolled from my fingers and thrashed from side-to-side in clipped staccato. "Not them. The others. Wilkinson knows who I mean."

"Wilkinson? Who else did he strong-arm into this madness? Because I'm sure his enemies could fill out a whole army."

Trece's eyelids fluttered and closed. "Find Wilkinson. Tell him."

"Tell him what?"

But unconsciousness claimed Trece once more. I checked his pulse and tried not to think about entangling my fingers with his while I held his wrist. I still woke up from technicolor dreams where Trece did all sorts of sensual, delicious things to me. Oh, I was embarrassed when I recalled them upon waking, but in my fantasies, I moaned and screamed and throbbed with pleasure. If he ever really touched me, I feared I'd combust like a firework: showy and glittering and gone.

I mean, he had his allegiance to Wilkinson, but he was a capable, hardworking refugee who wanted to use this assignment to gain access to the American Dream. He told me as much before Wilkinson even appeared. In his shoes, I'd probably serve Satan himself if it meant a better life.

The only thing that stopped me from acting on my attraction was one cardinal rule: volunteers were not allowed to date. Like the forbidden wasn't sexy as hell. I thought about Trece even more.

I hated myself for this weakness. It reminded me too much of my mother. As a madam, she was able to prey on uncontrolled lust to get what she wanted. I dropped Trece's arm and slipped it under the thin sheet. I didn't want to be like my mother. Not even a little.

Standing, I pushed through the tent's opening to find Manuel and thank him for his help. The sun streaked in steamy vertical lines through the air. I could almost see the atmosphere dancing. A tapir caterwauled nearby, and clouds of insects shimmered in the light. With a quick glance down, I realized the error of going anywhere near the mess tent. I was still covered in blood.

Not very appetizing for anyone eating. With a quick pivot, I scurried toward my tent to scrub off and change. I was halfway there when burnt tobacco fouled the air behind me.

"How long were you going to wait to tell me about Trece? Instead, I had to find out he was shot from a child." Wilkinson's snarl slithered along my nerve endings. His voice still transformed me into a nine-year-old castaway.

I stood firm and turned to face him. He was in the same camouflage as the last time I saw him, his pistol gleaming from a holster by his hip. Why didn't I shoot him with it when he gave me the chance?

I swallowed a choking lump of fear and twisted my expression into a mask of nonchalance. "Don't other refugee camps have oodles of victims for you to convert to your puppet army? We're the smallest outpost. Why do you spend so much time here?"

"I've haven't shown my face here in over a week, and I've left your people alone. What more do you want from me? Now stop whining and tell me about Trece."

"I just finished sewing him up. How was I supposed to call you?"

"Wait. You removed the bullet? As in surgery?" His face softened. "That boy is our best refugee recruit. You endangered his life with your first-aid-kit level skills. He needs a doctor."

"Yeah. Well, he needed help, and I was the only person available."

He blew a trail of smoke and stepped toward me. "I managed the thirty miles from Catacamas in my jeep without a single flat, only to stroll into camp and find out everything's going to shit. But no matter. I'll turn right back around and take him to the infirmary myself. Get him checked out by the doctor there."

"Why do you care so much about Trece? What's he doing for you?"

Wilkinson chewed on the tip of his cigar and smiled. "What? You think I'm too riddled with rot to care about my subordinates?"

"I'll admit it's a facet of your character I haven't seen."

"Because you only see what you want. Good leaders care about their men and women."

"By denying their quests for the American Dream."

"Bullshit. Every single recruit will end up American citizens, including Trece. I told you. He's the best we've got. With his knowledge of this unfathomable labyrinth, he's led more terrorized humans from Nicaragua than anyone else on our team. Everybody admires Trece. He's a real hero, and he risks his life willingly, just like everyone else."

His speech was persuasive, but still. He was Wilkinson. I couldn't believe he'd ever let concern for others get in the way of achieving his messed-up goals.

I thought back to Trece, naked on a cot and desperate to see Wilkinson. He made up my mind. "Well, Trece told me to give you a message."

He flicked ash to the wet ground. "What's that?"

I leaned into him, close enough to see the tobacco stains along the edges of his front teeth. "Right before he passed out, he said to tell you they're closing in on us."

"That's correct. The damn Soviets are trying to get under every leaf and vine in these tropics, putting a lot of escapees in grave danger. Since you care about these brown skins so much, you want to know why I'm here?

To order you to clear out this camp and move everyone to Catacamas. I'm protecting them, see?"

I glanced around the area, making mental notes about what to pack up first. I hated Wilkinson, but if the refugees were endangered, I wouldn't argue over taking them to a more secure location.

One loose end remained. I threw my shoulders back and stood toe-to-toe with him. "You already know he wasn't talking about the Sandinistas. I made that mistake, too. He said 'Not them. The others. Wilkinson knows'. So what do you know that I don't?"

WILKINSON

Emmaline stood there, fists clenched at chin level and eyes aflame, and once again I equated her with my lost Ann, the love of my life. She might've been petite, but Ann once ran off a whole band of thieves from our Frankfurt, Kentucky homestead with nothing but a broom. Like Emmaline, Ann was bred a city girl, but she took to the frontier like an addict to his preferred vice. Whenever I faltered or one of my schemes failed, I carried on because of her obstinate belief in me. She never doubted my value, even on her deathbed.

"Find me again, Jimmy," she croaked, her chilled hand clinging to mine.

But as I took in the funnel cloud of emotions in front of me, I knew Emmaline was possessed of a spirit imbued with both passion and reason. People were too complex for their own good sometimes. I wished I could see inside her, discover the hidden ingredients in her unique cocktail.

Instead, I maintained eye contact while I breathed another lungful of burnt tobacco. Once my nostrils ejected a warm blanket of smoke, I retorted, "I could have you charged with disrespecting an officer of the United States government, but I'll cut you some slack."

She lowered her defenses an inch. "I don't like being kept in the dark."

"Oh, others might see it differently, especially with your belligerent attitude and backtalk. You don't have the right to demand answers from me." I took another drag and turned my head to let the muggy breeze carry the offending odor away from her.

In response, she stood there, her expression a mixture of defiance and uncertainty.

I decided to throw her a raft just to show her I wasn't the ogre she thought me to be. "Look, you're a teenage volunteer at the ass end of nowhere. I realize you may have matured a decade or more since you arrived. Giving to others'll do that to a person. But when it comes to who's lurking in this rain forest and how to vanquish them, you don't have a fucking clue. You're a civilian, an amateur, and female. You need to recognize your limitations, stay in your place, and do your job."

I expected her to cower a little. Women and even some men usually retreated when I smacked them with my General voice from the old days. But not Emmaline. She expanded, volatile and breathtaking, like a firecracker about to ignite.

Her voice was a low growl. "Insult me however you like, Wilkinson. I've already survived you once, remember? And I'm not an idiot. The Mosquitia is littered with Sandinistas and Americans, Soviets and Cubans, Contras and mercenaries of all sorts. I'm pretty sure you fall into the last category, but I'm trying to figure out who Trece meant by *the others*. Who's out there that I don't know about?"

"I think you covered every possibility."

"Look, you—you asshole. An unidentified unit attacked us during the hurricane. Nobody has uncovered anything about who they were or what they were after, at least, not that they've shared. And even weirder, I can't remember what happened to one of them. Do you? I mean, you were there."

My brain strained to replay the scene, but it was blank like every other time. It was almost like her gunfire coupled with lightning erased a few moments in time. But I wouldn't show her my confusion. Instead, I conceded with, "It was an unusual death."

"Unusual? Come on, Wilkinson. Tell me what you saw."

"I think you're being a bit melodramatic, Emmaline."

Swampy goo speckled my pant legs when she stomped her foot. "I don't care what you think of me. Especially since Trece was shot by a mystery unit this afternoon while canvassing the perimeter."

I forgot her insubordinate outburst and started across the clearing with her on my heels. "Where is he?"

"Not so fast, Wilkinson. I want answers. Are these others to whom he's referring the soldiers who showed up the day of the hurricane? The ones you and Trece were supposed to bury?"

Damn her nosy mind. I stopped fast enough to cause her to bump into me, lose her footing, and fall backwards into a particularly juicy bit of slop. Rather than offering her a hand, I let her struggle to stand and blew elaborate smoke rings in twos and threes to buy myself some time.

Emmaline Cagney was putting things together too fast. What would she do when she found out the entire unit was a Nowhere assault team looking to end my final Nowhere life, and she eliminated one of them, someone I was certain had been a mortal enemy of mine? It was the only possible conclusion. I still couldn't recall a name or a sex or recover anything in my wiped-clean memory, no matter how much I thought, how many phone calls I made or questions I asked. The person never existed. Everything was hazy, like I blew my own stale smoke in front of it. Did Emmaline's bullet erase them from history's timeline?

How could I test my theory?

I flung my cigar toward the trees and extended a hand to Emmaline. Helping her to her feet, I said, "You're perceptive, Emmaline. I'll give you that. But haven't you noticed how unconventional Trece is?"

A frown fluttered across her lips and up to her sunburned brow. "Unconventional?"

"While he spent most of his life in Nicaragua, he was born in one of the wildest parts of the Honduran Mosquitia."

"Like there are wilder parts than this?" She fanned a slime-encrusted arm around the unruly clearing.

"Yes. In some places, tree cover is thick enough to block all light. One can stand on the jungle floor at high noon and be convinced it's midnight."

"I've been to places like that." She nibbled her lower lip, unconcerned about her filthy appearance, a sign she cared more about Trece than she let on.

I bookmarked that observation and let my description settle before continuing. "Imagine spending part of your life in a place like that." I gestured to the perimeter of the camp and lowered my voice. "He's descended from the ancient ones."

"You mean the Maya?"

"No. Millions of inhabitants from divergent tribes populated this place until a few hundred years ago."

Confusion etched awkward planes in her face. She took a step back, hands on hips, a cauldron of fiery rage once again.

"Are you insane? Do you think I am? Because nobody, let alone millions of people, could exist in these rain forests for long. I mean, look at it. This vegetation is untamable. We can barely keep snakes and lizards and insects out of our tents. Every morning when I wake up, it's like the vegetation has reclaimed another ten feet of our clearing. The edges have grown in on us while we've been standing here. We're living in a perpetual Death Star trash compactor scene from *Star Wars*."

I scratched my head. "What?"

"Never mind. Anyway, keeping this place semi-habitable is a constant, wearying war against pests and glop and disease. How could an entire civilization choose to make this a life?"

"I don't know, but mysteriously they did. Trece is part of their remnant. If you'd quit ogling his pecs, you might learn something from him."

She reddened to her hairline but didn't protest. Gotcha, Emmaline. Something else I could use against her when necessary. Her posture no longer brimmed with vexation.

I pointed to her clothing. "You need to clean off that gunk. It's unsanitary. Go wash up and assemble the camp. I need this place packed up and ready to go within two hours."

Before she could spew more questions, I turned my back on her and marched toward the medical tent. Outside, Emmaline's little refugee child shadow played with two stick figures clothed in banana leaves. I stopped when her questioning eyes met mine.

"I told Emmaline you were a nice man."

I chuckled. "I'm sure she didn't want to hear that."

"But you tried to help me the day of the big wind. You've got goodness inside you somewhere."

Speechless, I nodded and stepped through the flap.

Trece dozed on a low cot near the back. As I navigated between sealed medical supplies stacked in neat rows, I marveled at how well they kept the place. Emmaline made sure every tool and supply, weapon and foodstuff, was ready to move at a moment's notice. So much like my Ann.

As I approached Trece's cot, he stirred and opened pain-ringed eyes. Gesturing toward his bandaged side, he groaned. "How'd you know I was shot?"

"I didn't. I came to move the camp. All hell's broken loose in Washington. Damn plane carrying Contra weapons was shot down in Nicaraguan airspace."

Trece rocked himself to sit and threw his bare legs over the cot's side. With a hitch in his breath, he muttered, "So? They lost a few weapons. America has plenty to spare."

"You don't understand. Congress didn't know about the CIA dealing arms to the Contras. For a few years, patriots have been raising private money and making filthy deals all over the globe to keep the Contras fortified. What they've done is heroic, but our liberal Congress'll cast it as treason."

"Why?"

"Because they passed a law forbidding the whole arrangement and we've been lying to Congress for much of this decade. That damn plane crash puts our whole mission in jeopardy."

Trece clutched his patched-up side and wobbled to stand. Fresh blood stained the bandage but stayed within its square. He swayed like a hobbled kapok, one of those mythic rain forest trees that takes a thousand years to mature. As he lurched sideways, I hooked his arms over one of mine and guided him to rest on the cot.

Squatting next to him, I put myself on his level. My voice low, I bent toward his ear. "We're both Nowhere men, Trece. We can level with each other, can't we?"

WILKINSON

"A downed plane full of weapons handed us a full-on crisis with the Contras. Sandinistas and drug runners are threatening our training camps all over this shit hole, and even worse, a specialized Nowhere team is prowling around this wilderness."

His eyes fluttered open. "Somebody from a Nowhere group shot me. They sported the same green-and-white patches on their left shoulders as the ones who disappeared the day of the hurricane."

"I anticipated as much, but I'll deal with the living first. Given everything that's happening, this area is getting too crowded. We don't need to add a bunch of dead refugees to the mix, killed on the wrong side of the border. I can't even imagine what the unhinged American media'd do with that story. We've got to clear this place today, Trece, and get everybody to Catacamas."

I stood behind him and supported his agonized move to sit. Tropical life mocked us, a chorus of whoops and cackles beyond the tent. Unnerved, I spat, "How did humans ever survive here?"

Trece guided one arm into a sleeve, then the other, oblivious to the noise. "You Europeans never understood us."

"I'm American."

"But you're descended from Europeans, no?"

I nodded. "If you call the British Isles Europe. My ancestors cropped up in England right after the Norman Conquest."

"And mine already thrived in these tropical swamps by then. We flourished until the Spanish invaded this hemisphere." His brown fingers fumbled with the buttons along the front of his shirt, but he fastened them in proper order and picked up a pair of pants. He gawped at them mystified, like he didn't know where they belonged. I yanked them from his hand and knelt at his feet to guide his legs into the openings.

When he snapped the pants closed around his waist, I chided him. "I don't think you're being fair to the Spaniards. They saw plenty of bounty open for taking, something most human beings would do."

Trece snorted. "The Conquistadors and their ilk decimated us with their diseases and greed, their thirst for plunder. Untold millions of us died where we fell all over these parts. History will never have a proper accounting of our numbers. Our rotting bodies became part of the slime faster than the vines overran our mounded cities, making our deaths unsolved disappearances and banishing us to Nowhere. We were history's losers, relegated to the scribbled ramblings of a few zealous Conquistadors. Nobody took their writings seriously, and our broken remnant couldn't correct the story. We can blame your long-time friends in Spain for everything that befell us."

He was wrong about the last bit. An accomplished spy is friendly with all but a friend to none. The Spanish were never my friends. To them, I was Number 13, their most important double agent. I took millions from them to sell American military secrets but history never gave me credit for what I delivered to the United States in the bargain: enough intelligence to rout the Spanish on much of the North American continent. With secrets I provided, American patriots were eventually able to overrun Texas, consume Spanish Florida, and push over the Rockies to California. I ushered in those events by sending Zebulon Pike to chart Pikes Peak and stationing eyes all over the frontier. Narcissistic racists like Thomas Jefferson and Andrew Jackson took credit for the United States becoming a nation *from sea to shining sea*, but I sowed the seeds that yielded the bounty, and I did it with money the fucking Spaniards willingly contributed.

But why waste hot air explaining my actions to Trece? He had every right to hate Europeans in general and the Spanish in particular. I nodded. "We European-types don't have a commendable track record in our treatment of others. And that's one reason I'm here, fighting to free Nicaragua from oppression. If any of your blood flows in these collective veins, I want it to live free, and I'll fight to the last breath of my final Nowhere life to see it happen."

"Right. That's why you're conscripting my countrymen to go back to Nicaragua and fight."

"If you don't like our tactics, then why are you working with us?"

He trembled through another wave of crippling discomfort. When he spoke, his jaw clenched and his teeth ground together. "To be true to the descendants who even today fill this thin wisp of land with life. For now, working with you is the best route to accomplish my own Nowhere mission to free my homeland from persecution. But if I ever see another way, I'll take it, as long as I can remain true to myself." Trece winced as he sat on the edge of the cot and braced himself to stand. "Whenever I need to recall who I am, I hack my way to the White City, my forgotten home, and commune with the spirits." Sweat bubbled on his forehead and flowed down his cheek. "I wish I could go there now. Ask them how to tackle these challenges, especially on the Nowhere front. We don't need the added static of afterlife adversaries right now."

"Impossible, Trece. You're in no shape to take off for some jungle seance. As soon as I get you to Catacamas, I'm hauling your ass to the doctor. We need you back in the rain forest as soon as possible."

Trece slipped his feet into gook-encrusted boots. "If anyone can help decipher the aims of these Nowhere soldiers, the spirits of the White City can."

"I'll figure out what to do about the mysterious Nowhere force. They're after me. I'm sure of it."

"But they shot me."

"Yeah, most likely because they know you work for me. You focus on recuperating, and I'll figure them out. In the meantime, I'm more interested in Emmaline. What's she to you?"

"She's special here, sir—the key. We didn't start seeing Nowhere teams in these parts until recently, when she arrived. Maybe the two are connected. Once we have answers, we'll know how to use her to lure them in."

I flicked the lid on my lighter and watched orange flame set my cigar afire. After a long drag, I spewed smoke and studied him. "How many were out there?"

He finished with his boots and eased to his feet. "Four or five. Fierce, they were. I got off a half-dozen shots before one hit me. Little guy. Almost girly."

"Between the Contras and the Sandinistas, I've got too much shit to handle already. The last thing I need is some wretched Nowhere army kicking up trouble. Do you think you tagged any of them?"

"No way to tell, sir, but nobody got chewed up by thin air. What the hell is that about? Other than how it happened, I can't reconstruct anything else about it. Do you think it was a fluke of the hurricane?"

I chomped the tip of my stogie and squinted at him. "Between us, we'll dig to the root of it. You work with her as best you can to scuttle this place. I see those longing looks she fixes you with when she thinks nobody's looking. Take her. Maybe getting into her pants'll open the trapdoor to her secrets."

Trece rolled his eyes and limped past me toward the exit. "You're disgusting, sir. Fooling around with her won't open the vault of whatever power she has. Besides, it's not like I haven't been trying ever since she arrived. Not anything blatant, because I don't want to get her in trouble with Sisa and Abroad Together, but she'd be an idiot not to know I like her." He pointed to his bandaged side. "Especially since she may've saved my Nowhere life. But she's frozen me out ever since she found out I take orders from you."

"Yeah, she hates me."

"She probably should."

"Well, she's writing revisionist history. I'm a patriot, not a pedophile."
I bit the tip of my cigar. "Look, in my experience, women still go for
an attractive face, even after she's seen his weaknesses. Hell, some women
practically fall down with their legs wide open in front of the broken guys
who need fixing, like their vaginas combined with their own personal
improvement plans can cure the most broken men."

"I think Cagney's smarter than you're giving her credit for. Sure, she's
passionate, but her passion made this camp a success. She knows how to
apply it to causes without burning out or turning herself into a shrieking
shrew."

"Then maybe she'll succumb to your genuine attraction to her. I can
see you aren't faking, and I'm giving you permission to go for it."

He sighed and raked his fingers across his handsome, even-featured
face. "I'll have to be careful, but I'll think about it, okay?"

"Good. Do that."

He pushed back the canvas and leaned through the opening. "No
promises, though. Cagney sort of scares me."

"Spoken like the genuinely besotted."

He flashed his middle finger and turned toward my vehicle. "Between
Cagney, Sisa, and the refugees, this place'll be loaded up in under an hour,
sir." We began to walk side-by-side, me waiting to catch him if he stumbled,
him treading gingerly.

"That wound isn't hurting too much?"

"It's burning like a mother fucker, but I'm good for making sure we
give the area a full sweep. What're you going to do?"

"I'm heading deeper into the overgrowth to try to suss out this
Nowhere enemy. Command's got a handle on bands of Sandinistas and
drug traffickers roving through this maze. But I need to know who we're
dealing with on the Nowhere front. With the shit storm from DC getting
ready to flatten us, we can't afford any other surprises." My boots glopped
along the ground next to his. We stopped and stood in the half-dismantled
camp and squinted into late afternoon sunshine. Whenever I glimpsed a
shard of sky, I spent an instant convincing myself I wasn't swimming at

the bottom of a lake. Dampness distorted everything in this place, made it grow to cartoonish proportions, kept us ever-drenched.

Maybe I liked it because of my tenure in Louisiana. After all, I ruled New Orleans. Really ruled it. I liked dressing up in my uniform spangled with medals and gold braid, prowling the cobbled streets with my revolvers drawn, telling terrified citizens what to do. The cowering assholes had to obey me or be shot. Thanks to President Jefferson, I presided over the only time in history America ever declared martial law.

Same rules applied in these twisted rain forests. I was forced to carry out my Nowhere mission in the midst of a totalitarian paradise. Temptation teased me at every turn, but my Gravedigger's looming pickaxe always hewed it back. I wasn't here to put the whole world under my thumb; no, I existed to rout the communists from Nicaragua. Once I completed my mission, I was done with Nowhere.

I wouldn't let some damn Nowhere unit stop me. And if Trece helped me to divine Emmaline's mysteries before I moved on, so much the better.

We saw her then. Emmaline directed a line of six refugees ferrying food stuffs to the waiting trucks. Tents and other supplies were already disassembled and loaded. On the other side of the mushy expanse, Sisa worked with a group to get the last of the weapons cache from the bunker before she set the building on fire. We couldn't leave anything behind for an enemy to use against us.

When Emmaline saw me, she stomped in our direction, stiff-backed and chin elevated. Ignoring me, she zeroed in on Trece's side. "You shouldn't be up and about. We've got this covered."

His smile was radiant, even with his torment. "I wanted to thank you for fixing me up."

She softened a little, especially around her eyes. "Glad to help. Oh, I cleared you a place in the last truck. You can lie down and be reasonably comfortable until we can get you to a real doctor."

Trece never took his attention from her face. "I don't need a real doctor. I'll be okay. You saved my life."

She flushed and turned away from us. Sisa beckoned her across the almost empty camp, and Emmaline hurried to her side, leaving Trece and I alone.

I put a hand on his shoulder and squeezed. "You'll have her by nightfall."

He winced and clutched at his side. "You're giving my virility too much credit, sir. I'm about to faint from suffering."

"And some women find vulnerable men impossible to resist."

He stepped backward, protecting his wounded side with his elbow, and waved with his free hand. "Good luck, sir."

"Thanks. I'll canvass this area, mow through those Nowhere mercenaries, and beat you to Catacamas."

EMMALINE

"What am I doing?" I whispered to myself as I picked my way along Catacamas' pudding-like roads on foot. In twenty-four hours, I went from dressing a gunshot wound to dismantling an entire refugee camp to lying, useless and discarded, on a mildewed mattress in a rundown dormitory.

So much for volunteering. My assigned refugees, including Maria, were stripped from me and lodged on the other side of the base. Sisa spouted something about vetting them for spies and processing the rest for immigration into the United States, but I didn't believe her. Why couldn't I help get them ready for their journey to the U.S.A.? She didn't have a good reason for being secretive, which meant they could've just as likely been headed into battle. Given the paranoid mood around Catacamas, maybe my volunteer days were done for good.

But I wouldn't take being thrown aside. My new stuccoed, adobe-style dormitory was topped with a flimsy metal roof. Leaks stained the concrete floor like spilled tea, both ancient and recent. Every time I rolled over on my mattress, mold spores crawled up my nostrils. My throat burned, and if I had scratched my eyes any more, I might've dislodged them from their sockets. I'd take a tent any day. At least I could zip open a few panels and keep air moving through the screens.

I didn't think it'd hurt to check on my former charges and ask whether they needed anything. I needed to make sure Wilkinson wasn't shipping them all to their deaths.

Or maybe I could wander to the infirmary and look in on Trece. While I could think of ways to make myself useful to him, none of them were honorable.

With a burst of resolve, I got up and went in search of something productive to occupy my time.

But as I trudged around the base, I couldn't buy a scintilla of welcome. CIA types buzzed around like sand flies while Contra forces shot targets and played war games in the vegetation around the perimeter. I couldn't get past the guard at the gymnasium where the refugees were sequestered.

Restless, I sneaked past the filth-grimed windows of the main gatehouse and entered Catacamas-proper. Beyond the base's barbed wire fence, the city was composed of one-story block structures strung along a checkered grid that stretched as far as I could see. Bigger than I expected.

The American base was nestled in a secluded area near the start of the Mosquitia rain forest. Equipped with a paved landing strip and around twenty other concrete and metal-sided buildings, it served as the hub for whatever the U.S. government was leading in Nicaragua. While I was learning more about those shenanigans, I was in Honduras to help people who saw their loved ones slaughtered, fled their homes, and lost everything they owned to authoritarian rule. I couldn't leave them.

Wilkinson's presence changed me from a cowardly-but-caring humanitarian to—what? What was I? A tool in whatever badness Wilkinson was executing? A scared orphan who wanted to go home, only she had no home to return to? How could I stop him?

And when the refugees became my family, I couldn't even keep them. They were stripped from me and sequestered across the base. What would happen to Maria? Would anybody care for her like I did?

Sunlight beamed from Sisa's smile as she sauntered along a side street and saw me. I waited for her to cross the divide and fall in step beside me. She linked arms with me and squeezed. "Hi, friend."

"Hey. Do you know what's going to happen to volunteers like me now that we're here?"

"Yeah. You need to get ready to fly back to the States."

I circled on her. "What?"

"Things are too risky here. The leaders of Abroad Together don't want to be responsible for the lives of volunteers when we're under such blatant threat. You need to be ready to leave at any time."

"I don't want to go home," I fumed. "There's still so much I can do here."

"Look, I don't like it either, but it is what it is. You've got no choice."

A faded beach ball bounced across our path, and I picked it up and flung it toward a threadbare little boy, his black eyes headlights in a dirty face. He looked to be about Maria's age. Tears stung my eyelids. I couldn't leave without Maria.

"But I didn't even get to say goodbye."

"And I hope the order will be rescinded and you won't have to leave. The situation is sort of unusual, Emmaline. We had an evacuation order, imminent threats of attack. Hell, Trece was shot by some random Sandinista guerillas. Desperation doesn't leave much time for sentiment, you know?"

My heart unclenched. "You're right. I just, I've lost a lot recently. It's hard to keep caring for people only to have them taken from me."

Sisa stopped, hands on hips. "Isn't that what life is? Stop wallowing in your own pity party. Couples have children. They spend every spare drop of energy from the moment their offspring are born preparing them to leave. Maybe those new adults find a tribe and eventually someone to love. Only life takes a hairpin and disappoints. Tribes change. Many members aren't there for us when we need them, or they become people we no longer like. And the ones we decide to keep? We can't cling to them forever. Eventually, death robs us of everyone we've ever invested in. The biggest hearts love anyway, knowing they'll lose all in the end."

I glanced sideways at Sisa's proud profile, her sculpted cheekbones, pierced ears, and fierce eyes. Who was she really talking about? Me? Or her?

Knowing how losing my father shredded my heart, I couldn't imagine signing up for that kind of unconditional love again, let alone multiple times. Even losing Merry at the age of nine still stung. Their absence sapped my will like thousands of unseen parasites. I wished I only grappled with missing them for who they were, but it was more than that. I still needed their guidance, their ears, even their protection sometimes.

Now, I couldn't ask either of them what to do. No matter how much I filled the pages of Merry's journal, he'd never scrawl an answer. Being an adult meant filtering what happened through the sieve of life experience and figuring things out on my own.

But I knew Sisa was right about where to put my energy: in the present. I turned sideways and hugged her. "Thanks for giving me my father's words. Exactly what he would've told me. For a minute there, I thought his spirit spoke through you."

She squeezed my arm and steered me back to base. "You'll never stop missing him, you know."

"Yeah. I can't imagine a day that won't be a picture with his image cut out of the frame. The hole he left is still taunting me. Coming here, giving of myself, it helps, but it doesn't color in the Dad-shaped void."

"It gets easier. I went through the same things when my father died."

I whirled on her. "Your father died? How?" When her smooth face crumpled, I stammered, "I mean, I'm not trying to pry or be insensitive. It's just, wow, I didn't know we had dead fathers in common."

Sisa's inky eyes scanned the uneven rooflines of our new home. "My papa was like an ancient tree. Anchored and soaring. Deep roots. It's been a while since I lost him. He, um, fell into the flooded Missouri River and was gone. The current was like a waterfall running horizontally that year in Montana. Nobody ever found a scrap of clothing or anything."

"It was sudden. Like my dad."

She nodded. "Yes. I foundered for awhile after it happened. Eventually I started working here because I didn't know what else to do."

I pulled her to me and held her in a solid hug. Sometimes, a friend knows when to shut up and let the other person be heard. I hoped a hug was what Sisa needed.

After a long pause, she swiped a tear and walked us through the outer gate of the compound, really an opening in concrete block topped with razor wire. Clearing her throat, she said, "Have you heard how Trece's doing?"

"The doctor complimented my surgical skills. I got all the bullet bits and sewed him up well enough. They gave him some pain meds and antibiotics and told him to rest a couple of days."

"That's a problem. We're drilling to pick up more refugees waiting at the border. The order to go to them could come at any time, and Trece needs to lead the way."

"Now? When Wilkinson claims the jungle is overrun with Sandinistas to the point that we had to be evacuated? How will you both ever lead anyone through all those guns and snakes and death?"

She dropped me at the dormitory door and saluted. "Give us some credit. Trece is a magician. Besides, he's haunted these swamps a hell of a lot longer than those pieces of communist trash."

But I wasn't assured. They could die. Trece could die. And Wilkinson would be responsible. What could I do to protect Trece? And Sisa? Because I was determined to do something.

EMMALINE

I stormed through the ordered bunks of my temporary home and went straight to the shower. I needed to figure out how to make a stand against being sent back to the States.

Cold water flowed along my scalp and ran down my back. Why couldn't it wash my mounting concerns down the drain, too?

I didn't want to go home. There was nothing in Nashville for me. I needed to help Sisa and Trece rescue more Nicaraguans at the border and guide them through the Mosquitia to safety. Since arriving in the tropics, I learned how to carve a path through impossible greenery. Rain fell like a Niagara, a blinding wall of water and froth, but I got used to it. Mysterious lizards and life-ending snakes and clouds of biting insects swirled every few feet, but hadn't I proven my mettle? After all, I beheaded a deadly *fer-de-lance*, something both Sisa and Trece admitted they'd never accomplished.

I turned off the water and wrapped myself in a thin, scratchy towel, more brillo pad than terrycloth. Without stopping to dress, I found my cot and collapsed. For now, the dorm was blessedly empty. Nobody said how many other volunteers might be coming in from the field. By nightfall, I expected all thirty beds to be occupied.

I rolled over and fished Merry's leather journal from my knapsack.

Every time he had a few minutes to himself, Merry scribbled in this book. I wished it contained his notes and observations, anything that might give me a sense of where to go from here.

When I picked up the journal, it throbbed between my hands. The tips of my fingers sizzled and I dropped the book.

My pulse thudded against my temple as I studied the pebbled cover. I was dead weary, no question, a spent mind playing tricks on my sluggish senses. Tentatively, I brushed my fingers along the cover only to jerk my burned digits away from the steam left in their wake.

Was I imagining the book's muted glow? Avoiding it, I flicked a fingernail along the shut pages. When nothing happened, I touched them with my thumb. The cover's light strengthened, but I wasn't burned.

I undid the leather cords that kept the journal shut and flipped it open to see my first message to Merry.

Alien ink sparkled back at me. The paper was covered in handwriting I'd never seen before, lines and lines of entries I didn't pen. Frantic, I flipped through more pages. All were filled with someone else's writing. Ink pulsed and vanished like a strobe light.

Shocked, I dropped the tome on the concrete floor. It shimmered there for a couple of moments, while I stared at it.

I reached over the edge of the bunk and picked up the book with quaking hands. Its cover was still warm, but it didn't singe me. Slower this time, I opened the pages and turned them one-by-one. The first few sheets were covered with tiny scrawl that didn't dissipate.

Leaping from the thin mattress, I shouted, "Who wrote in my journal? Who?" Maybe I wasn't alone in the dormitory. I got no answer save the drip-drip-drip of water from the shower. Vacant mattresses were still stripped. No telltale duffel bags littered the floor.

Who could've pilfered through my backpack on the way to Catacamas? But that wasn't really possible, either. I kept my pack slung over my shoulders the entire time. And why wouldn't I? It contained every physical thing I valued.

I turned back to the book, thumbed to the first page, and started reading.

Dear Emmaline Cagney

I crabbed backwards along the mattress. My heart rattled against my ribcage hard enough to double me over. When was the journal last unguarded? I scrolled through my final hours at the refugee camp and saw myself take the book from my foot locker, re-read my first entry, thumb over many blank pages, and stuff it into my backpack. For the rest of the evacuation, I kept it zipped a few inches from my heart. I didn't shrug off the pack en route to Catacamas or when I went to the hospital to check on Trece or before exploring the small town. No, the only time I took off my backpack was in preparation for my shower.

A few nights ago, I wrote in the book and asked for advice. "Is this my sign, Merry?" I whispered.

No, the very idea was lunacy. I didn't believe in magic anymore, even though I wrote in the blasted book thinking Merry might answer, didn't I? No, magic was for children who were too innocent to know better, not for grown orphans mourning dead fathers.

But my name still taunted me from the first page. I crawled across the mattress, settled as close to the book as I dared, and started reading.

Dear Emmaline Cagney:

I'm sorry to have abandoned you until now. Several times over the past nine years, I wanted to spell out a message on these pages, but I feared you were too inexperienced to properly digest it. Recent events in your life forced me to act.

Whether we like it or not, your time has come. You cannot be expected to navigate the coming days without a map. Too much is at stake.

Well, duh. Of course, a lot was at stake. My very existence was on the line with Wilkinson once again trolling my life.

Could he have written this?

I smacked the book shut and closed my eyes to stop the room from spinning like the time I sat in the middle of a merry-go-round. When I crawled off, I couldn't stand on my own and threw up in my lap. Stomach acid lurched up my esophagus and burned my throat. Through clenched teeth, I whispered, "Wilkinson, are you doing this? It won't ever be funny, preying on a grieving teenager who's trying to do good in the world. Why can't you leave me alone?"

When I opened one eye, I leaned toward the book and almost retched. The journal I closed a few minutes before yawned wide at the last paragraph I read.

Incensed, I vaulted off the bed and crawled across concrete on hands-and-knees. "I know someone's here. Stop doing this." Not only was the space under my bed empty, but I found the same nothingness under every other bed. No one crouched in the shower or cowered within the lone metal cupboard or lurked outside either the front or side exits.

I galloped back to my bed, pounded the open page, and yelled, "Why are you doing this to me?"

In response, another sentence sparkled on the page, written by an unseen hand.

I know you have many questions.

I crumpled on the bed in front of the book. "You bet I do," I whispered.

You've always been an inquisitive spirit. Please keep reading. I'm confident I'll answer most of them, but first, I want to show you something. You've been craving more time with your father. What if you could see him again?

"Who are you?"

I can't reveal who I am, but I can take you to your dad.

I dropped the book again and stammered out loud, "That's not possible. That's not possible. Not possible. My father is dead. I touched his lifeless body and memorized his face before they shut the lid of the casket. Do you know what skin feels like on a dead body? Like a million ice cubes consumed the father I loved. When they put him in the ground, I threw the first handful of dirt into his grave."

I picked up the journal and clawed back to my place, *not possible* ringing in my head like a chant. But the handwriting seeped underneath my heart and found my life force. I couldn't stop reading, even though the tale offered nothing but inexplicable nonsense.

Hold this book to your chest and state your intention aloud.
Say you want to see your father, and he will appear.

I closed the book and cradled it against my flat boobs. I mean, come on. I knew I'd open my eyes and find myself sitting in the same stifling room in Central America. Books and chants didn't conjure dead people, no matter what psychics would have us believe. And besides, I was no medium.

But the abandoned little girl who once believed a message she wrote on a two-dollar bill would find its way to her father forced me to suspend my disbelief. After all, he got that money, and he found me. What if I really had a chance to hug my dad one more time, and I blew it? Closing my eyes, I took a deep breath and spoke out loud.

"Show me my father."

WILKINSON

"You clean this shit up, Wilkinson, or you'll be one of the fattest rolling heads in this formerly secret little war." The director of the CIA smashed down the receiver. The sound rocked through my skull like he'd boxed my ear with his fist. Exasperated, I replaced the sat-phone in its black cradle and stormed across the abandoned clearing of Emmaline's former refugee camp.

Brown puddles denoted sites where tents once stood. The remains of the bunker smoldered in the far corner. Once I reconnoitered the perimeter, I needed to head to Catacamas and engineer the beginning of my end in Nowhere.

I hiked up my waders, unsheathed my machete, and chopped my way into the maddening vegetation. Jungle creatures pelted me with berries and sticks and clumps of their own shit. I told myself suffering was part of my toll.

And I had plenty of impending hellaciousness to consider. The director of the CIA never paid for his fuck-ups. He was kind of like Jefferson. Our third president kept leather-bound volumes charting every conversation he ever had, skewed to make him look good, of course. "Contemporaneous records are always best, Wilkinson," he told me as he inked another quill and scribbled a few words. "In a court of law, they always trump recollections, especially when someone else certifies their authenticity. And those witnesses can always be bought."

The CIA director would have his records in order. Besides, I knew this was coming. If my escapades through life and death taught me anything, it was that I should never leave a trail that leads back to me.

A plane crashing while loaded with questionably-acquired arms bound for the Contras was a beacon burning from somebody's ass, most likely mine. I was a recent addition to this conflict. I gave the order for delivery. The whole cluster happened on my watch, even though almost a decade's worth of covert personnel could be blamed.

For most of the 1980s, the Communist-fearing Reagan administration found ways to supply their beloved Contra fighters with training, manpower, and weaponry. When Congress voted to deny federal support to the Contras, people within the administration cultivated private donors and foreign governments willing to pay for the chance to influence other state-side policies in the future. Every time a Congressional delegation flew down to Central America to investigate, somebody managed to convince them nothing untoward was happening, even after a Contra plane crashed into the Managua airport and almost killed two visiting United States senators.

I wish it had offed the hawkish, unpatriotic bastards. Our subversive fight protected their worthless, road-blocking asses. Despite this setback, the United States of America still needed a free, democratic Nicaragua. I knew Cuba's duplicity; we couldn't allow another puppet government for the Russians in our hemisphere.

How could it ever happen now, with the Democrats circling like buzzards over fresh roadkill?

I took out another Cuban cigar and guillotined its tip. Tobacco tickled my nose and swirled along my synapses. "Ah, smoke to help me think," I muttered, flicking open my silver lighter and setting the stogie's eager tip aflame.

The wreckage of an illicit plane wasn't the only thing I had to ponder.

I couldn't shake the feeling that something was off-kilter in Nowhere, a shrieking crescendo that gained momentum as it cascaded around my gut.

As I slopped along the narrow path, a bullet whizzed by my ear and shredded a low-hanging leaf ahead of me. Hitting the ground, I unhitched my other knife and wallowed in the muck to coat myself in sticky camouflage. I had to blend in with the terrain long enough to drag myself off the path and submerge myself in a soupy mud puddle.

Machine gun fire pockmarked the soft ground all around me, though how well a bullet remained on its trajectory in this bursting foliage was anyone's guess. I couldn't hold my breath in this glop forever. Blind, I jettisoned both machetes and swam toward the last direction I recalled, using buried roots to pull myself the last few inches and onto the opposite shore. Slime slid down my throat when I forced in air, and given how I was coated in it, I didn't know how I'd clean my eyes to aim and fire.

Another spray of Nowhere-ending finality fell all around me. One bullet grazed my cheek, a bloody trail through my muddy mask. With both machetes lost, I ripped open my holster, pointed my pistol, and rapid-fired into the darkness until my magazine clicked empty.

High-pitched laughter harmonized with roars from big cats. Patient footsteps squelched through the gloop. A familiar female voice shouted, "You're surrounded, Wilkinson. Your reserve ammo is ruined. We've commandeered your jeep."

My gasp was loud enough to reveal my position. I bit my lips together and tried to keep from giving myself away, but my temples throbbed. Could it be my afterlife's greatest cancer, Theodosia Burr? Hell, I ended at least two of the hag's Nowhere lives that I could remember, not to mention ruining her precious daddy's career when he failed in our scheme to invade Mexico. The two of them were putrid cancers on my life. Theodosia Burr couldn't bump my final Nowhere life. She was the last person I'd allow to kill me.

Drying mud cracked and groaned as I hauled myself to my hands and knees. My fingers found a banana leaf, and I used it to wipe as much dirt from my eyes as I dared before darting further into the twisted flora.

"There he is!" Theo shouted.

More gunfire peppered my position. Staying low, I was able to push myself through a few tangled vines and crawl behind a thick tree trunk. The density of the growth dulled sound. I found my next position, another tree a foot onward, and howled, "You can go to hell, Theodosia Burr!"

"My Nowhere mission is to send you there, and this time, I won't fail," she retorted. I looked around the tree trunk in time to see her remove the pin from a grenade and lob it my way.

Before I felt its percussive bite chew into everything, I left the shelter of the tree and tore my way through the thickets. The sound of the explosion masked my thrashing, but I didn't stop or look back. I didn't need to. I could hear Theo panting a few yards behind me.

I zigzagged through the flora to keep from giving her a clear shot, but that didn't stop her from firing. Every few feet, she fired a kill shot from her pistol, but given the terrain, she never hit me.

If I had a weapon, I could've shot a fatal hole through her opinionated skull. As it was, my side ached. I couldn't keep up this performance much longer, not without rest.

Pivoting right, I dove into a clump of vegetation, put my head between my knees, and tried to keep my breathing quiet.

In the distance, Theo's frustration colored the edges of her voice. "I know you're there, Wilkinson. You had to be involved in the disappearance of our hurricane strike team. What happened to them? Come on. You can tell me how you were involved before I finish you."

Parting vines just enough to glimpse the team, I counted four men in my line of sight, dressed in uniforms similar to the men we killed the day of the hurricane. Unarmed, I didn't have a chance to take them, but as they checked potential hiding spots further from mine, I decided to take another risk and crawled from my cocoon. Sufficiently rested, I sprung to my feet and ran deeper into the jungle.

Thorns tore into my skin and clothing, and vines slapped my face and arms, but I stayed upright as shouts from the team rang out behind me. The overgrowth muffled their pursuit, but I didn't mistake the percussive beat of machine guns spraying the foliage. Shredded leaves and twisted bark rained on me like shrapnel, but I kept pushing through the snarl until an unexpected light blinded me. With a surprised gasp, I tumbled headfirst into murky water. Liquid filtered into my airways, and I kicked and fanned my arms to find the light.

As soon as my head popped to the surface, I wheezed in as much air as I could.

"There he is!" Theo shouted. "I can take him!"

A deluge of bullets fell around me. I sucked in as much air as my tobacco-stained lungs allowed, and I dove deep, hoping the current would carry me beyond range.

When I surfaced again, coughing and dizzy, I approached a bend in the river. I looked back to glimpse Theo and her team hacking at the impenetrable tangle of bushes on their side of the shoreline. One soldier ran into the river, chest-deep, and continued to fire until I slipped behind a spit of land and out of sight.

They wouldn't be able to follow me without a boat. The sides of the river were too overgrown.

But I couldn't celebrate my escape. Not yet. Crocodiles lurked in this river. I wouldn't see one until it seized me with its teeth and rolled me underwater. I floated along with the swift current, trying to make as little disturbance as possible lest I attract unwanted attention. Through the opening in the trees overhead, the sky darkened, and fat drops of tropical rain began to fall.

Around another bend, a narrow lip of sand floated into view. I kicked toward it, oblivious to threat. My boots hit bottom as a splash parted the water from the opposite bank. I didn't stop to note whether it was human or reptile, though I suspected the latter. Theo's team couldn't get downriver this fast. Once I was free of the river, I didn't stop running until my sides throbbed and my lungs pounded, until I was entombed in an uncharted stretch of rain forest with no idea which way I'd come or how to get out.

WILKINSON

At the top of a rise, I finally stopped, put my hands on my knees, and huffed until my heart rate slowed and it didn't hurt my ribs to breathe.

Damn Theodosia. It was just like her to try to fuck up my best chance at success. The woman blamed me for everything that went wrong with her worthless life, but it was she who ruined mine. I'd always remember what she and her ass of a father Aaron Burr did to me in that out-of-the-way room on a forgotten island. A guy never forgets the people who thwarted his biggest dream.

God, I didn't have time to relive ancient history now.

Still, she was close. I bet she savored the scent of my final Nowhere failure. Well, I had some news for that bitch: I'd relish eviscerating her first.

When I raised my head and stumbled from the hill, my boot caught on a sharp protrusion, and I tumbled head over foot to the bottom. Prostrate on my face, I felt around my head, trunk, and appendages for any scrapes or breaks. Though I was sore all over, every part of me was intact.

Relieved, I pulled myself to sit and came face-to-face with a cracked monkey face made of clay stranded in the mire a few feet from me. Holding my breath, I dragged my eyes over the rest of the area.

I fell into a ruined clearing surrounded by hills. When I blinked again, I realized those hills were manmade mounds covered in trees and undergrowth. The monkey was some sort of idol. My knees popped when I pushed to my feet and turned in a slow circle.

I knew this place. I stood where even the jungle prostrated itself. Trece told me all about his mystical upbringing in the White City, but I'd never experienced its rumpled abandonment. One-quarter-of-a-million people once occupied this snarl of earthen platforms, obliterated terraces, and tree-choked plazas, until the Spanish brought smallpox to the New World. I didn't blame Trece for fleeing his home after watching everyone he knew and loved perish via a disfiguring, brutal plague. Too many people died to pass down a coherent oral history, and the poor bastards didn't have an alphabet to write. There was no record of what happened, so Trece and a whole civilization of unresolved deaths wound up in Nowhere with me.

Despite the storied curse, Trece told me he came here to commune with his ancestors. I tramped through the echoing expanse and couldn't fathom what this forlorn ruin might say. The humid air hummed with loss and grief. Sweat salted my lips and stung my eyes, but I kept fighting through the thicket until my arms turned liquid. Spent and sore, I massaged my upper arms and shouted, "Hello!"

Raccoon-like kinkajous barked through vines, accompanied by the thunderous noise of an insect sonata. But behind their piercing cacophony, another sound burbled. I tore into the bramble and strained to reach its source through the bog and muck. "Hello!" I called again.

With a final burst, I broke through matted vegetation and fell face-first into another clearing. Wet ooze plugged my nostrils. Suffocating, I rolled onto my back and pulled out my canteen to rinse away the grime.

Two bare feet grew into tree-like legs inches from my head. At first, I thought its humanity was an illusion, but I followed the trunks to their source: a living obelisk capped with an ocher-painted face. Two charcoal eyes blinked down at me.

Never knowing whether natives were friend or foe in these parts, I swallowed my scream of surprise and lay still, returning her intent stare. After a few blinks, she offered me a hand.

"Please. We are many. Let us help you stand."

Their voices echoed like thousands of persons talking at once. I grasped their palm and used it for balance to keep from slipping on the soggy ground. When I was steady, they flashed white teeth. "Trece told us about you."

"Trece?"

"Yes. Whenever Nowhere overwhelms him, he comes back here, to the spot where the remnant of his society buried their broken idols before vacating their city. Do you know why they mutilated their offerings?"

"No."

They rooted through the sludge and pulled out another monkey idol carved from stone. A jagged scar punctured its right ear. "We leave pieces of our spirits in everything we make. Those remnants inhabit every kind of vessel. They smashed these things to release those spirits as an offering to cleanse and protect their forgotten city. We are those spirits, personified. We can help the worthy or punish the ignoble."

"My objectives here are noble."

"Trece tells us you are a selfless leader, a true patriot of your country to the north, but we're not so certain. Your anima emanates a rancid, pestilent odor."

Perceptive spirit. I poured on some flattery. "Because you're a god, you know my name's Wilkinson, but I hope you'll tell me yours."

"We have many names. Trece calls us Ku. Please enlighten us. What do you seek here?"

I smacked an engorged kissing bug before it bit into my neck. Venom from one bite could swell my liver to bursting.

"I'm not here on purpose. I was running from a rogue team of Sandinistas, and I sort of wound up here. But I know where I am. Trece is always carrying on about how the jungle is wise at the White City. That's where I am, right?"

Ku nodded their collective head.

"I never realized he was actually communing with it."

Kohl-rimmed eyes stared back at me, and I saw hundreds of faces behind them, cheetahs and cougars, sloths and parrots, mixed in with countless humans. Comforted by their wisdom, I stumbled on. "Because you talk with Trece, I assume you know your remnant wound up in an in-between called Nowhere, a place where people with unresolved deaths are doomed to spend a few lives and help the living accomplish something meaningful. While I haven't always made the best choices in Nowhere, I've spent this life focused on my mission. We're this close to freeing the nation next door from a tyrannical regime."

"Do you think we don't know about your country's meddling in the private affairs of another?"

"It's not private when what they do impacts the lives of our citizens, threatens their safety, and gives them reason to fear."

"Your kind use fear to line your pockets and maintain power, and you mock the misguided beings who place their trust in you."

I waved my muck-caked hands. "Look, you're right. Lots of my countrymen snort money and power like lines of cocaine. I'm not interested in those things. I want to be finished with Nowhere and find out what's on the other side. To do that, I must help some rebels defeat their authoritarian leaders and establish a free country. We're so close to victory. I can sense it."

"Then why are you troubled?"

"A couple of Nowhere teams are opposed to my ultimate success."

They nodded again.

I rushed on. "One shot Trece yesterday."

"He will heal. Besides, you don't care about Trece. Why are you really here?"

If she could see the future, the witch ought to know what I wanted, but I thought it might be ill-advised to mention my motivations. I swallowed. "Today, a similar group came after me. While I made an army of enemies in my other lives, I've done everything aboveboard in this one. No double-dealing."

"Don't lie to us, Wilkinson. We heard the cries of the young blonde child you harassed in a former life. We've seen her here, too young for such a load of grieving. Yet, she is confronted with you, an obstacle in her path once again, almost like you're her destiny."

"I don't care about her. I just want to get the hell out of here, I swear. Am I going to succeed?"

I bit my salty lip and waited for Ku to confirm what I already suspected, a reality I couldn't afford. My mission with the Contras was screaming toward a murky conclusion, but we could still deliver. Trece was bringing hundreds of trained Nicaraguans into our fold. In the coming days, we'd have enough troops to coordinate damaging strikes from ground and air. We could still win. We had to.

My horizon teased the glistening beaches of a new world. If I strained, I could almost touch my final destination. I already heard my Gravedigger's disappointed shrieks as I stepped through the membrane and found out what lay on Nowhere's far shore. I couldn't let an unexpected storm sink me, not when I was so close to success, my reward for a single well-lived Nowhere life.

Ku's voices merged into the deranged catcalls of my Gravedigger. I ducked to avoid the steel point of his pickaxe and cowered in a ball. Each word of Ku's pronouncement landed as a separate blow. "Stay focused on your mission, Wilkinson. Forget the girl. This small faction of Nowhere mercenaries doesn't concern you. Whenever temptations arise, rebuke them."

"But two of them tried to kill me! This is my last Nowhere life. I've got to complete this mission before they get to me."

"To protect this hallowed place, we feel out every presence lurking in the Mosquitia. These mercenaries don't care about you. They seek the girl to use for a purpose we cannot divine. If they can kill you, they will, but they're doing it to protect her."

"Emmaline."

"Yes. Because they don't emanate malice toward her, we chose to let them proceed."

"What if I try to protect her instead?"

"She cannot hide anywhere. This contingent is a determined, skilled force pursuing a young woman with no concept of her own power."

Unrest gurgled through my lips. "Her power?"

I longed to find out more about Emmaline's bullets, but I thought I was being fanciful. And here was a god confirming her as a source of unknown gifts without my even asking.

Ku's howl picked me up and flung me against the side of a vine-choked mound. For an instant, I saw a pristine series of ordered terraces stepping down to the river, a wide walkway leading into trees, and wooden buildings arranged at exact angles around a pyramid. Whatever power Emmaline possessed, it was nothing compared to Ku's.

But when they spoke, I knew I didn't have a hope of harnessing this god. "Don't be disingenuous, Wilkinson. You've pursued her through multiple turns in Nowhere. Clearly, she wields power over you."

"I just want to keep her safe. I swear it. She lost her father recently, and her mother's long gone."

"You deal in the superficial. She's a special part of Nowhere."

"But she isn't part of Nowhere. She's actually alive, not in-between."

"You're wrong. You're wrong. You're wrong." All of Ku's voices spoke to me then, many eyes condensed into one blazing pair. I flickered under the force of their stare. Then darkness crushed me.

I came to face up, eyelashes singed and nose blistered. When I hobbled to stand, I was back where I started in the refugee camp clearing. Ku, the one voice-of-many, was gone.

EMMALINE

When I asked to see my father, I didn't expect the dorm's edges to blacken like someone had set fire to a painting. Uprooted trees and smashed concrete swirled into a charred vortex. I closed my eyes to keep from seeing wads of brimstone rain down from the unknown I had summoned. Smoke tore at my eyes and burned my nose. I stuffed the journal into my waistband and wrapped my arms around my head, fearing my flesh would slither off my bones like tender meat.

The silence was louder than the faulty fluorescent light buzzing in the dormitory. Opening my right eye to a slit, I peeked at my surroundings. Rich wood paneling marched to a ceiling crowned with plaster molding. I padded across polished floors covered with cushiony rugs.

"What is this room?" I murmured aloud. I didn't recall ever seeing my father in such an environment. Maybe this was a weird office where the dead and the living converged.

Wavy sunlight flooded the antique desk against the wall, its roll top open to reveal various papers scattered across a dark green leather top. As I approached, the door crashed open, and Merry hurried in.

"Merry?" I shrieked. "What are you doing here? Where's my dad?"

I longed to crawl into his lap like I did when I was nine, wrap his neck with warm love, and tell him what a hero he was. He risked his life to guide me along the Natchez Trace, teaching me about self-sufficiency and strength with every mile we covered. It was funny how I never felt like he was really gone until my dad, Lee Cagney, died. I'd been without them both for interminable months.

But now he was standing inches from me. I couldn't believe my luck.

"Merry." I said his name again, but no sound reached his ears. No matter how I screeched, he never glanced my way or broke his determined stride toward the window.

I waved my hands in front of my face and pinched myself and even tried to knock an inkwell—an inkwell?—from his desk, but my hand couldn't get closer than an inch above its surface, like an invisible shield hovered there.

"What's happening?"

I staggered toward Merry and tried to throw my arms around him, but his aura interacting with mine was like trying to touch two north ends of magnets together.

Oblivious, he ratcheted open the window, threw one suit-clad leg over the sill, and sat on the ledge. He rested his head on the wooden frame and closed his weary blue eyes. "Dammit. I'm not meant to be trapped between four walls, hustling natives for their land."

Wait a second wait a second wait a second. What natives? Whose land?

He clenched a letter between his fingers. Tiptoeing toward him, I leaned over and tried to read the loopy, old-fashioned handwriting. He wadded it up and threw it into the dirt road two stories below. Before I registered anything else, he was on his feet, following a faint worn line in the carpet to his desk. With supple grace, he sat, took out a sheet of paper, and raised a quill—a quill?—to its blank face.

Sidling up beside him, I said, "Merry, why won't you talk to me? Aren't you happy to see me? Because I'm thrilled to see you. Where's my dad? How long will we have to wait for him?"

In the next breath, I forgot my father. Merry's compact penmanship filled the top of the page.

Dear Sir:

I am writing regarding my denied request for reimbursement of expenses incurred for the Mandan delegation. I beg your administration to reconsider this most profound mortification of the governor of Upper Louisiana.

Huh? When did Upper Louisiana have its own governor? Didn't the whole state share one? I inched closer to Merry, bent over his shoulder, and kept reading.

Before they set out for Washington DC, I promised to return them to the Dakotas in a style befitting them, and I borrowed from my own meager savings to remain true to my word. Furthermore, I swore they would be allowed to remain on their tribal lands along the banks of the Missouri and told them their hunting grounds wouldn't be plundered. I may be many unfavorable things, sir, but I am not a prevaricator.

Dipping his quill in the open inkwell, he covered his face with his hands and muttered, "I'm ruined. All my money's tied up in speculative land deals. I don't even own a place to lay my head here in St. Louis, and I'm the damn governor. If the administration doesn't reimburse me, I'm finished."

In slow motion, he retrieved the quill and closed out his letter.

I am coming to Washington DC to make my case. Please expect me within the month.

Yours sincerely,

Meriwether Lewis

My jaw popped when my mouth sprung open. Meriwether Lewis? Merry was Meriwether Lewis, captain of the Lewis and Clark Expedition to the Pacific, leader of Thomas Jefferson's Corps of Discovery? I rifled through my mental file cabinet. I mean, I liked history well enough, but I was more interested in the seedier aspects of historical characters. Memorizing dusty dates and places wasn't interesting.

And nothing from this bygone scene had anything to do with my father. Where was he? I mean, the journal definitely transported me someplace, but it didn't deliver what was promised.

The only possible truth hit me then. "What year is this?" I mouthed the words, searched the top of the desk, and spotted a calendar in the jumble of discarded paper. A date strobed from the center of one haloed pile: 1809.

I collapsed into the chair on the opposite side of his desk and yelped when I fell through it. My behind hovered inches from the floor. I took in that impossibility of physics and catalogued the other bizarre happenings one by one: the way the dormitory dissolved and this room appeared; how Merry couldn't hear me speak or even see me; the way I couldn't touch objects and floated slightly above anything animate; the long-ago date on Merry's calendar.

Did the journal send me back in time?

No. Time travel wasn't possible. I mean, I loved reading science fiction, because it fired my imagination, not because I thought it could ever be real.

Still, I took in my surroundings and couldn't argue with myself any longer. I must have travelled back in time. Or a shard of concrete hit my head and caused me to have one hell of a hallucination.

Merry put down his quill and marched to the walnut sideboard. Rainbows of light glimmered on cut glass. He unstoppered a bottle and poured a shot of amber booze. Steeling himself with one shaking hand rested on the sideboard, he picked up the drink with the other and knocked it back. I expected him to pour himself a second and maybe a third, but he stoppered the bottle and stalked toward a matching walnut cabinet on the opposite wall.

"Going for something stronger, Merry?" I asked, though by now I knew he wouldn't answer.

My voice wasn't even a breeze. Once again, he didn't acknowledge my comment. Instead, he flung open two doors. The hinges squeaked as they parted to reveal stacks and stacks of books. With a sigh, he picked one up, unwound the leather string, and opened it.

Gobsmacked, I reached along my back and swiped Merry's journal from my waistband. The book he held was just like mine, which made sense because it was his, but how he had one and I also had one didn't compute at all.

Holding the journal to his forehead, he shut his eyes and spoke through clenched teeth. "It's time, Meriwether Lewis. You're seeking scientific perfection in these scribblings, but Jefferson doesn't care about that."

The room wobbled a little, but I gripped my journal, determined to see this hallucination or whatever it was to its conclusion.

Lewis flung his book onto his desk and stalked to the window. When he rubbed his hands over his face, I longed to throw my arms around him, like I had when I was nine and he was still my Merry. I knew that move, that rubbing away of annoyance. Every time he got frustrated with me on the Trace, he deployed that gesture to settle himself.

His chest expanded with air. As he let it out, he spoke. "Jefferson just wants the damn things published, no matter how amateur they make me look. But I need more time! Nothing is ready."

Whirling to face me, his proud back crumpled. I swore he saw me, but if he did, he gave no indication. He murmured, "But I can't delay any longer, because I need the money."

In two steps, he was in front of the open wardrobe, shoving journals into canvas sacks. Once the wardrobe was empty, he moved to the desk, found a blank piece of stationery, and inked his quill once again. I crept around the desk to read over his shoulder as he wrote.

Dear Clark:

I'm leaving St. Louis in your hands and embarking for the District of Columbia in the morning. You know my perilous financial situation. Perhaps I can convince the President to reimburse me in person.

And of course, Jefferson is rabid for the publication of our journals. I'm taking the final thirty-five with me, the ones our publisher cannot account for. After I meet with President Madison, I'll deliver these journals to Philadelphia and collect the balance of our publication advance. Those two influxes of cash should save my poor mother from the mortification of a bankrupt son.

I shall return by mid-October. Please keep me apprised of

developments here.

Your loyal servant,

Meriwether Lewis

While he finished packing, I studied him. I wasn't an expert on Lewis's life. In school, we learned Lewis and Clark followed Sacagawea to the Pacific Ocean. They came home and that was the end. It was a tiny, boring paragraph in my eighth-grade history book. I didn't know what happened to any of the men after the expedition ended. Nor did I learn how they died.

I paged through his journal—my copy—and scanned the first page again.

Dear Emmaline Cagney:

I'm sorry to have abandoned you until now. Several times over the past nine years, I wanted to spell out this message on these pages, but I feared you were too inexperienced to properly digest it. Recent events in your life forced me to act.

Whether we like it or not, your time has come. You cannot be expected to navigate the coming days without a map. Too much is at stake.

Wait a minute. What happened to Meriwether Lewis? How did he die? And where was my father? He was supposed to be here.

But before I got an answer, wind whooshed in my ear. Startled, I opened my eyes and found myself standing in the middle of the vacant Honduran dormitory, Merry's journal hugged to my chest. Glancing at my watch, I choked.

No time passed. It was like I never went anywhere.

EMMALINE

However I dissected the prior scene, I couldn't cast it aside. Not yet. It was real. Merry was Meriwether Lewis, an outsized explorer and adventurer.

But why did the journal take me to Merry when I asked to see my father?

Sweat drizzled down the small of my back. Rattled, I opened the journal to where I was sure I left off, only to find several pages of new writing. Same style. A few drawings popped from among the compact words.

> *You're probably still reliving the scene you witnessed, where you asked to see your father and were transported to an episode in Merry's short life.*
>
> *Allow me to help you grasp what's happening.*

"You lied to me, book. You promised I could see my father if I held you to my chest and asked, but he wasn't there. I mean, I was glad to see Merry again after so many years. Why didn't he know I was there? And why did the calendar read 1809?" Questions bounced along the pulse of my stuttered breathing. I hiccuped, "What does any of this mean?"

Ink rearranged itself on the page in response to my barked queries. My eyes crossed when I tried to follow its streaks and swirls. After a few moments, sentences coalesced, and I settled in to continue reading.

This book is your guide to the world of Nowhere. It's a real world inhabited by real people who once lived. You've even met a few of them, but I'm getting ahead of myself.

But I was already lost. What was Nowhere? And what did it have to do with Merry? Curiosity conquered my fear. I walked a finger toward the lower-right-hand corner and turned a page. More inexplicable sentences greeted me.

The people who inhabit Nowhere are those who were unfortunate enough to die an unresolved death.

I scratched my nose. "Unresolved death?"

Yes, an unresolved death, meaning no one knows how they died. Maybe there's a dispute about the manner of death, say murder versus suicide, and the mystery was never solved. Or perhaps a person disappeared, and no one ever discovered what happened to them.

"Wait. How did Merry die?"

Suicide. Or murder. I know which, but I don't count. A living person has to uncover the truth.

I gave Merry this journal a long time ago. He carried it with him through each of his thirteen Nowhere lives. Nowhere inhabitants must accomplish a mission to move on to a true afterlife. Though he meticulously recorded what happened each time, each Nowhere failure erased the entries. Nowhere people start each life from the same place, but usually at a different time.

I flopped backward on the mattress, my mind whirring with questions. Merry was a part of this place called Nowhere? And he interacted with me when I was nine? The book indicated he died young. "Gosh, I wish I'd paid more attention in history class," I sighed and sat up. Was this what happened when a *fer-de-lance* bit human flesh? Radical hallucinations? Crazed sightings? A lonely teenager talking to a book in the middle of the tropics?

"What does any of this have to do with my father?"

I know you have questions. This narrative will answer them. Patience, please.

Patience? After what just happened? I picked up the tome and hurled it across the room. It hit the rough wall with a *thwack* and landed spine downward on the floor. More handwriting crisscrossed its pages. I balled up my fists, rubbed them against my eyes, and shouted, "I have just returned from 1809. This is 1986. I spent at least ten minutes in a room with a man I loved as a child, a man you're telling me is some sort of zombie or ghost or not human or something. I asked you to take me to my father, and he wasn't even there. Now, you're telling me about a weird world called Nowhere, refusing to show me where my dad is, and lecturing me on patience? Seriously?" Tears scalded the corners of my eyes, but I flicked them aside before they poured down my face.

Instead, I breathed. In. Out. Deep and refreshing. I focused on the rise and fall of my ribcage until I could speak without yelling, crying, or cursing.

I crept toward the journal, staying low behind the cots. What did I know? A magic book might shoot out a death ray and consume me.

When I pulled up a few inches from its pages, I whispered, "I just wanted to see Dad. That's all."

You're not who you think you are. You're much more special. You are the child of two Nowhere souls. I took you to your dad. Merry was your father.

And with that revelation, my world turned black, a colorless, shapeless nothing.

I came to with my left cheek sweat-pasted to the concrete floor. The journal rested inches from my nose, still open. With monumental effort, I lifted my head enough to see the traitorous pages, the lies printed there.

Merry was your father.

I rolled onto my back and stared at the stained ceiling tiles. Coupled with going back in time, this revelation was too much to absorb in one day.

Lee Cagney was the only dad I ever had. He was there as far back as

I could remember, taking me for walks in Jackson Square, filling my fat toddler hands with beignets, and throwing pennies into the fountain. I could even see the world from his eye level, because he carried me so much when I was really small. I called for him with every nightmare and ate the peanut butter-and-banana sandwiches he fixed and danced to his music and risked my life to find him.

And he was just as thrilled to see me. I knew he was. Certainty burrowed through the fissures in my heart, all the way to my marrow. I mean, I loved Merry, but he couldn't be my dad. Kids know their parents in cosmic, unexplained ways, and my essence was sprung from Lee Cagney's.

When I ratcheted to my side, the journal loomed once more. I rested my head in my left hand and read fresh psyche-killing words.

> *I know you want to believe Lee Cagney was your father. You still cling to his memory and miss him every breath, as you should. Perhaps someday you'll discover how he became involved in your life, but those revelations are beyond the bounds of my instruction. My focus is on revealing who you really are. Merry was your father. You're a child of Nowhere. And you need all of your wits to encounter an even fiercer Nowhere man, your true enemy.*

"Who's my enemy?"

But his jowled face already materialized in my mind's eye. For once, I wasn't floored to read words in the infernal book.

> *James Wilkinson is your Nowhere nemesis.*

"Wait. Wilkinson is a Nowhere man? He's caught in the same weird world as Merry was?"

> *Yes. You must stop him, Emmaline, before he tries to harness your unique powers.*

"My powers? What powers do I have?"

> *You can travel backward in time, not forward, and you can only witness scenes that actually occurred, not interact with or alter them in any way.*

"Like what just happened with Merry?"

Yes. And you can also—

Before the writing finished, the room was consumed with a sucking sound. It raced between my ears, tugged at my clammy clothing, and fanned the journal's pages. In less than a second, the book smacked shut and vaulted across the room. By the time I got to my mattress, it was already there, closed with the outer tie done up in a knot. No matter how I tried, I couldn't undo it.

Exasperated, I thudded onto the bed and bellowed, "What else can I do? How can I fight Wilkinson if you don't tell me what to do?"

WILKINSON

"I don't know, Emmaline. How do you plan to fight me?"

Emmaline looked up from her bunk as I charged towards her.

I was still trying to unpack all the revelations from my White City trip, and in the short time I was gone, Emmaline had found her own ways to play. As I approached her bunk, she adjusted her pillow and sat taller, eyes defiant.

"I'm not going home tomorrow or the next day."

I halted. "I'm sorry?"

She stood and crossed her arms over her chest. "Sisa told me the volunteers are being sent back to the States on a special airplane. Your orders, she said. But I'm not leaving."

Well, this convenient outburst wasn't what I expected. Intrigued, I sat diagonally across from her on the opposite cot. Hands open. Expression solicitous. "Why do you believe you should be allowed to stay in a theater of increasing peril?"

"I care about these people. I mean, I put off a year of college to help them escape and build better lives. Because of that, I don't want to go home when I can help Trece and Sisa move more refugees to safety. Plus, I want to protect them from you."

I wagged my head from side to side. "Protect them from me? What a load of bullshit. You can't do anything without my say-so."

"And I understand that. Why do you think I'm begging you to let me work with Trece and Sisa?"

"Absolutely not. He's an expert on these jungles. She's been down here three years, while you've only been with us a few months. Granted, you've taken to this life, but you have no concept of the dangers."

"How are they any different from what I faced at the refugee camp? I mean, people shot at me. I had to defend others and kill deadly snakes and beat back vegetation that practically sprouted fourteen new limbs every time I lobbed off one. I can help them. You know I can."

My nostrils twitched for a cigar, because my brain was sharper when it was infused with smoke. I clenched my hands together and shifted on the cot. "The Mosquitia is diabolical the further you go toward Nicaragua. No place for an American teenager, regardless of how much you want to help. I can't allow it."

"Look, I don't care whether I live or not. My dad's dead, all right? He won't be there when I get home. He's gone forever. I'd rather lose my life rescuing people who are fighting to live than go back to the empty wasteland of my old life."

Could she be serious? Of course, I knew the face of true grief. It studied me every time I looked in a mirror and thought about my beloved Ann. Like Emmaline, I knew what it meant to leave my whole world in a worthless patch of ground, to wander the earth with a hole where my heart should be. Death and loss and grief were the cords that bound us together.

I sat slightly forward and cleared my throat. "Emmaline, I know what it's like to lose life's one true light. Your dad was yours, just as my Ann was mine."

She shrank backward. "I'm not her."

"I know you're not. But that's what barren grief does to a person: it convinces us we're seeing things that aren't there. An angle of the chin, perhaps. A knowing look behind the eye. The same stubborn turns of phrase. You remind me of my lost wife, but you could never be her. I understand now, because I've had more time to sit with her absence."

Emmaline swallowed hard. "You mean, it gets easier?"

Raw hope settled into the planes of her young face. I wished I could tell her the sting of loss faded with time, but whatever life I was on, it had a habit of leaving me off-kilter. Just when I got used to living without something vital, I had to exist without another precious thing. Since she was looking to me for advice, I decided to be honest, maybe capture a tiny portion of her trust.

"Not easier. Not exactly. We learn to see in the dark, but that doesn't mean we don't bump into things. Fall over. Get lost. Without our loved ones, our compasses, we'll always make mistakes. I can't let you make the error of staying here when it's too dangerous."

"But I just said I don't care if I die."

"And I'll have to answer for your wasted life."

She got up and sat on my cot beside me. Her hands hovered above mine, but she jerked them away and sat on them. "When you took this job, you knew you might die anytime."

I nodded. "Yes. It's part of the deal when one serves his country."

She turned on me, blue eyes flashing. "And I'm serving my country here, by aiding the refugees. If they stay in Nicaragua, they'll be tortured or murdered or both. I don't blame them for dragging their children through a jungle crawling with dangers for the chance to be free. America is still a shining light, a home for immigrants from all over, and I can't wait for them to get there and love it as much as I do. We're preparing them to succeed, and I'm proud of that. I signed up for this. I want to see it through to the end, even if it means my death. Please, Wilkinson. I don't want to leave so much undone. Let me stay and do what I can to help these people. They're all I have. I don't care what it costs me."

I held her red-rimmed stare for a few moments before giving her a single nod. "Even if some of them choose to go back and fight?"

She nodded.

"Fine. Meet me in my office. It's in the administration building near the main gate. Fifteen minutes. I've got reports of an unidentified group patrolling the swamps to the northeast. We'll go over the intel together first, and when I give the signal, you can tag along while I track them down and confront them. I need to see how you handle yourself. I must know that you are prepared to do whatever is necessary for our work to succeed. And if you fail, I'll send you home on the very next plane out of here."

I stepped into sheeting rain and congratulated myself. Because we wouldn't be tracking any ordinary band of Sandinistas. We were ambushing Theodosia's Nowhere gang. I'd soon know whether her bullets were as special as I thought they were.

She sprinted headlong into my trap. I couldn't wait for the whoosh of the spring to ensnare her.

WILKINSON

I locked myself in an office and paced enough to carve out a ditch in the concrete floor. The sound of my footsteps bounced off cinderblock and metal. As fifteen minutes ticked past thirty, I began to wonder where Emmaline was. Did she realize her future in Honduras was riding on her performance? How did I fail to make that clear? I didn't have time to nurse her second thoughts. One downed airplane in Nicaragua was plenty for the time being.

A rap sounded on the pressboard door. In two strides, I opened it, Emmaline's name already on my lips.

Emmaline's volunteer coordinator, Sisa, blew into the room instead. Her She-Rambo look always unsettled me. She was more bull-dyke than female. No tits. Did her best to look like a man, though she was too short to pull it off. I couldn't wait to put her on a plane and send her back to America.

She fixed me with a steely glare as she folded her arms across her flat chest.

"Where is Emmaline Cagney?"

I refused to take a step backward, no matter how much my feet itched. "You ought to have a better handle on that, Sisa."

She sniffed, her chin rising a notch higher. "What do you mean?"

"The girl has always been your responsibility. You're her direct superior. Yet from what I can tell, you let her snoop around a military operation unsupervised."

"You know she's our best volunteer. With all the other Abroad Togethers trickling in over the next twenty-four hours, I've got loads of shit to do. Flights to coordinate. Meals to plan."

"You've always been good at pivoting. Why are you so worked up?"

"Because we don't have enough beds in the dormitory, which is an even bigger problem given that we only have one dorm. Male and female will have to sleep together. Policing those amped-up teens on their last night here will be impossible. I can already see the goodbye hook-ups."

"Still, you left her completely without supervision. I ought to report you."

The woman threw up her hands, and I waited for them to close around my throat and squeeze. Instead, her fighting balloon burst. I could almost see the wind seeping from her.

She stalked past me and sank into a metal chair on the far wall. "Look," she breathed, "Everyone's rattled, Wilkinson. Hell, I am too. Word is spreading that an arms transport plane crashed. Is it true?"

I sank into my vinyl-covered swivel chair and grabbed my smoking paraphernalia from the corner of my metal desk. My hands stopped shaking when tobacco swirled through my airways. "Damn. I was convinced the director'd keep it quiet for a few days."

"And that's not all. Washington's hunger for refugee recruits for the Contra cause has been crushing. We can't get them turned around fast enough to fill the spots of the ones who die." She swatted one impatient backhand toward the window behind her. "With Emmaline self-sufficient here, I chose to focus on my main mission of supporting the Contras. After all, we both know this Abroad Together shit is my cover. I won't say I'm proud of it, but we both prioritize every day, right?"

I got up, circled the desk, and planted myself in front of her. "I'd buy that argument if we knew where the damn girl was now. But she was supposed to report to this office over a half-hour ago. Have you seen her?"

Sisa leapt to her feet, nose-to-nose with me. "Not in a couple of hours. I met her wandering around Catacamas and preyed upon our friendship to steer her back to base."

Friendship? Was Sisa friends with Emmaline? Maybe she learned something useful about the damn girl.

In one deft move, I whipped out my pistol and held it to her temple. Her brown eyes widened, but she didn't scream. I bet Sisa only screamed while bent over a chair being screwed from behind with a strap-on. With Theo prowling the jungle, I didn't have time to be nice. Through clenched teeth, I grunted, "Friends, huh? Why didn't you tell me?"

Her body stiffened, but her voice was steady. "Isn't this a bit of an overreaction, Wilkinson? You've never cared about my relationships with volunteers before."

"I want to know everything you've got on Emmaline Cagney. Now."

"You know as much as I do. Hell, you know more given that you met her when she was a prostitute's child in New Orleans."

"Yeah. But you handpicked her to come to Honduras. Why?"

"Get off it, Jimmy. You know how Abroad Together works. We run applicants through the usual paces: grades, community involvement, high school extracurriculars. But what we're really looking for, as you know better than any-damn-one, are exceptional kids. In Abroad Together's version of the SAT, Emmaline tested higher than any applicant we've ever had."

She was right. And Emmaline had another trait that made her well-suited to this mission. With the death of her father, she had nothing to lose, so she would give everything.

And she didn't pine for anyone back home. When she arrived, she devoted herself to her new life with a singular focus I found rare in people of any age, living or Nowhere. I almost felt a twinge of sympathy for a kid so alone in the world. Almost.

I clicked the gun's safety off and snarled, "I think there's more to her being here than the usual bullshit explanation, Sisa. She's different from the other recruits."

Her throat worked through a swallow. "Other than out-testing the others, she isn't."

"Sure she is. And I'm willing to bet one of your Nowhere lives you know what that is. So, what'll it be? A bullet through your noggin, or you tell me what you know?"

Her defiant eyes hardened, but I sensed fear behind the facade. Even ruthless agents like Sisa preferred a designed life, however fractured, over starting afresh in Nowhere. She didn't want to go back, have her memory erased, or wind up on some other mission. No, she preferred to be right here, right now, where we all agreed toppling communists was noble, right, and good.

"I told you. I don't—"

My silenced gunshot turned her sentence into an agonized fragment. She crumpled over, screaming. A gash smoked in the floor between her feet. I bumped the hot tip of the pistol into her temple and sneered, "I missed on purpose. Next time, I'm firing right here. Now tell me. What drew you to Emmaline Cagney? What secrets has she told you?"

Sisa's face and neck were mottled red, but she didn't cry. Instead, her shoulders relaxed as she replied in dull monotone. "Take the fucking gun away, Wilkinson. I'll spill what I know."

I moved it a couple of inches but kept it in full view. "Go on."

She chewed her lip until it bled. "I can't recall who brought me her file, but that's not unusual around here, right?"

"Where'd this happen?"

"In this very office almost a year ago. It's like her file appeared on the corner of the desk there. A note inside read *I think you'll find this application significant.* I have no idea who left it there."

I leaned into her. "What about what she did during the hurricane? We both saw Emmaline fire a shot, but other than a load of gore, I can't conjure a single speck of a detail about it now."

"Do you think the two are related?"

I tapped her forehead with the gun. "Do you?"

"How the hell should I know? I'm shackled to Nowhere just like you.

If I were omniscient, I wouldn't be here. I'd already be lounging on a beach sipping a frothy umbrella drink on the other side of this fucked-up purgatory."

I stepped away from her and opened the drawer of a metal file cabinet. It screeched wide, revealing molded files wrinkled by constant clamminess. I pulled out the first one and scanned it. "Is her file here?"

"You know I don't keep the special ones." She tapped the side of her stubbly head. "I commit those to memory and burn them immediately."

I knocked the butt of my gun into the back of her skull. Not hard enough to render her unconscious. Just enough force to scare her. She snapped back and moaned, her breath halting. I put my wet lips close to her ear and teased, "Tell me what you learned from that file."

"I swear, the only unusual thing the file revealed is she's special. But I don't know how."

"Like you're supposed to pay attention to her?"

"Yes. And don't ask me what I was supposed to be looking for. I befriended her, taught her everything I know about life in these parts, but other than the speed with which she adapted, I never noticed anything truly unique about her. Except for what we both saw at the other end of her bullet, of course."

A knock sounded on my door. I marched to the peephole and saw Emmaline there, her matted frizz framed by the outside light. I turned back to Sisa and said, "I order you to stay right there while I take this urgent communique. I won't be a minute."

Opening the door, I stepped into the hall and mopped my brow. "Emmaline, I'm glad you're here. I was interrogating someone who's infiltrated our system, and they've barricaded themselves in my office." Releasing the safety and checking the silencer, I handed her my pistol. "Here's your first test. Loop around the outside of the building and take a position under the back window. I'll force the door to divert their attention, and you use this gun to hobble them. Don't shoot to kill. Just administer a cripple shot. Go now."

"But I can't shoot—?"

"We both know you can. Now hurry!"

I gave her enough time to get around to the open window of my office, then I rammed open the door.

Sisa was still sitting in the chair, her shaved head backlit by the window frame. Because of course, she knew she couldn't leave without being insubordinate.

Right on cue, Emmaline stepped up to the opening and pulled the trigger. Her very real bullet smashed into Sisa's back and sent warm blood and innards cascading over my pristine floor.

And just like the last time Emmaline fired a gun, her body broke free of the chair and levitated a few feet above the floor. Emmaline and I both watched, transfixed, as molecules rearranged themselves into a void that consumed Sisa's corpse bite-by-bite. In less than a minute, she was gone. I was already forgetting her.

Emmaline fell to her knees, her eyes a flood. "On my God, you said it was an exercise. The gun wasn't supposed to be real. She was my friend, and there wasn't any lightning this time, and what is going on? I didn't mean to kill her." Confusion flicked across her face. "Wasn't she my friend? What just happened?"

I shrugged. The woman's face was disintegrating into a featureless blob. I couldn't remember her name. In a few minutes, I was certain I'd recall nothing about her. It was like she never existed on any plane. Was it even a she?

Emmaline's bullets were two-for-two.

Which likely meant her ammo erased someone from history, as though they were never born.

I wiped my forehead on my sleeve. Since I already couldn't recall the details, I decided to make some up. "I confronted the—the person, because my sources revealed them to be a Sandinista spy trained by Communists. You knocked just as they were resisting arrest."

"That can't be true." Her shoulders slumped a little. "I mean, I don't believe it, but I know I'm a murderer. This day has been so confusing. I don't understand what's happening."

I took one hesitant step toward her. "You're a hero. You snuffed an enemy spy from our midst. You've still got to complete your other tests, but there's no way I'm sending you back home now, not when you've proven you'll kill to protect your country."

EMMALINE

I had to get free from Wilkinson, out of the suffocating sunshine, and alone to think. I backed away from him and hurried down the road, but his clipped voice followed me. "Six hundred hours, Emmaline. Advance training for our mission on the exercise field at sunup tomorrow. You're doing well."

I didn't have much time before I had to run my next gauntlet, though he obviously thought I did something right with my bullet. I wasn't so sure. The exercise wasn't supposed to be real, and I couldn't recall anything about it now, other than the same body-chomping scene from the hurricane. Would the journal finally tell me what that meant?

I couldn't risk taking it out on base. Not again. Hanging a left at the mess hall, I ran toward the smaller rear gate of the compound. A lone sentry raised his hand and waved me through when I flashed my Abroad Together identity card.

I followed a worn trail and wound my way deep into the rain forest. Greenery swallowed me. I only crept far enough for all sound from the base to fade behind cat calls and shrieks and buzzing and lizard feet scurrying along branches overhead.

Finally, I could think.

I sat on an exposed tree root and rested my head against its swirling trunk. Once again, a human being evaporated feet from me after I fired my weapon. Was it because Wilkinson, a Nowhere man, was there like the other time? I mean, I couldn't blame it on lightning this go 'round, because there wasn't any.

I didn't believe Wilkinson for a minute. I was no hero, but I needed to stay in Honduras and find out what the journal wanted me to do, so I'd have to play along. At least, he wasn't locking me up for shooting someone. He meant for me to do it, and if they really were the enemy, I suppose he was right.

Standing, I clutched the book to my heart, closed my eyes, and whispered, "Can I see where Wilkinson starts every Nowhere life? You said he uses the same place every time. Take me there."

When I opened my eyes, cinder swirled around me. The Mosquitia, unfettered by gravity, rose up in a big splash like a giant meteor had struck its core. The ground fell away from my feet. I tried to scream, but whatever sound I made was lost in the whirling drain. Maybe I fell upward or downward. I couldn't tell. But I spun like a toy. Everything became a blur.

And as fast as it happened, I was still. A hot breeze stirred my unruly mop, and the air smelled of freshly dug dirt and mold. When I opened one eye, I couldn't mistake where I was. I mean, I didn't know which cemetery I was standing in, but it was definitely a cemetery, a boundless one. Above-ground crypts like in New Orleans marched down either side of the unpaved avenue, ornate tributes to the dead, too close together to even peek between them.

Where is this place? Has Wilkinson been here?

I dragged my eyes across the moonlit crypt in front of me. Its stone flourishes were broken near the top, and the iron gate was unlatched. Inside, a dusty urn was lashed to the altar by cobwebs, and bouquets of moldy plastic and silk flowers littered the marble floor.

When I stepped back from the door, I noticed the tarnished copper plaque: *Castillo*. Was I in Spain? Or still in Honduras? Though I didn't know of such an elaborate graveyard in Honduras.

A man cleared his throat behind me, and I pivoted toward him. Restless fingers fiddled with the front pocket of his soiled overalls, but he didn't have the face of a manual laborer. It was smooth and sun-free, almost effeminate in its delicacy. He carried a pickaxe.

"Do you work here?"

He dipped his head toward me, drove the metal point into the ground, and leaned on his tool. "Something like that. I wasn't expecting anyone today. Especially not at this grave."

I clutched Merry's journal behind my back. "And I'm kind of surprised to be here. Where am I?"

"This is the National Cemetery in Mexico City."

"Mexico City?" The journal took me from Honduras to Mexico City in less than a minute. I swallowed. "Um, that's—interesting."

"Is it now? Because I think you're being here is pretty damn interesting myself."

"Why? Lots of people visit cemeteries, right? Particularly prosperous ones like this."

"Yeah, but they don't meet me as part of a casual walking tour. I'm only here to greet special visitors, but like I said, I wasn't expecting you."

I stuffed the journal in the waistband of my filthy pants. He must've thought I was some sort of sick grave robber, given my grubby appearance. I gulped. "I'm not here to disturb anything, Mister. Um, what's your name?"

"Now, isn't that a riveting question?"

"Why? Everybody's got a name."

"Well, I used to, but I don't anymore, so you can call me Gravedigger. What's yours?"

"I'm Emmaline. Emmaline Cagney. Nice to meet you, Gravedigger."

"And how'd you find Nowhere, Miss Emmaline Cagney? Because you're not dead. I've dealt with these hopeless in-betweeners for some time now. They transmit a certain code. Oh, not like vampires or zombies or the rest of the ridiculous tales humans create to explain what comes after death. But they stand out. I can always feel them right here." He pointed to his heart and tapped. "In the center of my chest."

I touched my ribcage with one hand and thought about Wilkinson, about Merry. Even people like Sisa and Trece. Was everybody around me part of Nowhere? "Yeah, I feel them there, too."

"So, if you aren't starting a stint in Nowhere, what're you doing here?"

"I, well, how do I say this without sounding like an idiot?"

"Just spit it out, girl."

"I'm looking for the place where James Wilkinson starts his lives."

"Jimmy? That worthless bastard better be on the upside, finishing Nowhere life number 13, his final one." He chuckled. "I took most of them."

"Took most of them? What do you mean?"

"I whupped his ass and buried him in a grave more than a half-dozen times, right where you're standing."

"You can do that?"

"We gatekeepers aren't supposed to harm our charges, but I figured I'd get a pass because of all the rules Jimmy's flouted. And I'm still here, so I guess I was right."

My head was saturated with too much information, like being clobbered by a brutal sinus attack. I rubbed the bridge of my nose and closed my eyes to ease the pressure, but it didn't help. I squinted through two slits, and queried, "So when he fails a Nowhere assignment, this is where he starts over?"

"Yeah. I'm his Gravedigger." He eyed the pickaxe and shrugged. "Well, I don't really dig graves, except his a few times. But every Nowhere victim has a kind of mentor, somebody who meets them when they fail and helps them pick everything up and start over."

Merry's face danced across my mind. "Kind of like a parent?"

"Oh, I wouldn't go that far, but maybe. These goobs are a ball-and-chain, but I guess it's only fair. It's the job we get when we botch thirteen assignments."

"You mean, you didn't complete a mission by the end of your thirteenth Nowhere life?"

"Nope. And it sucks. I used to be somebody, a vibrant person with a family, a job, a story—at least I guess had those things—but because I failed my assignments, I fell from life's timeline. I'm a nameless non-existent nobody who's stuck being a gravedigger for all eternity."

"But that's terrible! Surely there's a way out."

"If there is, I sure as hell don't know it."

I jumped from foot to foot. "Does that happen to Wilkinson, too? If he fails this last assignment?"

"Far as I know, but like I said, I worked hard to put the fear of failure into his sorry ass last time he was here. Nobody wants to wind up like me."

I took a step forward, close enough to see moonlight reflected on his tobacco-tinged teeth. "Could you tell me about him? You know, Wilkinson and his assignment?"

The Gravedigger scratched his close-cut scalp and frowned. "I'm not sure Jimmy'd want me weaving yarns about him. Why don't you ask him who he was?"

"Because I don't think he'd be honest. He doesn't realize I know about Nowhere."

"Then I can't tell you, either."

I ground one foot in the dirt and bit my lip. I didn't come all this way only to leave without something to help me uncover Wilkinson's secrets. Maybe they'd reveal the one weakness that would help me deal with him.

I removed Merry's journal from my waistband and held it toward him. "This book helps me travel through time and visit places like yours. It's weird, because when I witness an actual scene from history, I can't interact with anyone. It's like I'm a ghost. But here, in the in-between, I can talk to you and feel things with my fingertips. I wonder why it's different."

He stuck out his smooth, unworked palm like he expected me to hand over the book, but when I hugged it to me, he laughed. "Look. You can't pull that out in my presence and not expect me to be curious. Besides, if you let me read a few pages, I'll send you back with some reading material of your own." He felt along his back and produced a similar leather-bound book. Tapping its Coptic spine of intricate knots against his right temple, he smiled. "Wilkinson's secrets. All the way back to his first outing here."

147

I lunged toward it, but the Gravedigger thrust it behind his back, taunting. "You let me read a few pages of your book, and I'll tear out a few pages of this one and send them back with you."

"I can't let you read my journal. It's the only way I can do anything."

"You're pretty naive, girl. I'm sure you can do more than you think."

I gulped. At least, the Gravedigger hadn't heard what happened when I fired my gun. Standing straighter, I thrust my chin out, "Well, Wilkinson can't make me do anything. I hate him."

He stepped back. "Hate? Nah. Look at you. You're the sweetest looking thing I've seen in a while." He pushed a golden tress from my cheek. "But if I were you, I'd be careful with old Jimmy. He's crafty. And even though you won't do anything for me, I'm giving something to you." Tearing out a page from his tome, he crumpled it up and put it in my front pocket. "Don't work with him if it feels wrong, and knowing Jimmy, it'll probably be wrong."

He slung the pickaxe over his shoulder and whistled down the lane until the darkness swallowed him. I took one last look around, and when I closed my eyes and clutched the journal to my breast, unsettled air consumed me again. But instead of watching the commotion, I waited until everything was still to open my eyes.

I was leaning against the same tropical tree. Like I'd never been anywhere.

EMMALINE

A red-haired stranger looked up from her cot when I charged into the dorm with the Gravedigger's single page flaming through my shirt pocket.

I surveyed the room. Most of the other beds were taken by departing Abroad Together volunteers, college-age teens from all over the United States. The air was filled with clashing accents and self-conscious laughter.

Great. No more dormitory opportunities to play with Merry's journal until everyone flew out the next day. I mean, I could've gone back into the matted overgrowth, but I didn't want to slip back outside to speak privately to a book – as insane as that sounded – and end up trapped in the wild Mosquitia after dark. Plus, I had my looming physical test the next morning, and I was determined to check on my former refugees, including Maria, no matter how many times the guard denied me.

Fuming at my lack of privacy, I stood taller and forced myself into a slow turn around the room. "Hi. I'm Emmaline." I smiled and shook hands and said my name again and again. One slight girl needed an extra coverlet. Another was nursing an open cut on her hand. After I delivered a second blanket to the first teen, and I dressed and bandaged the wound of the other one, I made sure everyone was supplied with enough netting to keep most of the night insects from chowing on their blood and flesh.

By the time I fell onto my bunk for a quick nap, I wondered if Merry was proud of me. I was sure he didn't have time to brood or feel sorry for himself on his western expedition. He probably behaved the same way then as he did with me: confident, caring, fearless.

I was trying to be that way in Honduras. I always wondered where I got my restless heart. My mother never left New Orleans. Running her brothel took every shred of her time and energy.

I shot upright. Ew, did Merry sleep with her? Was he one of her clients? Was that how I happened?

Did Nowhere children require one Nowhere parent? Or two? I collapsed into my thin pillow and rubbed my temple. Too much to keep straight, and no privacy to scour the journal for the answer.

The front door opened and Trece walked toward my cot. I sat up and yelped, "Trece. I thought you were still in the infirmary. How's the wound?"

His fingers fluttered along his side. "Barely hurts. You did a great job fixing me up."

My eyes clouded. Shouldn't we be talking about something else? A death maybe? What was I forgetting to tell him?

He sat down on the end of my cot and rested his arms on his knees. Leaning toward me, he quipped, "Why didn't you come and check on your patient?" His eyes were lit like sparklers.

I rolled over onto my stomach and avoided getting singed. An unsettled feeling gnawed at my gut. What was it? I should've been more upset about shooting someone in Wilkinson's office earlier, but I wasn't. Who were they? What did they mean to me? It was like walking into a room with an intention to do something and arriving at a blank. I might've been bothered for days over a task I couldn't recall.

I shrugged off the lingering twinges. "You know how it is. They've kept me pretty busy. I had some things to check out around the perimeter."

"Just as well. Your favorite person was here earlier." Trece put a hand on my arm. "Wilkinson."

I sat up, melted into the wall, and pulled my coverlet around me. "Did he ask where I was?"

"Nope." He fanned a hand around the overpopulated room. "How could he find anyone in this melee?"

I scooted closer to him. "What was he doing then?"

His teeth flashed in the harsh light. "He told me you wanted to stay behind when everyone else flies out in the coming days and asked me what I thought about you helping ferry refugees through the deep jungle."

"I hope you told him I can do it."

"I tried. I'm sure he's considering it. But he shifted into a lengthy discussion about the uptick in mercenaries scouring the area. How we needed to be extra careful. Asked if I'd seen any suspicious teams of men and women."

"Women? That's weird. Why that last question? The Sandinistas are chauvinists. They don't have women in positions other than sex object or slave."

Trece bounced over to my mattress and settled in beside me. I almost couldn't focus on what he was saying, because the heat from his body was twisting my insides into a craven furnace. I hugged my pillow to my chest and studied the far wall when he said, "I know, right? I'm glad you picked up on that one, too."

My head a mass of need, I scooted from my bed, slipped into my boots, and stretched. "Look. I've got some paperwork to fill out, you know, for staying. I'm going to head over to the administration building for an hour or so."

He popped to his feet. "Great. I'll go with you."

No, no, no. How would I review the Gravedigger's pages with Trece in the room? Especially when I'd rather have him haul me up on a desk and kiss me until I—

I reddened and squeaked, "No. I need to focus."

He grinned and brushed his fingers along my arm, leaving a trail of flame along every nerve ending. "But I might be able to help you. I'm sure it's a lot of the same stuff I filled out when I got here."

No matter how much I wanted to be alone with him, I couldn't trust Trece. He reported to Wilkinson, whether he liked it or not. Plus, he couldn't know about Nowhere or Wilkinson's role there. What might happen if an ordinary person found out about it? Would I do the same thing to him with a few sentences that my bullet did? I couldn't risk it, not with Trece.

"No, Trece. Really. I need to do this by myself, okay? Some of this information is kind of sensitive."

"Then I'll be waiting for you when you get back. Maybe we can go for a walk or something."

Why was persistence so attractive in a man when I liked him?

I put my hand on his forearm and squeezed. "I'll probably be too tired. It's been a day, and I've still got to complete a physical test in the morning."

He ducked his head and nodded, hurt etched along the corners of his fetching eyes, the downslope of his luscious mouth. He shifted topics. "I know. I'm running you through the paces on the first part of your workout."

"The first part?" I echoed.

"Yeah. Expect a bruising." He stepped closer. "Sure you don't want to spend the next few hours trying to get me to tell you how to prepare?"

I ran my gaze over his parted lips, the dimple next to his mouth I longed to taste. "I can't," I muttered. Before I changed my mind, I bounded into sunlight and followed the main gravel road to the administrative building. I never looked back, or I probably would've turned around and spent the night with Trece.

And I couldn't be irresponsible, not when the Gravedigger gave me such a potential gift.

One window glowed from the inside the office building. Being a hub, the place was always occupied. I let myself in the metal entry door and hurried past bland offices to a vacant one at the rear. Back when I'd first arrived, someone assigned me and other volunteers a space to plan refugee activities, make inventory lists, and escape when we needed time alone.

As an only child, I thought I'd love being surrounded by people. Life growing up was sometimes lonely, no matter how much backstory Lee Cagney added. He tried, but it was like pouring sand into a sieve. Grains stuck to me here and there, but a lot was swept out to sea. Connections were tough to make when I didn't trust anybody.

I pushed through the door of the office and closed it. A single cot sat forlorn in the empty space. Whenever the dormitory overflowed, someone ended up spending the night here, and I decided to go ahead and claim it.

Stretching out on my stomach, I took the Gravedigger's wadded page from my front pocket. It crackled and scratched as I untangled it and tried to press it flat on the pillow. The edges were tea-stained, and the paper's surface was whispery between my fingers. It smelled like a library of old and rare books. Spidery handwriting covered the page, interspersed with what looked like symbols from calculus or trigonometry, subjects I barely grasped in high school. I settled in and tried to read.

1812

In life, a man never outgrew his predilections, did he? Despite certain unpleasantries with—

There was an upside-down triangle printed carefully after the word *with*. I couldn't fathom what an upside-down triangle might indicate, so I skipped over it and kept reading.

I received a new military commission, a major general. I made a stop on my way to—a combination of two unknown symbols. I found myself standing on a beach. Salt spray stung my eyes as I trained them toward the yawning shoreline. I never imagined myself in this position, at this moment, waiting for scraps of a ship to wash ashore.

Nobody knows it was I who ordered—more weird symbols—to push off from Charleston ahead of a hurricane and drown a ship full of passengers.

Including that whore Theodosia Burr.

I stopped. Who was Theodosia Burr? What kind of name was that?

I rolled onto my back and followed the edges of water stains around the top of the walls. I needed to find out what this revelation meant.

But how?

EMMALINE

I'd finished mulling over the Gravedigger's single page late last night, but I didn't have any answers. This morning, my body was wracked with fatigue from hours spent flipping through Merry's journal without conjuring any additional clues about Wilkinson or Nowhere or anything else. The book was silent in the face of my questioning. It revealed nothing more.

And now Trece was trying to kill me for rejecting him the evening before.

"Keep going! If you drop, you die! Move!" Trece nudged my flaming shoulders with a stick. Where was the guy who wanted to go on a romantic late-night stroll? I was such a lovesick idiot. I probably projected my intentions onto him. He wasn't really attracted to me.

And in that moment, I hated him. My legs were liquid lava, and I'd sucked enough water out of the moist air to drown twice. Still, I strained against my hundred-pound pack and kept my eye on the makeshift finish line: a pull-up bar glinting in the sun on the exercise course.

When I insisted on staying to help ferry a bunch of refugees into Honduras, I didn't realize it meant enduring a boot camp meant for a Green Beret. Sure, I expected more training, but not a morning of running swampy trails with an overweight pack, fording saturated expanses where I sunk up to my neck, and clearing waist-thick tree limbs with Trece shouting at me the whole time.

I tried to tune him out and focused on the stakes. Wilkinson. Whatever he was up to in Nowhere. Discovering the other secrets of Merry's journal. Besides, I wasn't going to let any refugee be disappointed when a slight blonde American came to lead them to freedom.

As I stayed ahead of Trece, the journal still nagged at my subconscious. The scene in Merry's office called to me. I needed to go back, but I couldn't when every hour was consumed with preparing to prove I could ferry refugees through a hostile rain forest. Using a book to flit through history did little to save lives today, and the refugees were more important. So, I strapped the journal next to my skin, threw on my shirt, and told myself I'd go back soon.

I was afraid of what I'd see next time I dissolved into the journal's world. Fearful of who I'd meet. Unsure what these haphazard episodes would mean for me. When I arrived in Honduras, I was just Lee Cagney's daughter, and I was more than okay with that. But shouldering the mantle of someone more powerful, a Nowhere offspring with a responsibility to defeat Wilkinson? I mean, I wanted to see him dead, but I wasn't ready to kill him, regardless of what Merry's journal said.

Trece's breath stung my right ear. "Sandinistas are right behind you, Cagney. They've got machine guns trained on you and your refugees." How could he be on my heels and not be out of breath? Especially since he was recovering from a gunshot wound. Was he a cyborg, like in *Terminator*? He hurried in front of me. His spittle stung my face with his yelling. "If you aren't at the finish in three seconds, everybody dies. Do you hear me?"

Rage boiled to my surface. Why was he being such a jerk? Trece's personality shifts were maddening. Sometimes, he still harped on how lazy and entitled Americans were, but underneath the bluster, he could be thoughtful and attentive. Like the earplugs to help me sleep amidst the booming of the tropics and candy bars for midnight snacking. Once, he slipped a small rectangular package into my hand.

"What's this?" I wondered as I tore at the twine.

"Soap I picked up from a village. It's like showering with lemons. Not expensive or American, but I thought you'd appreciate it."

I rubbed my fingers along a rough surface studded with lemon zest, an uneven rectangle. When I flipped it over, I found a fingerprint, proof that it was handmade.

I mean, I wasn't someone who fell for men who berated and then rewarded me. I saw what Trece was: an expert fisherman, arrogant enough to think he could use his reel to tease me into taking his bait and sacrificing my life by becoming a footnote in his. The woman labors to support her man, and he's the only one who's remembered. Nope. Not for me.

I shoved him out of my way and streaked toward the finish. When I touched the pull up bar, I didn't stop. Instead, I sprinted around the course once more for good measure while he waited on the sidelines. I'd show him how much I could do under pressure.

When I rounded the last bend, he stepped in my path and grabbed me by both shoulders. "Enough. You proved your point. You're a badass, Cagney. I pushed you, because I don't want to lose you out there. The Sandinistas'll be ten thousand times worse than I was, and you can't break under that kind of pressure."

"I think I just proved I won't."

"You did well enough to earn a decent meal. Now, let's go eat."

The vegetation spun, but I wouldn't let him see how close I was to fainting. "Just let me catch my breath, and I'll meet you in the mess hall."

"I've got food for us here."

"Huh? Oh, come on. I don't want to eat mission rations before I have to."

"Neither do I. You're working hard. That's why I decided to share my lunch with you."

"What? I don't want your food."

"I bet you will when you see it. Over there." He motioned to the verdant snarl behind me. "Sometimes, I get my pick of provisions. You might want to check them out before you decide."

Questions died on the tip of my tongue when he took my hand and led me along a tangled path to an opening a few feet away. A tarp was spread on the mushy ground, and a cooler anchored one end. I shrugged from my backpack and settled on the opposite side of the covering, while he dug through a satchel and produced a woven blanket. "Cloth makes this plastic a little more tolerable," he said as he slung one end my way. I got up and helped him spread it out and tucked a paper napkin under my chin.

"What's on the menu? Are you going to impress me with roast *fer-de-lance* or some other delicacy you killed?"

He flashed a lop-sided grin. "Not this time." He opened the cooler and pulled out a crumpled white bag. "I didn't know whether you liked Big Macs or Quarter Pounders, but given how far you've extended yourself physically, I figured you might eat one of each."

My taste buds warred with my emotions. Five minutes ago, I was ready to kill him, but when he told me he didn't want anything to happen to me, I melted. I couldn't remember the last time I had fast food or a decent kiss. Every molecule of my being screamed to tackle him, slip my fingers into his shirt, and put my trembling lips on his skin, but instead I blushed to my hairline and studied the greasy bag.

I will not fall for this. I will not. I didn't owe him favors for his thoughtfulness, sexual or otherwise.

I swallowed. Was I being too tough on him? His eager fingers tore into the paper, his intention focused on one thing. He was craving junk food enough to scarf a whole Big Mac in two bites.

"Where did you find McDonald's?" I had to keep talking, or I'd do something like lick the mustard from the dimple at the corner of his mouth.

He shrugged. "I'm sorry it's not the freshest. Mess guys heated it up and brought it out here, but I've had it since yesterday."

"Yesterday?" I reached for the familiar yellow paper of the Big Mac and tore into it. The seeded bun was decadent against my lips, and the meat was ecstasy on my tongue. I closed my eyes, chewed a little bite of home, and forgot how much I missed it.

He unwrapped another Quarter Pounder with cheese and talked through a bite. "Yeah. I get to make special requests sometimes when people are flying in from the States."

"That's surprising."

"Surprising? Why?"

"From how you talk sometimes, I got the impression you hated America. I mean, I know you'll probably wind up an immigrant there after this is over, but I'm not sure that's what you really want."

"Oh, I'll have plenty of opportunities in America, even though I hate the way some Americans act. There's a difference."

I shoved a fat bundle of salty French fries into my mouth. "How?" I mumbled though wads of tasty potato.

So much for seducing him. Like I'd ever do that anyway.

He stretched out his legs until his boot-clad feet touched mine. In one deft move, he scissored my ankles between his and left them there. I swallowed, afraid to break the spell.

"I've never been to the United States. At least, not that I, well, never mind."

I nudged his ankle. "What?"

His hesitated and took another bite of his sandwich. "Oh, it's nothing. I got to ride along on a delivery once, but I wasn't allowed to leave the plane. No passport. I'm getting my papers at the end of my mission here. So, I've flown into Miami, but I guess that doesn't count."

"We export a lot of images of who we are through movies and music and stuff, huh?"

"Yeah, if somebody's never met an American, they're pretty likely to form opinions from what they see and read and listen to. But for me, it's more than that. You know the people running this refugee operation are American. Some of the refugees sign up for Contra training. They want to go back to Nicaragua and fight their former overlords. You know, free their country. I'm trying to give them choices, you know? Claim asylum in the States or train to go home and fight."

"I can't even fathom what that's like. If I escaped an intolerable situation, could I go back and try to overthrow my former tormentors? Gosh, I don't know."

He finished his burger and stretched out on his side, facing me. A lock of black fell into his eyes, and I itched to brush it aside. Before I embarrassed myself, he pushed it back and squinted up at me. "What do you mean?"

"If America were ever taken over by a totalitarian regime, I don't know that I'd be bold enough to risk my life, to speak out, to fight back. So much of what you said about Americans is true. I'm afraid we're too spoiled, too comfortable, too bloated and lazy. I think we're too easily discouraged. We expect life to always unfold with possibility, like petals on a rose, only I think we've forgotten that even the loveliest flowers shrivel and turn brown and die."

"But their deaths make way for more flowers."

"Right, I guess in the coming days, I'll find out if I have what it takes to sacrifice my life for a cause." I toyed with the remaining fries splayed on a napkin between us. "Some of the people I've met here are fiercer than I'll ever be. I don't know how they do it, but they believe in freedom so much, they left everything behind for the chance to learn how to go back and die for it."

His finger drew a fiery line up my neck and turned my face toward his. An inferno consumed my heart, but I didn't care what he saw. I locked eyes with him and didn't resist. "I'm sorry for what I said about Americans, for how I've treated you. You're acing this, Cagney. I meant it earlier when I said you're a badass." He stroked my cheek and sent me tumbling over the precipice.

His lips parted, and I tilted toward him. What a pushover. Against all practical advice, I was ready to devour his beckoning mouth. As I readied for the shock of his kiss, the jungle quaked.

Wilkinson crashed through the overgrowth and stood over us, hands on hips, his eyes two coals. "What are you two doing, out here necking in the flora?"

Trece rolled away from me and popped to his feet. "Sir. We were just, you know, taking a break. Cagney ran fifteen miles today. I'm letting her rest."

He took a step toward the cluttered trail. "No fraternizing here. You both know that. I've got an urgent appointment today, Trece, and you're needed elsewhere. Be at the airstrip in five."

I stood up. "Take me with you."

But he walked into the tangle without looking back. Trece stuffed everything into the cooler and took it with him, another wordless exit. Airplane engines churned up the trees. "What just happened?" I whispered.

But as I flopped onto the ground and took out Merry's journal, shame turned my heat for Trece to shards of ice. I was letting hormones consume me when I needed to figure out how to vanquish Wilkinson. Because I only fought to remain so that I could work with the journal and divine how to get rid of him for good.

I squeezed the leather. I never thought this would be so confusing and complex. When I came here, I expected to hand out clothes and settle people into new lives, not uncover another world and a whole new identity. What a simpleton I was. I took a shaky breath and muttered, "I promise to make you proud, Merry. Show me how you'd move forward. Give me an example from when you were alive."

The frame's edges burned away. Invisible flames consumed the trees until they were smoky ether. And when everything cleared, Merry was there. I took out a pencil and opened the journal to a blank page, determined to record what he revealed. If I didn't use my forays to make an accurate record of history, how would I ever interpret it for the future.

WILKINSON

A private jet engine thrummed in the background, ready to fly me to Air Force One. The President was on an official trip to Mexico. When he demanded a conference, I had to go to him. Flight time was what he had available. I was headed to DC from Mexico City, but Trece wasn't going with me. Not this time.

I patted him on the shoulder. "I want you to ratchet up your wooing. You were doing great back there."

"Cagney's tough. It's not an act. I actually respect her." His jaw hardened as he stood.

"Well, *respect her* all you like, but I meant what I said back there. Keep your feelings out of it. This is work. Understand?"

"Yes sir." He wheeled around and stalked toward the door.

"Go back there and finish what you started. Nothing wrong with leaving her a little off-kilter. And keep me apprised of her progress. I need her ready as soon as possible."

With a nod, he ducked under the doorframe and clanged down the metal steps. The pilot sealed the door and flew me to Mexico City in under an hour. We landed next to the President's jet, where I hurried from plane to plane.

A steward led me up the front steps, guided me along a warren of screens and chairs, and left me in the President's office. While I waited, I smoked my stogie and tried to relax my fevered brain.

I expected Air Force One to be supreme luxury, but the President's office was wedged into one side of the plane. He had a small wooden desk with the ubiquitous jelly beans in a dish as its sole decoration, plus a narrow sofa where I assumed he slept. Nothing elaborate for our commander-in-chief.

A summons like this wasn't a good sign, especially not in the wake of the plane that crashed carrying a shipment of illegal arms. Nobody knew where the Sandinistas took the guy who was flying it. That one plane blew up the national news. Every operative was scrambling. I needed to drag this thing back on course or risk having my Nowhere outing deemed a failure.

Failure number thirteen meant the end: erased from history's timeline. Forgotten forever. A nameless gravedigger in a Shakespearean yarn.

But that wouldn't happen now, because Emmaline was going to fire her gun and help me finish. After all, her bullets seem to be able to erase both the living and the dead.

As I waited for the President to appear, I finalized my story. I just hoped I could sell it to the most powerful man on the planet.

A few agonizing minutes later, a buzzer sounded, and the President strode into the cabin. His papery face lacked the usual Hollywood smile.

"Jimmy. Jimmy. Jimmy. The Nicaragua thing's a mess. This plane crash, it'll annihilate our Contra program. The press is already nosing around in the wreckage. Damn pricks don't care that one of our boys almost died, do they? No, they just want to find enough dirt to finish me." He dropped into a chair opposite, his shellacked head in his hands. "The boys at CIA told me you've been a covert advisor to several other presidents."

"Yes, sir."

"I don't want to know any more about it. They assured me of your sound advice and discretion."

God, I always relished these moments with powerful men. That's the thing about power. For some, it's as addictive as a shot of heroin. But when the high wears off, presidents were just ordinary men who could be broken by falsehoods, disloyalties, and failed schemes. Helping them pick their way through misfortunes cemented my own dominion.

I sat taller. "If you're asking for my advice, you need to come clean with them, sir."

"With whom?"

"The American people. Take responsibility. Tell them whatever truth you can. You'll disarm the media. They expect politicians to lie. Bastards won't know what to do with an elected official who tells the truth."

"But I can't admit I knew about it."

I got up and flung my arm around his bony shoulders. Underneath his suit of armor, he was thinner, frailer than I expected. I greased my voice with an extra dash of reassurance. "Sir, the art of lying isn't the lie; it's seasoning the lie with enough truth to sell it. For example, did you know about this specific mission?"

"Well, no."

"All right. Your underlings ran the mission and kept you in the dark. Perhaps they did it to protect you, to give you this exact moment of deniability. Run with it, sir. That's my advice."

He stared into space for a few moments, and I wondered where he went. It was almost like he forgot I was in the room. I cleared my throat and brought him back. After a brief gape of confusion, he shook cobwebs from his head and pumped my hand with his. "Thank you for your counsel. You're making your country proud, Jimmy. God bless America."

He ferried me into a secret chamber adjacent to his office until we landed. After everyone else exited the plane, I crept from my closet and found a limousine waiting at the foot of the stairs. My driver made quick work of zipping across the tarmac to another private jet. Two private flights in one day cost the taxpayers buckets of money, but it was necessary when a person wasn't supposed to be seen anywhere near the President.

I took the steps two at a time and settled into a pliant leather chair, comfort I had expected on Air Force One. The steward brought me a whiskey and a clipped cigar before we lifted off, and I accepted them without a glance and lit up. The web of DC fell away underneath me while

I sipped my first cool drink to celebrate.

Four hours later, I landed on the airstrip in Catacamas.

The base was bedlam. The exposure of our covert activities obviously ratcheted up refugee desperation. Tents were pitched on every available surface, all the way to the tree line. New Nicaraguan families huddled along the base's main artery in twos and threes, awaiting the opening of the mess hall. I counted at least a hundred potential Contras in the mix, because from teenagers on up, any upright body could hold a gun. And I didn't give a shit how many we sacrificed, as long as we got rid of the Soviet-sponsored regime next door without loss of American life and I finished with Nowhere.

Bleeding-heart Emmaline must have figured some of her charges were being recruited to help our cause, although she would certainly make a scene if she found out her volunteer work was actually feeding healthy refugee bodies to Sandinista machine guns along the Nicaraguan border. But every death brought us closer to ending communism in Central America without sacrificing white ass American lives. My mission mattered.

Trece sped around the corner of a concrete barracks. My lungs collapsed when he hit me head-on. I leaned against the building, gasping like an asthmatic, while Trece filled the air with apologies and waited for me to recover. As soon as I could stand, he stuck a hand under my elbow and steered me into the alley between the mess hall and infirmary. Sun shifted to shade, with my dull eyes fighting to bring dirty tile pavers and drying laundry into focus.

"So, Trece. Update me on Emmaline."

"I didn't get very far, sir."

I led him further into the alley and lowered my voice. "What do you mean?"

"Look around you, sir. People everywhere. They started tottering from the snarl right after you left. At one point, the line stretched from the main gate and halfway along the primary artery in town. We didn't guide them here, which means nobody vetted them."

"You think the enemy could be hiding among them, waiting to take down the base?"

"It's probable. I disregarded your orders to check stories, verifying identities when I could. I put the remaining Abroad Together volunteers on it, the ones we didn't fly home earlier today, including Emmaline. Still, we didn't have enough people to handle everyone, even with me."

I took his arm and led him into the open. On the way, I whispered, "Don't worry. I'll plant several plainclothes patrols, even join them myself if necessary."

As we mingled with the rear of the food line, Emmaline stepped through the back door of the mess hall and ambled toward the secondary gate. It opened to the tree line running along the back of the base. Looking left and right, she waved her credentials at the solitary guard, walked across the dirt road, and stepped into the thicket.

"She's supposed to be working with her beloved refugees. What's she doing?" I hissed in Trece's ear.

"I don't know, sir."

I grabbed him by the shoulder and started running. "Let's go."

We plowed into the gnarled vegetation. Vines and branches tore at my face as I led the way. Overhead, parrots cackled, and unseen wildlife pelted us with berries. The forest thickened, and I tripped over a root and fell into a small clearing. Trece tumbled and landed on top of me. As we fought to extricate ourselves, I stared across the expanse and gasped. Trece followed my gaze.

Emmaline shimmered there, her arms wrapped around her chest. Her lips moved, but no sound escaped, and her usually vibrant eyes were unfocused. My eyes cried for a refreshing blink, but I forced them to stay trained on her. In ten clicks or so, she was gone. Vaporized. Invisible.

I staggered to my feet. "Emmaline? Emmaline Cagney? Where'd you go?"

But I had a knack for sensing the essence of a thing. Like when I went to the White City, I expected Ku was there before I met them. Same thing with Emmaline's absence. Wherever she went, no part of her lingered here.

Trece whistled. "What do you think that's about?"

I felt around for a cigar, but when I fished one from my front pocket, it was crushed flat from my fall. Throwing it into the bramble, I sighed. "We're both Nowhere. Watching other Nowhere types vanish when they end a life is usual stuff. But this? I don't know. She's definitely living *this* life, not a Nowhere redo. Which makes me wonder."

"What?"

"I found your White City. Met your Ku."

Trece bowed. "They told me."

"Yeah, well, of course they did. They—I have such a hard time calling something that looks like a woman *they*—they told me Emmaline has special Nowhere powers. Maybe we just got another taste of them."

"Any idea what they are?"

"Disappearing into the ether, obviously, but for what purpose? Magic bullets that eat her victims. And another thing bothers me."

"What?"

"Ku said the Nowhere assassins are trying to protect Emmaline. I'm sure they're looking to whack me as part of their mission, too."

"Why would anyone eliminate you, sir?"

"Let's just say I've made a few Nowhere enemies enroute to this overly dank hell. If they already know Emmaline's secrets, they might force her to serve them, probably to some nefarious end. We've got to find out what this means, Trece." I took out my pistol, released the safety, and thrust it at him. "Stay here. Whenever she reappears, hold her at gunpoint and bring her to me."

EMMALINE

I hurtled through space like a comet. This time, the rain forest scattered and fell away, leaving me without a center of gravity. Brimstone flamed all around me. I'd asked the journal to show me an episode from Merry's life; I wasn't expecting a tour through hell.

A door fanned open in the distance. My body floated through its spotlit frame and into a sun-washed courtroom. Spectators clad in a mix of sweeping skirts, three-piece suits, and plumed hats filled every available seat, leaned against slate gray walls, and even stood in the aisles. Many of the ladies wore gloves and carried lace shawls, even though it was too hot for such covering. Multi-layered crinolines peeked from underneath their floor-length hems. Given the stifling heat, I was glad I didn't have to wear a corset like the women in the room. I craned my neck from the far corner of the balcony and tried to glimpse the show. Was Merry in the courtroom? Was he on trial? Was that why the journal brought me here?

As I melted between bodies and inched toward the loft's edge, I caught sight of the defendant. I'd never seen the man before.

But I couldn't mistake the first witness for the prosecution. Wilkinson sauntered up the aisle, his pudge stuffed into a general's uniform gaudy with tassels and gold braid. He sat in the wood-paneled box and puffed on his usual stinking cigar.

I scanned the defendant's table. No Merry. Several unfamiliar men sat there, scribbling notes and whispering in each other's ears. One of them rose and approached Wilkinson. I strained over the balcony railing, hovering above the ground floor. Wide planks marched horizontally toward the front.

A striking man, balding a bit with piercing eyes, paced in front of Wilkinson. Maybe he was the lead attorney. I settled in to watch.

"Sir." The defense attorney's tone was conversational, relaxed. "In your testimony for the prosecution, you swore that the defendant committed treason against the United States."

Wilkinson blew a plume of smoke and nodded. "Yes. By invading New Orleans, a city we'd recently acquired from Napoleon."

"And what evidence do you have that anyone planned to take New Orleans by force?"

"Come on, Burr. Everyone knew your intentions. You and your army of cretins were the talk of Louisiana, hell, the whole damn country."

Burr? Who was he? Where had I heard that name recently? Wilkinson spoke to this defense lawyer Burr like he was the one on trial. I floated closer, stopping a quarter of the way up a side aisle, and settled into an alcove halfway up the wall. Wilkinson couldn't see me, though I swore he studied me with one eye while he smoked his cigar and awaited the next question.

"So you only present rumors and hearsay?"

"Newspapers printed missives on your crimes."

"Based upon what evidence?"

"People claimed—"

"What one hears others say is the definition of *hearsay,* my dear General." Burr smirked to the judge, while Wilkinson seethed in his seat. His face reddened with rage, and his eyes squinted with murderous fury as the man named Burr carried on. "Unless you have an unfortunate letter I wrote to someone citing my alleged desire to topple New Orleans or multiple witnesses to a treasonous act or perhaps a concurrent log where you recorded detailed happenings from that time, you lack evidence of my guilt. Charges in publications are not incontrovertible proof of a crime; they could just as well be propaganda. We can unravel the ownership of many of our rags and discover the underlying aims of their publishers. I've already done it for you in the case of one: *The American Citizen*."

Burr stalked toward his table, snatched a sheaf of papers, and cried, "Permission to approach the bench?"

The baggy-eyed judge nodded. "Proceed."

The accused handed the judge his evidence and turned to face the room, his back to a smoldering Wilkinson. He tented his hands in front of his chin and smiled at the crowd. "I submit Exhibit A, Your Honor. As you can read, *The American Citizen* is a periodical of recent provenance, founded in 1801."

I blinked at the date, still not quite believing I floated someplace in the early nineteenth century. Gripping the journal as anchor, I focused on Burr's next reveal.

"My colleagues and I researched the ownership of *The American Citizen*, home to a former features editor named James Cheetham."

The judge yawned. "Do you have a point?"

"Yes, Your Honor. I'm getting to it."

"Do hurry."

Wilkinson smirked behind a smokescreen while Burr proceeded.

"The Irish are adept at drinking, but they're also masters of written vitriol, and Cheetham is their apex-god. Since 1804, he has been listed as the publisher of *The American Citizen*, but in reality, the paper's majority owner is a shadow company registered in New York. If you turn to page three, you'll find a roll call of several companies and their ownership percentages. Do you have it?"

Papers ruffled, and the judge took out a magnifying glass. Holding it over the page, he murmured, "Yes. Yes, I see it."

Wilkinson tamped out his cigar on the sole of his boot and craned his neck toward the bench. "What? What do you see?"

Burr ambled to the other side of the courtroom, his posture one of a theatrical performer. He twirled on Wilkinson and cried, "The company with the largest ownership in *The American Citizen*, the rag that destroyed my political reputation with colorful libels subsequently proven false, is none other than a Virginia outfit called the Paris Exchange."

"What does that have to do with your treason?" Wilkinson countered.

"The Paris Exchange's primary business is importing cases of French wine on credit and transferring them to the Monticello Company, sole legal owner of the Paris Exchange."

Wilkinson's face purpled at the same time the judge flashed a satisfied half-smile. "And who owns Monticello?"

"One Thomas Jefferson, Your Honor. President of the United States. Why else would the President own a newspaper—he owns at least ten, by the way—other than to influence their reporting, both to spit shine his image and to shit on his enemies?" He bounded to his table, whisked up more papers, and dropped them in front of the judge. "Exhibit B, Your Honor. Articles about me clipped from *The American Citizen* during my run for governor of New York, a list of no fewer than two hundred essays assassinating my character and accusing me of crimes I did not commit. Several articles even insinuated that I engage in carnal relations with my own daughter!"

Bedlam broke out across the claustrophobic room. The judge slammed his gavel, repeatedly shouting, "Order! Order! Come to order!"

After a minute of confusion, the crowd quieted.

"The evidence I present firmly establishes that stories can be spun to suit any point of view. We have deposed multiple parties to these prevarications under oath. Both their testimonies and presented evidence counter much of what *The American Citizen* printed about me. Still, this misinformation persists. It's why a man who wanted to start a quiet farming life on Louisiana's Balstrop Tract with fifty other men stands before you today accused of treason."

Wilkinson lumbered to his feet. "You had no such intentions. You told—" His face turned white, and he crashed backward into his chair. When he groped for a fresh cigar, his hands trembled.

"I told you my intentions? Is that what you were going to say?"

Wilkinson leaned forward, one big hand on the wooden barrier, and spat. "Don't put words in my mouth, Burr."

"Ah, but you have no problem repeating all sorts of nonsense when it means you might see me hang. Is that right?"

Burr didn't give Wilkinson time to answer. He turned on his heel, spread his arms wide, and thundered, "I therefore assert that gossip repeated at parties and bought-and-paid-for propaganda printed in newspapers cannot be relied upon as incontrovertible evidence of guilt, in this or any other courtroom in the United States of America."

Wilkinson leapt over the barrier and ran toward Burr, his fists flailing, but Burr's team of lawyers rushed between them and held him back. He waved one fist in the air and yelled, "How dare you twist my actions and humiliate me in front of my fellow citizens? I've served my country faithfully for over two decades. I'm not the peddler of treason on trial here! You're a national disgrace, Burr!"

Burr stalked to his table, opened a folder, and scanned papers like Wilkinson wasn't there.

The crowd rocked like one body, conjoined and continuous. No matter how many times the judge banged his gavel on his desk, spectators shouted and spat, nodded and even laughed. Wilkinson's testimony was a shamble. Everyone saw how Burr picked his testimony apart and goaded him into losing control. He kept shouting threats at Burr until the judge ordered him withdrawn from the courtroom.

Wilkinson threw one last volley. "I won't ever forget this, Aaron Burr. You deserve to hang, and by God, I'll do everything I can to see it happen."

As much as I relished his red face and deflated stance as he was being led down the center aisle, another sight attached itself like a fish hook in the corner of my eye. It pulled my head around in time to see Meriwether Lewis—my father, though I still couldn't believe it—exiting via the front double door. I only glimpsed profile, but I'd know him anywhere. His head was tilted toward a slender woman, her face obscured by a broad brimmed hat festooned with feathers. Still, I didn't miss it when he put one arm around her narrow waist and drew her close enough to burn a kiss into her cheek. Lust and longing were potent chemistry. The atmosphere crackled between them.

What was Merry doing here? Who was his female companion? And what did they mean to Wilkinson? His fiery scrutiny threw javelins into their backs from his walk of shame down the center aisle. He wasn't just furious with the man called Burr. From the way his face morphed when he saw Merry, I knew Wilkinson hated him even more. But why?

EMMALINE

A shroud twisted around my body. I levitated above the scene and rode its cosmic cloth back to my point of departure. I heard the sweeping insect music before crashing into the ground exactly where I left. I slipped the journal into my waistband and tried to get to my feet, but I slipped on saturated ground.

A sturdy hand appeared over my shoulder. "Here. Let me help you."

I gasped and rounded on Trece. How long had he been here? What exactly had he seen? It mattered. I didn't know what a witness saw on my return, and it wasn't something I wanted to explain. Plus, I needed time to process what transpired in the long-ago courtroom. Wilkinson and Merry had a long rivalry, but what did the courtroom scene mean?

Trece stood over me, his hand still extended. I wasn't sorry to see his friendly face. Memories of our last encounter rocked my heart a little. I gripped his palm and let him pull me to stand. My nose stopped inches from his. I gave him a rueful half-smile. "Thanks. I lost track of how long I've been wallowing there."

His eyes didn't leave my lower lip as he moved in, cupped one hand behind my neck, and kissed me. My mouth parted, and he deepened the kiss with his tongue, igniting a bonfire that tore through my core and soaked my crotch. He pulled back and threaded his fingers through my tangles before yanking me to him and devouring me again, his hands roaming from my head to my back, and I felt his muscles tense when I teased my fingers along his spine. God, I wished I could feel his skin through his shirt. I groped toward his waistband and tried to free his hem, delirious with desire.

Abruptly, he pulled back. His breathing haggard and raw, he gasped, "Wait. Not here. Not like this. Anybody from the base could stumble upon us. Plus, after he caught us with McDonalds yesterday, General Wilkinson ordered me not to get involved with you."

"And you're going to follow that order?" I outlined his jaw with my finger and almost combusted when he let out an animal grunt and covered my mouth with his once more. After a few heart-quickening minutes, he broke the kiss and encircled me in his arms. Goose bumps skittered across my skin when his breath hit my ear.

"Of course, I'm not listening to Wilkinson. I've wanted you from the time I first saw you." He pulled back and followed the outline of my breast through my work shirt. "Let's do this, Cagney. Let's do it now. I know where we can go."

"Where?" I didn't recognize my sultry voice, but I was ready to follow him anywhere.

He wove his fingers through mine. "Come with me."

Our boots splashed through fresh puddles as we ran along the path to the compound's rear gate. He pulled his hand away from mine until we cleared it, but as we ran into an alley between two storage buildings, he backed me up against the block wall, worked his fingers under the hem of my shirt, and kissed me again. A low moan escaped my lips when his skin touched mine. "Hurry, Trece," I panted.

With one hand, he reached diagonally behind me and released a lever. Picking me up, he twirled and kicked a door open wide enough for us to tumble through. I couldn't see much before the door clanged shut. I shuddered when his hand cupped my breast through my bra.

"That'll be enough, you two." Wilkinson's voice boomed through shrouded aisles from the room's far corner.

Trece and I jumped apart and stood there, breathless and guilty and more than a little disappointed. At least, I was.

Wilkinson flicked his lighter to the cigar stuck between his disgusting lips. I glanced sideways at Trece as Wilkinson bit into the tobacco and barked, "You're excused, Trece."

"But sir—"

"I said that'll be all. Go to my office. I'll deal with you there."

Trece didn't say anything or even look my way. Instead, he abandoned me with a few footfalls and a slammed door. Its echo pinged across the hard surfaces of the interior.

A blink later, my head snapped backward when Wilkinson threw me onto the unyielding floor. "It's time for the next round of your training, Emmaline Cagney."

Realization and horror overcame me. "Did Trece lead me to you?"

"Immaterial. All that matters is what you are going to tell me." With a feint to the left, he flipped me on my stomach, pinned my aching arms behind my back, jerked me to my feet, and forced me across the room. At the far end, he flung me against the wall. Rattled, I bit the inside of my cheek. Salty liquid filled my mouth and slid down my throat. I was afraid I'd lose a few teeth when I spat. With a shaky hand I tried to reach Wilkinson's boots, but he was too far, and I was too weak.

His voice quivered with the menace of my childhood. Bulldog-faced Wilkinson, corrupt judge with hideous plans for me, was reborn. His jowls shook. "You're not leaving this building until you tell me how you did that."

"Did what?" I pulled my knees into my chest to shield myself from him. Like that'd work when he started swinging again. I was such an idiot. I sighed and stuck trembling fingers between the bends in my legs, hoping he didn't see. I would not let Wilkinson scare me. I would not.

"I was there, Emmaline. In the swamps a while ago. I saw what happened."

I thrust my chin in the air and scowled. "You mean, you were basically a peeper while Trece and I made out? Still a pervert, Wilkinson?"

The back of his hand smashed into my cheek. My world flickered, and fresh blood oozed along my teeth. I lay on my side, curled up in a ball, and tried to protect my organs from a full-on assault.

He blew out cigar smoke with his chuckle. "I've got to hand it to Trece, he moves quickly. When we saw you vaporize or whatever it was you did, I told him to haul your ass here at gunpoint as soon as you reappeared. And you must've returned almost as soon as you disappeared, because I left him not ten minutes ago."

A lead weight ripped through my stomach. "That's not true."

But part of it had to be. Wilkinson described what he saw when I ordered the journal to transport me. I didn't doubt that I dematerialized like a feat from science fiction. Still, I recalled the heat of Trece's kiss and his fevered caresses. He couldn't fake that. Could he?

He probed my leg with the steel toe of his boot. "He doesn't matter now. Tell me how you did it. Where'd you go when you moon-beamed out of here?"

"Tobacco smoke is rotting your brain, Wilkinson. I don't know what you're talking about."

Wilkinson's words machine-gunned through his snarl. "Don't be such a little fool, Emmaline. I know all about your special powers. And I'd be willing to wager you know all about mine."

I stiffened and tried to scoot backward toward the wall, but he picked me up by my neck and shook me. My brain stem smashed into my spinal cord, an agonizing, nerve-fired heat that spread like lava along my torso and through my limbs. Gray matter smacked inside my skull with the force of his shaking.

Warm spittle peppered my cheeks. He foamed into my face. "You don't have to answer. I'm not even going to pretend you don't know I'm a Nowhere man. I've already confirmed what I need to use you. And from now on, you'll pull your disappearing acts and fire your weapons whenever I demand."

I was losing feeling in my face, my arms and legs. The winds of what lay beyond this life whooshed between my ears. Did Wilkinson read Merry's journal? Did he know I was a Nowhere child? If I was a Nowhere child, did I go to heaven? Or hell? Or did a frightful plain of nothingness sprawl before me?

He released my neck, and for a moment, I knew what it might be like to jump off a ledge. I hung there, suspended between floating and splatting, and for a beat, I hoped I might soar. Instead, my knees crunched underneath me when I hit the floor. I collapsed onto my side, my eyes streaming with tears of hopelessness and torment.

Wilkinson kicked me in the ribs with the toe of his boot. "Tell me how you vanished in the clearing. Where did you go?"

"I won't!" I wrapped my arms around myself to ward off any further beatings, my stifling world pulsing and fading to black.

Wilkinson's words tugged me back. "You're a worthless, prick-teasing whore just like your mother."

The sheen of my mother's long curls cloaked my vision. For a few seconds, I was with her again. She pulled me to her, picked up her brush, and ran it through my tangles. "Don't you ever forget, Emmaline. You're more powerful than you know."

She kissed my cheek and cradled me in her lap, and I basked in her glow. But any instant, the lights would go out. Her love would morph into criticism, regimented demands, and petty meanness. It always did.

Everything she did propelled me to live without her.

"Who was my mother?" I rasped through swollen lips. "I mean, before she had me?"

Wilkinson's harsh laugh pinged around the claustrophobic space. "Believe me. Your mother was always just a whore."

He turned and skulked through the door, leaving me in the dark. I had more questions, and I couldn't see anything. Water dripped somewhere further back in the space, echoing its torture, driving me mad.

I dragged myself toward the door and pounded on it until my fists were bruised and swollen, but nobody came. Wilkinson had locked me in a tomb and left me to die.

I must've passed out. When I woke, one round bulb burned in the ceiling. My hands were bandaged, and what was left of me was spread on a low cot. I turned my head and cried out in agony. The simplest movement hurt like I was a thousand years old.

I tried to sit up, but my back was locked, my legs numb. Before I passed out again, a singular face blocked the light and peered down on me, its stringy head sheathed in a halo of artificial light.

Confusion submerged me in a restless coma, one where Wilkinson kept telling me about my mother but I couldn't make out the words.

EMMALINE

My eyes fluttered open to a bamboo mat ceiling and tropical noises booming loud enough to vibrate the dirt floor. I tried to turn my head but moving sent volcanic waves of agony along my spine and through my battered limbs. Once my eyes focused, a small face coalesced, child-like and familiar.

"Maria," I stuttered. "I've missed you."

"Don't try to move. You've been unconscious for several days." She smoothed a lock from my cheek and cradled my head in her lap.

"But where are we?" I coughed. "Wilkinson ambushed me in Catacamas." Fresh agony squeezed my heart. Did Trece really lead me there, as Wilkinson claimed? Was everything he said and what we shared fake? I squinted up at Maria. Tight, tender skin throbbed from the effort. She was too young to understand.

Maria caressed my face with a cool, rough cloth. "The nice man did this?"

I nodded and winced. "Yes, Wilkinson. He beat me and locked me away and—and kept saying crazy things. He wants to control me, I think."

"Please don't try to talk about it now. You're still weak."

"Where are we?"

Maria fanned miniature hands around the makeshift space. We were cocooned in leaves and bamboo. A single camp lamp burned in the corner, casting dream-like shadows around the cramped space. The whole place smelled of kerosene and green.

"We're hiding. I'm very good at hiding, remember?"

I thought back to the time she was lost in the blasted foliage before Hurricane Paine hit.

"Yeah, I almost didn't find you out there."

"You only found me because I let you. I wasn't lost; I was hiding to track the man I told you about. He turned out to be Wilkinson."

"How long have I been here?"

"A few days. I brought you here—with help, of course."

"And where is *here*?"

"Deeper into the Mosquitia.

I fought against the sledgehammer pounding my side and achieved forty-five degrees of uprightness. Exhausted, I leaned against her shoulder and was grateful to feel sweat streaming down my back. My arms and legs pulsed, but I could still use them to push myself to sit and to balance. Despite my unceasing pain, I considered it a win.

When I was settled, I whispered, "So, Wilkinson is sure to be pissed, which is stellar."

I let one groping session with Trece demolish all caution. I mean, I should've been suspicious when I saw him standing there upon returning from the past. At least, I saved Merry's journal. By stuffing it between my waistband and the small of my back, it protected me from some of Wilkinson's savage blows, but still. How did I know Trece wasn't putting his hand up my shirt and copping a feel to steal my precious book?

My journal. Where was it?

Every muscle in my back groaned when I moved too fast. "Maria, where's my journal?"

"What journal?"

I mimed its size and shape with my hands. "Leather. About this thick. I stuck it in the waistband of my pants."

She offered me a piece of hard candy with tacky fingers. "There was a book next to you when I found you. I didn't know what it was, but when I looked inside it, it was empty."

The skin throbbed around my eyes and my cheeks were bruised and tight, but I still gaped. "Empty?"

"Uh-huh. So I left it in the building where I found you."

My hands hovered over her skinny shoulders, but I couldn't shake her, no matter how much I longed to. Wilkinson might have my journal. Right now. This minute, he could be reading the secrets of Nowhere and using them to destroy me. I mean, Maria claimed the book was empty, but a Nowhere soul might be able to read it. Especially one as perverse as Wilkinson. And how was I going to travel across time now?

Maria gently laid her hand on mine, treating my bruised brokenness with care. "I'm sorry. I didn't know it was important. I wanted to get you away from Wilkinson. He could've killed you back there, and it would've been my fault. I couldn't watch you die. Nobody has ever cared for me like you do.

Water pooled at the corners of my eyes. "I'm grateful for you, too."

She held me for a few breaths and pulled away, her small face determined. "We can't stay here much longer. Bad people are everywhere. The Mosquitia is buzzing with pirates, mercenaries, drug runners, and Wilkinson. You need to get out of Honduras altogether. Go home to America, Emmaline."

Merry's concerned expression rushed my imagination. He never would've left me alone in a tropical labyrinth when I was nine. No matter how much I bragged about my hiding skills and self-sufficiency, he would've snatched me up and carried me to someone who could look after me. I took her chin in my fingers. "I can't leave you."

A branch cracked beyond our hiding place. Maria put her a finger over her lips and extinguished the lamp. Scooting across the ground on her hands and knees, she whispered in my ear. "We've got to go. Do you think you can walk?"

Pangs fired through every extremity as I creaked to unsteady feet. "If I slow us down, save yourself."

"As if!" She snapped and guided me into the thunderous gloom. Everywhere we stepped, I expected to roust a deadly *fer-de-lance* or a crocodile or a hungry cougar, any of whom were better at hiding than Maria and I. Hobbled, I fought to navigate over root-studded ground. It was like trying to walk on wet sand where the surf breaks on the shore, oozing and sucking our feet into the muck. After a trek of sheer struggle, we came upon a hill covered in a tangle of vegetation. "Stay here. We're near the gate of an ancient city. The gods will protect you."

I tried to keep my breath even and quiet as she raced back into the underbrush. Foreign noises crashed through the trees, percussive and insistent, but the Mosquitia was a continuous curtain of insulation. Sound didn't travel very far, and what reached the ear was distorted by how many things it touched en route. I waited anxiously for Maria's return.

But the next face I saw wasn't Maria's. Beside me, a visage glowed. I wanted to scream, but no matter how wide I opened my mouth, no sound escaped. I tried to shuffle backwards, but my hands and feet were rooted in place like they were four vines growing from the mucky floor.

It leaned closer and spoke with a thousand voices. "You're the one. Your energy has disrupted this entire ribbon of land between two oceans. What you seek isn't here."

I gulped. "How do you know what I seek?"

"Go home, Emmaline Cagney. Go home, and you will defeat your enemies and see your mother again."

"But I don't want to see my mother," I whimpered. "I hated her. She—"

Maria crashed through the bushes and ran through the spooky image, shattering it into a mist of fireflies. They swarmed like a funnel cloud and vanished through the trees. A man's black silhouette stood in its place.

WILKINSON

The damn rain forest was the blackest black I'd ever seen. By the time I realized someone absconded with Emmaline, it was nigh on sunrise. Hell, I roughed her up as much as I dared. I was sure she wasn't in any shape to go anywhere.

And only one person could've helped her escape.

Trece rapped on the thin door and stuck his head into my office. "Come in," I snapped.

He pushed the door closed and stood until I motioned for him to sit in a metal folding chair. His pants were covered with dried goo all the way to his groin. More goop flecked his shirt and clung like thick pomade in his jet-hued hair.

I let him squirm while I took my time lighting a Cuban stogie. Smoke clouded his expectant face when I snarled, "I think you know why you're here."

"To be rewarded? After all, you were the one that told me to seduce her. I convinced Cagney to follow me willingly, without brandishing my gun, but I didn't expect you to know where I was taking her. You could've given me more time."

I slammed my fist into my desktop, sending stinging soreness through my knuckles. Pencils scattered across the metal top like I threw a fat wad of jacks. "And now she's missing."

Trece's eyes crackled with fear. "Sir?"

Burnt tobacco singed my fingertips. I put my Cuban into an ashtray and got up to pace. "You heard me. She's vanished. Gone. Like you or I would be if we lost a Nowhere life. And I want to know how she escaped."

Trece gulped. "Sir? I don't understand."

I stalked around my desk and leaned into him, cigar breath fanning his scared native face. For the sum of my existences, I was always saddled with these substandard humans, people who looked different, bowed down to alien things, roamed the globe like nomads. Trece personified them all in a package of brown skin. Therefore, he'd bear the brunt of my ire.

His head snapped backward when I punched him in the nose. Blood dribbled from one nostril, but he gripped the sides of the chair with his hands and didn't move to wipe it.

Leaning in, I snarled, "You're the only one who could've helped her. Nobody else knew she was there."

"You're aware of what I've been doing for the past couple of days."

"Am I?"

"Yes, I've been preparing to guide another big group of refugees through the Mosquitia. Given everything involved, I never had time to think about Cagney, let alone help her flee."

"Come on, Trece. What do you take me for? Do you think I haven't desired a woman or several in my time?"

"I'm sure you have," he muttered, his lips bloodstained.

"But you care about that girl."

His eyes flicked sideways. A hint of impatience crept into his tone. "She's human. I care about humans, remember? That's why I'm spending this Nowhere life helping them flee Nicaraguan enslavement, even if it means serving masters like you."

"But she's not the same. You can't fool me, son. I saw how you were devouring her."

The boy's dark knuckles turned white from gripping the chair. However he fought it, I could see the storm of resentment beneath his mask of respect. His chin hardened. "Lust is meaningless. Animal. Look, I brought her there, just like you ordered. What else did you want me to do? Torture her?"

I leered at him and licked my tobacco-scented lips. "You did a better job of that than I did, touching her that way."

Deflated, I went behind my desk and relit my cigar. Ashes. Without Emmaline, my plans were no better than the burned remains in my ashtray. I was so weary of fighting incompetents, serving ungrateful leaders, and having grenades explode all over my fucking plans. I was on the brink of fulfilling my mission, but Emmaline Cagney was my key to success. She could eradicate anyone who got in my way, and she could rid history of every Nowhere soul who ever maligned me on my way to a successful final mission, including Theodosia Burr. Thirteen always was my lucky number. I made it work for me back when the Spaniards made me Spanish spy Number 13, and now I needed to make it work for me in my thirteenth Nowhere life.

My temples throbbed. "Let's set aside all talk of Emmaline right now."

"You mean, you don't think I hid her away someplace?"

"For now, it doesn't matter what I think. We have a more urgent directive from Washington. What's the status at the border?"

"Hundreds of refugees are standing by at several checkpoints, ready to join the Contras."

"Good. I've got a team ready to go out there with you and assist with retrieval. About twenty highly trained soldiers."

"Thank you."

I whipped out another cigar and sliced off its tip. "We have close to two thousand trained Contras stacked along our side of the Honduras/Nicaragua border. Once we collect the new recruits, they're going to invade. The CIA has promised air support. Bombs. A couple of key assassinations. We'll deliver a death blow to the Sandinista regime starting tomorrow, wipe that downed plane full of weapons from history, and give the bullshit American media something else to misreport."

Trece pointed to a box of tissues on my desk. "May I?"

I waved him forward and studied him while he cleaned up another bloody mess I made. His nose was swollen on one side, bruised but not broken. Because I was a decent guy.

Once he soaked up as much red goo as he could, he tossed the soiled tissues in the garbage can and slumped his shoulders. "I'm behind on my preparations. May I go?"

Smoke massaged my lungs and leaked into the open air. "You just remember one thing out there. Emmaline Cagney's bullets raining from one of those planes could've permanently erased hundreds of Commies, because I'll bet you a bunch of them are Nowhere. If she could take them all out, we'd have a quick victory in this secret war. However we accomplish it, a win means muzzling those Democrat bastards in Washington. Hell, it might keep the good team in power for decades, give us a way to rewrite the rules of the country in our favor. If you abetted her in any way, I hope one of her bullets shreds you tomorrow."

Trece vaulted across my desk, seized my ashtray, and threw it across the room. It gouged a hole in the flimsy wall and clattered onto the cement floor. He didn't stop seething even when I blew smoke in his animated face. "You're out of line, Trece."

"And you're full of shit. I've been carrying water for you for weeks because I want to complete my Nowhere mission as much as you. You told me to bring Cagney to you, and as much as I didn't want to do it, I was a good soldier. I followed your order. It's not my fault my tactics were more creative."

"I'm just wondering what you might've done if I hadn't butted in."

"We both know I would've fucked her. I've wanted to do it for months. Afterward, I could've excused myself on some romantic pretense. Getting us some water, maybe, or a post-coital snack from the mess hall. And you could've sauntered in and taken over. The way you did it, she'll never trust me again."

"And why do you care what she thinks?"

"If we ever find her, you may need someone to get close to her again.

Great job, because now that won't be me. To think Cagney might've helped me be done with Nowhere forever, and you wrecked my chance."

"I've tracked her before. I'll do it again. She can't hide from me for long."

"I'm sick to here," he saluted, fingers to forehead, "of being in this place. Do you know how long five hundred years is? You haven't been here half that. I don't want to be trapped in this underworld for all time. I want to move on, but you're dicking around with my mission, risking my future and my past."

In two moves, I grabbed him by the front of his dirt-stained shirt. Dried sludge crunched underneath my fingers as I yanked him close to my face. The tip of my cigar burned less than an inch from his left cheek. It bobbed up and down with every word I forced through clenched teeth. "You know what? If I've learned one thing from my actual life, it's this: do not align yourself with anyone. Every bastard turns on you eventually. You've got to get your own ass out of Nowhere, Trece. Your success or failure has nothing to do with me." I pushed him into the wall and pulled at the hem of my jacket. I wished it were spangled with all the medals I was ever awarded. That'd show his squealy, thankless ass who he was dealing with.

But CIA operatives couldn't afford to be identified by the accolades they won. As much as I enjoyed them when I was living, in the end my enemies used them to hang me. Discharged from the army. Forced into retirement. Blamed for the failure of a war I didn't want to fight.

Kind of like this Central American circus. If it weren't for my madman Gravedigger, I'd choose a thousand other places to set up house.

I put out my stogie and strode toward the door. Indicating the spilled ash, I said, "Clean up the mess you made. Then, carry on with your rescue mission. I'll check the progress of the invasion from afar."

Trece's stared like one of those carved statues he worshipped. Hard lines. Dead eyes. "Where will you be?"

I rushed him. Our noses almost touched. "General James Wilkinson does not answer to you. Now, fuck off."

WILKINSON

Of all the instructions I issued, I was clear about one thing: Emmaline Cagney must be located. I called in every favor I could muster for the search effort, because I would not have anyone blaming me for the disappearance and/or death of a teenage American volunteer.

I didn't leave anything to chance. I blasted queries on the secure channel to every training camp in the Mosquitia. I demanded faxed copies of vehicle usage logs and boat charters. No matter how much I probed, I couldn't ascertain her method of escape.

One issue still niggled me: Emmaline's disappearing act. She never revealed anything about how she accomplished it, no matter how much I bloodied her. I planned to go back for another round of persuasion, but the bitch fled before I returned, and she took her magical secrets with her. Or maybe she used them to break free.

A knock sounded on my door. "Come in!" I snapped.

"Top secret communique for you, sir." A uniformed lackey with a close-cropped head held out a clipboard. "Please sign here to accept delivery."

I scrawled my name and snatched the brown envelope from his hand. "Dismissed," I barked.

When I slid my chrome letter opener under the flap and tore into the envelope, a single piece of vellum fluttered onto my desk. One side was covered in effeminate cursive, the words squeezed until the message was almost a continuous one-word sentence.

I flipped it over, got out my magnifier, read the signature at the bottom of the page, and howled.

"Theodosia Burr! Goddamn her to hell!"

With every fresh stab of her missive, I seethed.

Wilkinson:

I know you think you're the smarter of the two of us. You always have. I well recall the last time I stood up to your preposterous ideas, ideas that would've gotten me and everyone I loved killed.

My face flushed with rage. Because of course I knew what she meant. While we lived, I argued for one solution to a conundrum, but the bitch Theo stepped in and convinced the other men in the room to follow her womanish plan. Not only was I castrated in front of my colleagues, but I also lost my dream of governing a swath of Mexico.

It was Theo's fault. Women were all about applying emotion to every situation when brute action is required. And who followed women? Weak, pathetic men, like Aaron Burr. I hated her.

Lighting a cigar, I picked up the sheet and kept reading.

I won't let you threaten anyone connected to me again. While I don't know Emmaline Cagney, I believe I'm responsible for her. I'm not convinced she's my mission this Nowhere life, but I'm risking all to protect her. Why? Because I know you want her, and I'll do everything in my power to prevent you from having anything you want.

You won't find Emmaline Cagney. Not where I've taken her. Call in every tainted favor. Put the intimidating muscle of the government behind you. I don't care what you do. She's gone, Wilkinson. You'll never see her again.

But you'll see me soon, because I'm coming for you, and I'm going to erase you from history's timeline. Get ready to be forgotten forever.

Theodosia Burr

Enraged, I touched the tip of my stogie to the corner of the page. When flames crackled over Theo's handwriting, I pretended she was being consumed, a fiery hell she deserved for thwarting the one aspiration of my life: To rule men instead of being a good soldier to rulers. I craved the glory, and she took my best chance.

But she was mistaken. I wouldn't sit still, waiting for her to find me. Hell no. Emmaline wasn't the only one with a talent for disappearing. I'd use my connections and go underground.

A second later, I banged my fist on the desk. Ash rose like a plume from my ashtray. A thin film settled over one corner of my desk. While massaging my hand, I leaned back in my chair and stared at the ceiling.

I couldn't vanish. Our biggest Nicaraguan operation was scheduled to happen tomorrow, and I was mission leader. If I went AWOL, the whole thing might never get off the ground.

Breath flowed in tobacco-tinged wheezes. Why did I always allow myself to be sidetracked by the pull of power and money and revenge?

Despite the media circus, I was hours from completing my Nowhere assignment, and I needed Emmaline's bullets to do it. Our impending Contra invasion would tip the balance of America's clandestine war, and I would dissolve into my just reward. Maybe no one would ever know the extent of my contributions to history, but so what? Why did I care whether people fathomed what I did? Clinging to dreams from my life prevented me from making a noble exit into whatever was next. Nobody would rewrite history books to include General James Wilkinson just because I used a gifted girl to take out a few of my enemies. I could still do it without her.

"Focus, Jimmy. Focus on what matters," I whispered aloud.

Perhaps, my Ann would be on Nowhere's other shore. I didn't really believe in that horse shit, but the mere possibility of a reunion with her trumped my schemes. I could almost hear her whisper, "Finish this, Jimmy. Forget Emmaline. Forget Theodosia. Be done with Nowhere and come to me."

But if Theo made good on her threat, my actions wouldn't matter. I wouldn't finish my Nowhere assignment anyway. Plus, with every passing minute, I was giving Theo a sure target and losing time on Emmaline.

I looked at my watch. Its onyx-and-stainless-steel face read midmorning. Our Contra operation was scheduled to begin at 9am the next day. Troops and materiel were already in place. I only had to give the order to strike.

Meaning I had less than twenty-four hours to neutralize Theo and locate Emmaline.

My Gravedigger's crazed cackles wafted in the stuffy breeze. He already knew this Emmaline tangent would be my undoing. Bastard was already lifting his pickaxe, preparing to cleave my erased brain in two. Because that's what would happen. I'd become a nameless being without a history. Nobody would remember my name or accomplishments.

To hell with him. I picked up my cigars and stalked to the door. With a private jet at my disposal, I could go anywhere, but I had a couple of places in mind. I was certain I'd find both Theo and Emmaline lurking nearby.

EMMALINE

I shrank against the mound to hide from the approaching male figure haloed by light. Maria's voice penetrated the scrim of my dream. She burrowed in beside me and whispered, "Emmaline, we can't stay here much longer."

I licked my dry lips and slumped against the vine-choked wall. "Where can we go?"

"Cagney. I know you're here. Come out. I need to talk to you." Trece's clipped commands buzzed next to my ears like swarming mosquitoes. I didn't have to take orders from him. Maria and I clung together behind our screen of vegetation, mutually trying not to breathe.

Trece shook the leaves in front of us and stuck his head through an opening. His brown face morphed from anger to concern as soon as he saw me. Stepping through the foliage, he reached out to touch my face, but I shrank away from his outstretched hand. He bit his knuckle and said, "My God, I did this to you."

"You may as well have," I slurred, my tongue thick and sore. "I really wanted you, but I guess you knew how to take advantage of that, didn't you?"

Trece took a step toward us. "Cagney, I know you think what happened with Wilkinson is my fault, and I don't blame you. On some level, it is. I led you there on purpose, but I swear, I thought he'd show up much later. He said he was going to question you about your weird vanishing acts. He never mentioned torture or beatings."

I slid backwards. Every inch stabbed my muscles and joints with fresh torment. Locking eyes with him, I said, "I was afraid you saw me coming back, but as soon as you kissed me, I was swept into every sensation, because I wanted you practically from the moment I met you. Did you even know that? For months, I would've given you everything. Now, I'm glad I didn't share hallowed pieces of myself with a snake like you. I want you to leave Maria and me here. We'll get ourselves to safety. By the time you come back with Wilkinson, we'll be gone. You'll never find us."

Trece ignored my outburst and stooped next to me. "I'm not on Wilkinson's side here. Believe that. I don't know what your vanish-and-return thing is all about, but I've seen something like it. It's like what happens every time a Nowhere soul fails a mission and gets sent back to the beginning."

I sat up too fast. Pain twinged along my spine, but I gritted my teeth against it. "How do you know about Nowhere?"

He picked up a broken piece of pottery and ran his thumb along it. Standing, he looked around him. "I used to live here, next to this mound, along with a tribe of over a hundred thousand. Smallpox destroyed us. In less than a decade, almost one hundred percent of us were exterminated. We didn't have a written language, and as you can see, we didn't live in a hospitable place. Basically, we vanished, and because nobody knew what happened to us, we wound up in Nowhere."

"But that had to have happened hundreds of years ago."

"Almost five hundred. I've been in this hell, trying to successfully complete a mission, for almost five centuries. And I'm almost there, Cagney. I'm convinced this last refugee run is my ticket out of here. I'm on my way to the Nicaraguan border, because helping people who are being slaughtered is my mission. Wilkinson can go to hell."

"I'm sure he will," I muttered and winced.

"Look, Cagney. I'm an asshole. Wilkinson told me to get close to you, but I didn't do it for him. My attraction to you was true. I see that now more than ever. I wish I'd brought you here whole instead of doing Wilkinson's bidding, but if I go against him, I can't do my job. He'll lock me up for insubordination, or worse, send me back to Nicaragua to be executed by the Sandinistas. My boat's waiting in the river over there." He pointed over his shoulder. "But I always stop here and commune with the gods en route. I didn't intend to run into you and Maria." He turned to the little girl. "Did you help her escape?"

Maria's head bobbed up and down. "It wasn't easy, but I'm good at hiding."

I took his hand and pulled him down beside us. We sat in a line with our backs resting on the mound. "I guess you know Wilkinson's Nowhere, too."

"Yeah. He often reminded me he could end my mission at any time, send me back to the beginning, and I only have one life left if I fail."

"I'm sorry this whole world exists, Trece. It's not your fault you disappeared. You're being punished for something over which you had no control. Winners write history books and assign losers to shadowy bit parts."

He rolled his head my way and locked eyes with me, and I sensed lifetimes in his two black orbs. "I don't see it that way, Cagney."

"You don't?"

"No. I've been given multiple chances to make a mark, to do life right, and I'm not going to squander this one." He trailed his fingers along my bruised cheek. "You don't have to tell me anything about your abilities. I haven't earned the right to know. But Wilkinson won't stop until he finds a way to make you use whatever power you have to serve him. You've got to get out of Honduras, away from Central America, and lay low for a while."

"I suspect it won't matter where I go, and I can't leave Maria behind." I put an arm around her thin shoulders and squeezed.

Fireflies flew in from crevices in the mound. They ducked and swirled through the overgrown clearing until they congealed into one light. Out of the corner of my eye, I saw Trece bow his head, but I couldn't take my focus from the emerging face. It stared with a thousand discerning eyes that morphed into a feminine face and body.

Trece chanted, "Thank you for showing yourself to me, oh mighty god Ku."

"She's a god?" I fought to stand through darts of pain in my legs and back. But when she looked at me, I stopped hurting.

"We've felt your presence in these jungles for weeks."

"Mine?" I squeaked.

"Yes. It isn't safe for you to be here. I hope you'll forgive me someday, Emmaline, but I have to go. Ku will take care of you. This is goodbye."

"But the refugees—"

Ku's voices thundered, "The world will continue to suffer refugees, because some human beings are diabolical and cruel. When the persecuted come knocking, people are defined by how they respond—be it compassion and benevolence, or intolerance and callous indifference. What if God were knocking on the door, in need of food or shelter or protection, but because he took the form of a refugee, people rejected his pleas? Because you're fighting on the right side—you're actually helping people in severe distress instead of judging them, condemning them, or sending them away—we're going to hide you from Wilkinson. If he breaks you, countless refugees will be endangered."

I looked around the twisted mound. "You're hiding me here?"

Trece stepped between us. "No. Not here. I summoned Ku for you, because they can put you beyond Wilkinson's grip. All I can offer you is this gun, and it won't be enough." As I took his pistol in my hand, he stroked my lip with his thumb, and his black eyes teared. "I don't want this to ever happen to you again. You're such a badass, Cagney. I hope you'll always know how much I care about you. I'm so, so sorry."

I swallowed against a knot in my throat. "I am, too." I leaned in to brush my lips across his cheek. "Go and finish your mission. Be done with Nowhere."

He saluted, took a few steps toward the river, and stopped. Turning back, he said, "And if I fail, maybe I'll see you again."

I grinned. "I'll never forget you, Trece."

Maria slipped her hand in mine, and we watched the jungle close in around his retreating figure. Ku hovered into the frame.

"Close your eyes, both of you. Emmaline, I'm sending you deep into hiding."

I grabbed Maria's hand. "What will happen to Maria?"

"You came from a place that proudly proclaims *Give me your tired, your poor, your huddled masses yearning to breathe free, the wretched refuse of your teeming shore. Send these, the homeless, tempest-tost to me, I lift my lamp beside the golden door.* If you uphold that spirit at home as you do here, Maria will find a new life there."

I fell on my knees next to the little girl and pulled her to me. "Remember me, Maria. I'm Emmaline Cagney. Hold my name in your heart and I'll be with you always."

Wind whipped my hair, and I fought to maintain my hold on Maria as we swirled into an unseen whirlpool. I tried to open my eyes and couldn't. It was like they were wired shut. Still, the sensations were the same as when the journal transported me back in time. A furnace of heat blasted my body, and disembodied voices echoed without giving me any discernible words.

How was this possible without the journal? Would I wake up in another historical era? Or would my ultimate destination be different because of Ku?

EMMALINE

When I exhaled, my breath was smoke and fog. Water rushed in the distance, and overhead the navy sky sparkled with so many stars, as if a galaxy was falling on me.

I lay on a pebbled beach next to a churning river. I could just make out the other shore through the murk. I got up and approached the water line, hand outstretched. Liquid chilled my fingers.

"This isn't Honduras," I said aloud. "These trees are different." Those I could see were mostly hardwood and evergreen. I forgot they changed colors, lost leaves, and experienced rebirth every spring in my part of the globe, while in the Mosquitia, everything grew and grew and grew.

Thinking Ku might send me some sort of directive, I said, "Where am I?"

But all I heard was a rustle of breeze. With a sigh of frustration, I followed the beach until I was enveloped by the scents of juniper and pine, oak and cedar. As I picked my way along the faint path, I believed I was speeding toward my appointment with destiny. Around every bend, I braced myself for the stench of tobacco and the crack of Wilkinson's fist.

Would I survive? What was I here to find?

By now, I was growing used to these shifts in scenery, but I still didn't understand why a forgotten god from an ancient culture would protect me. Why not give me some instructions, maybe a map? I didn't even know where I was. Would I suddenly be yanked back to the rain forest? Or some other bewildering locale?

I put my hand over my heart and tried to listen to what my spirit said, but the space underneath the muscle was hollow and silent and still. Maybe broken hearts turned liquid, leaked all over the human essence, and snuffed out its light. I wished I could ask Merry if my very foundation would recover. Merry'd know better than anyone, but by now I was sure he was finished with Nowhere. I'd never see him again.

I bumped into an oak tree when I misjudged a turn in the path, and moonlight illuminated the fast-moving river. "Is that the Mississippi?" I whispered. I remembered floating its dark stretches on my flight from New Orleans with Merry. It reminded me of an oil slick reflecting the sky, but these waters churned with whitecaps.

My eyes prodded the darkness.

An owl's hoot echoed through the trees. I jumped and hurried along a narrower trail off to the right. It snaked along the riverbank and opened onto a sandy beach, free of river rocks.

I plopped down on the soft sand and stared at the roadmap of time. Everything that had ever happened was etched in the sky, millennia of twinkle lights extending to the dawn of the universe. How many of those stars still existed, how many flamed out millions of years ago? The heavens were full of ghosts, and I was witnessing the energy they left behind. Were they like Nowhere stars?

I massaged my sore calves and marveled at everything I'd been through in recent weeks. A hurricane. Wilkinson. The journal and its revelations about my father. Time travel. Beatings.

Where was Maria? If I survived, could I find her? Ku said she was transporting her to America, but would a brown orphan really be welcome?

And losing Trece. While I'd probably never trust him again, I still glimpsed a falling star and wished him well on his Nowhere journey. Were I stuck in a revolving Nowhere existence, I didn't know what I'd be willing to do to be free. He was desperate, doing the best he could with what he had. I just wished he'd told me about his role in Nowhere sooner. We might've helped each other.

A shout pierced the distance. I left the beach and hurried toward the woods. Effort warmed my face, and my heart raced. My shredded muscles didn't allow this kind of workout.

Without warning, I yelped as I stepped around a tree, gasping and gagging. A woman stood defiant in a clearing surrounded by three men.

And I knew her. I thought she was dead, but she was here, above ground and pristine. Like the Medusa crossed with an Amazon.

"Mother?" I shrieked.

I Am Number 13

EMMALINE

I rammed against a tree and my lungs collapsed. Gunfire popped through the clearing, and I scrabbled for breath like I drowned in midair. Crazed voices pelted my ears, but I couldn't make out any words.

My mother. My mother was a few feet away. My mother was shooting at me. What was *my mother* doing here?

I closed my eyes, yanked the pistol from my waistband, and clutched it in my right hand. Breath rushed into my deflated lungs. With my gun to my forehead like a modified prayer, I ducked around the tree and shouted, "Here's what you deserve for everything you did to me!"

And I fired.

The bullet left the muzzle in slow motion and I watched it follow a trajectory straight for my mother, but I never saw it hit its mark. With another sudden shift, I was transported into a wheat field that marched toward the tree line in golden waves. The sun burned my face, and the forest sported an early smattering of fall colors, reds and yellows and oranges peeking through green, not the crisp brown of a season already past.

I spun around. How'd I get here? I didn't ask the journal to take me anywhere or demand to see this place, because I didn't have the book. Didn't I need the journal to travel through time?

One instant, I was firing at my mother. The next, I was here. Where was my mother? And Maria? What happened to Maria?

I scanned the field in every direction, movement that didn't burn or twinge or ache. Pushing back my sleeve, I looked for the bruises Wilkinson inflicted, but my skin was clear and pale. I felt around my midsection for tender areas, but my body was whole.

Still, I was afraid to move. This instance of transporting was wildly different from seeing Merry, meeting Wilkinson's Gravedigger, and eavesdropping on a trial. The journal didn't bring me to wherever I was. What would I find if I left the field? Was my mother, Nadine Cagney, waiting to ambush me, aiming to kill me?

After all the other weird things I learned about Nowhere, I wasn't sure I had the strength to pull back any more layers. I mean, I was still grappling with the fact that Merry was my father and I was possessed of bizarre skills because of my Nowhere parentage, leaving no space to contemplate my mother.

My insides jolted with a euphoric thought. If Lee Cagney wasn't my father, then some other woman could be my mother. Because I preferred any nameless Nowhere womb to Nadine Cagney's. Plus, my head throbbed from thinking about what it might mean for such a depraved woman to operate in Nowhere without consequences.

Unless Wilkinson administered her consequences after I ran away from her New Orleans whorehouse when I was nine and found Merry. Was she why he stumbled upon me in that New Orleans alley on a stormy autumn night? Did he already know what sort of mother she was?

Too many unanswered questions, as numerous as the grains of wheat that hemmed me in. I parted the golden shafts and inched my way through the field.

In a hundred or so steps, I emerged next to a dirt road. I hopped across a narrow ditch and onto the pathway. Wagon ruts and hoof prints gouged the surface, like the road recently dried out after a shower.

I turned right and followed the lip of a cornfield, the stalks overburdened with bounty.

Trees formed a leafy ceiling over the road. Around the next bend, I stopped short when I saw a man leading a horse toward me. His clothes were similar to the ones the courtroom spectators wore the day I saw Wilkinson be humiliated by Aaron Burr. But how did I travel back in time without the journal?

From my prior experiences, I figured he couldn't see me, but that was when I carried the journal. This encounter might be different. I shouted, "Hey. Can you help me? I'm not sure where I am."

But he didn't raise an eye or alter his step. I parked in the middle of the road, incredulous, while he and the horse passed by on my right. Like everyone else I'd met on these forays, he didn't acknowledge me.

He continued his slow progress up the dirt road. Birds twittered in the trees, and geese waddled across the road behind him. "I'm really in the past again," I mumbled. "But when?"

A whitewashed mansion stood at the far end of the road. Sunlight sparkled on its bounty of glass-paned windows. Covered porticoes sprang from each corner and connected with smaller wood-sided buildings flanking the main house.

I turned toward the heavy back door and broke into a run. As I emerged from a tunnel of trees, the setting briefly tilted, and I glimpsed the mansion's future. A broken stair. A weed-infested lawn. The toothy foundation with its two broken wings.

But in one breath, I returned to the age when the house was impressive and haughty and practically painted with money. Gold leaf glowed against the black shutters and the impressive double entrance. A polished brass knocker glimmered in the sun, and marble lined the steps leading to the front door.

Smoke bloomed from the chimney of the structure to the right of the main house. I crept toward it, intent on peering through the wavy glass, when the wall dissolved. I was actually in the room with two men dressed in the same type of suit Merry wore the day I visited his office.

And like that time trip, I was a shade in a room and stripped of power to haunt the two men. I hovered above a window seat and took in my surroundings.

Whoever owned this place had vaults brimming with money. The entire room was lined with fragrant cedar, and overstuffed bookcases ranged from ceiling to floor on two walls. The books were all bound in leather, and some were weathered and scaly like a tome I once saw in a museum.

Who were these people? How did shooting my mother lead here?

The occupants sat on either side of a heavy desk, one with his back to me. Their voices flooded my ears. The man facing away from me was speaking. "I don't want to discuss anything until my daughter arrives here on Blennerhassett Island."

Where was Blennerhassett Island? Did Ku transport me here in the first place? I wished I could pull out a book with a map to explain my orientation.

Instead, I settled in to listen to the men. "She's my equal partner in this venture, and I respect and rely on her observations on all things."

His voice tugged at my synapses. I'd heard it before.

The other man's musical Irish filled the room. "The river bell clanged about fifteen minutes ago. I expect her any minute, along with our other guest."

"He made it? I didn't think he could get away from St. Louis this time."

"I'm sure he charmed his way into a legitimate meeting someplace to provide cover for our *tete-a-tete*."

"He's probably mesmerizing the President. Such a cretin. I'll be glad to be rid of Jefferson soon."

Jefferson? Thomas Jefferson? Again? What did he have to do with this?

The Irishman spoke again. "I wonder whether Jefferson hates you more than you hate him, or vice versa."

I moved toward the door to get a better look at the other man, the one whose voice niggled me. But as his profile came into view, he got up to pace, keeping his back to me. "I don't hate people, Harman. It only gives them power over me. And this entire venture is about asserting my own power, making my life, and sealing my legacy, not about exacting revenge on old Tom."

Footsteps sounded on the porch, followed by a knock. I was too confused to know what to expect and positioned myself next to the door. But when it opened, I reeled backward and screamed.

I knew why I was here.

My mother—Nadine Cagney, my whorehouse-running, abusive mother—stepped into the room, her long silk skirts skimming the floor. Her corset showcased her tiny waist to perfection. Dark spirals swirled in an elaborate updo underneath a perky feathered hat. She removed her gloves as she walked in, flushed and breathless, and dashed toward the man who wasn't Harman. He turned just in time for me to see his face before she dove into his awaiting arms.

He was the man from the courtroom, the one who humiliated Wilkinson. He was on trial for treason that day. It was Aaron Burr.

"Dear Theodosia!"

"Daddy!"

My head snapped forward. "Huh? Daddy? Aaron Burr is my mother's father?"

But nobody heard me. She rained kisses on both his cheeks until he collapsed into the chair in a fit of laughter. She moved to stand behind him, her hand resting on his right shoulder. Loving. Protective. Adoring.

Harman stood and approached a table spangled with several crystal decanters. Removing a stopper from one, he filled three glasses with amber liquid and distributed them amongst those present. Holding his glass overhead, he said, "I propose a toast. To our Theodosia, Aaron Burr's grandest success."

They clinked glasses and sipped, but I needed to press pause. I read that name on the scrap of Wilkinson's paper from his Gravedigger. But my mother's name wasn't Theodosia. It was Nadine. Aaron Burr, the man who shot Alexander Hamilton in a duel, couldn't be my mother's father. Because that would make him my grandfather, and I was not descended from one of history's most reviled men. And it would make me over a hundred years old. It wasn't possible.

A board creaked on the walkway just beyond the open door. I turned as James Wilkinson preened into the room. He wore a military uniform awash with gold braid and beribboned medals. I couldn't understand how he stayed upright under all that weight. Baubles tinkled as he moved, like he was a human chandelier. I mean, I wasn't exactly surprised to see him. When he was torturing me, he admitted he was a Nowhere man and kept hounding me about my mother.

She and Burr cut their reunion short, with her taking the silk-covered chair next to him. The golden tones blended well with the emerald dyes of her dress. Smoothing her skirts, she smiled. "General Wilkinson. It's a pleasure to see you again."

He bowed his balding head, exaggerating his bulldog chin. "Theo. Our venture clearly suits you. You're lovelier than ever."

Burr looped her hand through the crook of his arm, his voice clipped and tight. "What's the latest, Jimmy?"

"I've got news from the Mexican front, gentlemen. Texas could be ours. We need enough men and munitions to overthrow two of their forts on the eastern frontier, and we can use them as a base to penetrate the interior.

Harman nodded. "Aye, how many fully armed fighters might that mean?"

"A few hundred men and enough materiel for every man to have two guns, a knife, and ammunition."

Burr rolled his eyes. "More money I don't have."

Harman poured Wilkinson a drink and passed it to him on his way to his substantial walnut desk. Once seated, he flung his feet onto the marbled leather top, put his hands behind his head, and stretched. "No worries, comrades. I've got enough money to outfit an army or two."

Wilkinson took a swig of his drink and continued. "Many Texans settled there because they didn't want to be part of the United States, but they're already impatient with the Spanish crown. Madrid's another universe to them. Plus, nobody knows what might happen if Mexico declares independence from Spain and tries to govern itself, and there's plenty of talk that might happen soon. To sum up, Texans are ready for a new leader." He turned to Burr. "A leader like you."

With a nod from her father, my mother rose and walked toward Wilkinson, talking the whole time. "And we told you, Wilkinson, we're prepared to fully outfit the Balstrop Tract in western Louisiana. It's well situated to stage an invasion of Texas should the opportunity arise, and attractive because nobody wants it. On most maps, it's beyond the realm of Jefferson's Napoleonic Land Grab. With Harman backing the enterprise, we could promise settlers ample land and perks for moving. I think it makes sense to lure families and adventurers to the general area and let them get used to their surroundings. Once we're solid, we can assemble an army and invade Mexico."

Wilkinson never glanced at my mother or oriented any part of his body in her direction. He carried on as if she hadn't spoken and addressed the men. "Things on the Spanish front are unfolding too quickly. An effeminate plan is too patient. It'll take a few years, maybe even a decade to come to fruition. My sources insist the Spanish crown will cut Mexico loose before then. We've got to strike now while we have our best chance of success." He turned to Aaron Burr. "Surely you can see that?"

Burr got up from his chair and slipped an arm around my mother's shoulders. She nuzzled her head under his chin and wrapped one arm around his waist. I didn't know what to make of it. My mother was clearly closer to her father than I'd been to either of mine. A loving shorthand flowed between them, like they kept no secrets. Burr squeezed her and stepped away to address Wilkinson. "You're certainly persuasive, Jimmy. But empires aren't built overnight. They're erected block-by-block, stone-by-stone, deal-by-deal." He assumed the convincing posture of the attorney arguing his case. "We've got to get on the same itinerary here, gentlemen. Next year, I'm finished as Jefferson's Vice President. While I plan to run for governor of New York, I can't say whether I'll win. I'm confident Master Tom will marshal every libelous cretin in his arsenal to destroy me in the press."

Wilkinson whistled. "You've no idea how many newspapers and pamphlets he owns or controls. The man's a master of lies and distortions."

Burr's arms jutted wide like a preacher at a hell-fire-and-brimstone revival. "Exactly. Let Master Tom and his band of southern slave holders have America. They've imprisoned the Africans and are beginning to displace the natives. I'd like to build a different legacy. For myself." He waved toward Theo. "For my family to rule fairly."

He exchanged a knowing look with my mother. She nodded her head once, a slight cue, and he stood taller and thrust out his chest. "I say let's decide our course by democratic vote."

Wilkinson rocked from toe-to-heel, his hefty cheeks reddening. "But you and I already cancel each other out, leaving Harman the deciding voice. It's too much pressure on our relationship to put him in that untenable position. Maybe over the next few days here on Blennerhassett, we can work together and craft a compromise."

My mother gathered her flowing skirts in one hand, putting her trouser-clad legs on display. "I also get a vote, Jimmy."

Wilkinson's careful mask fell away, and his visage was etched with incredulous loathing. "But you're a woman. Women can't vote."

Aaron Burr stepped between them. "She's a human being. I reared my daughter to believe her voice is equal to any man's. That's one reason I want to leave America and start anew. I'm tired of being told my daughter is less-than-human because of her sex, and I'm weary of the arguments for continuing to enslave the living for profit. In our future realm, everyone—woman or Negro or immigrant—gets a vote."

Harman spoke up. "And I also get a vote. Frankly, I should get several votes because my money's financing this venture, but that wouldn't be very democratic, would it? When voting for the best needs of a populace, money shouldn't influence the decision. Lord help us if America ever degenerates to the point that politicians can be bought." He stopped and took a sip of whiskey. "But I'm also for a more cautious approach. If we establish ourselves and make sound investments, the fruits of our new territory can finance a future invasion. I vote with the Vice President and his daughter."

Wilkinson rearranged his mask, but I didn't miss the raw fury boiling there. His smile was thin and bloodless when he snapped. "I can't believe you men are siding with this know-nothing woman."

My mother stepped forward, hands on hips. "You know better than anyone how my father hired tutors and educated me better than most male children. I'm not ignorant. But you, Jimmy—I know you send rocks and skins and whatnot to President Jefferson, because you think the scientific endears you to him. He knows most of what you send him is misidentified, pathetic attempts to elevate yourself. He tells everyone what a boor you are, Jimmy."

"Education doesn't make a person smart," he snarled and wagged a finger at each of them. "You sit on your pedestals with your elitist swagger and look down your noses at people like me, but you don't understand. I'm in the thick of it. While you sit here in this money-lined room and develop your neat theories over expensive scotch, I'm taking fire in the trenches, fending off enemies, and making the connections that will bring our dreams to reality."

My mother folded her arms across her chest. "Then why don't you make everything happen yourself? Take the lead instead of throwing stones from the shadows. Or are you really that much of a coward?"

Wilkinson lunged for my mother's throat, but her father and Harman jumped in his path and restrained him. He writhed against their grips on his arms and rained spittle on the carpet.

"Coward? I'll never forget this humiliation, Theo. You poisoned them with your emotional pleas before I arrived, and you castrated me in front of my colleagues. Rest assured, I'll make you pay."

I Am Number 13

EMMALINE

After the men hauled Wilkinson out the door, I followed my mother along the starlit portico, expecting her to step through the gold-leafed front door and take her usual place with the women. Instead, she glided down the front steps and flew across the terraced yard. I struggled to keep up. Though my feet didn't touch the ground, I couldn't match her pace. How did she move so quickly and stay upright without a flashlight?

My bones froze when I realized she was running toward the spot where I fired on her a few minutes before.

Crickets and frogs warbled a nighttime chorus all around me as I reached the clearing a few steps behind her. I expected the noise to pick up the trees by the roots and slam them into the ground. Why did Nadine, I mean Theodosia—gosh, I'd never get used to that name—why did my mother come out here?

As I took my place beside her, another figure materialized from the cover of trees. His face was shrouded in shadow, but I'd memorized his casual, confident stride long ago.

My mother was meeting Meriwether Lewis. Merry. My father.

Her confident voice wafted back to me. "I hoped I'd catch you before you pushed off."

Merry kept his distance, arms folded across his chest, though I could wrap my hands around his fight against her magnetism, a tangible, living thing between them. Love emanated from the softness around his eyes. It traveled across the clearing and merged with her adoring expression. He dug his heels into the dirt to keep from going to her and rubbed his hands over his face before speaking, a familiar tic I knew from our time together. "You know this situation, it's insufferable. Of all the available people in this country, you and I can't love each other."

Theo took a tentative step toward him. "But we already do."

"You're married."

"I married for money. I've never loved my husband. Everyone knows my father needed access to someone else's fortune to realize his political ambitions and to gain the support of a powerful southern state." Her chin jutted higher. "My husband had a mistress when we married. He knows I have my dalliances, and he doesn't care."

"I'm not a prude, Theodosia. When we started this, I was in it for a casual romp. I admit it. You were unattainable, because even if you left your marriage, your father despises my godfather and benefactor. Aaron Burr would never consent to a relationship between his only child and Thomas Jefferson's *protégé*." Merry spun on his heel and faced the hardwood. He stammered his admission into the empty air in front of him, as if he couldn't say to her directly. "I never expected to love you."

My mother closed the gap between them and put her hand on his arm. Her small palm burned there while he kept his back to her and exhaled anguished breaths. She put her head on his arm and whispered, "And I love you. Why can't knowing you possess me to my very foundation be enough? You've conquered me to my root, stripped away every logical defense against losing myself. I love you as much as I adore my son and worship my father."

My mother had a son? I had a brother? I floated across grass overburdened with frost and floated at their feet, determined not to miss another layer, a single revelation of the complex woman my mother was turning out to be.

Merry yielded, and she melted into his arms and buried her face in his chest. He kissed the top of her head and stroked her hair, his blue eyes so very like mine glistening with tears. The night noises went silent when he spoke. "No matter how long I live, I'll never love anyone as profoundly. I don't know how they failed to notice the last time we dined here. You floated into the room, and I wanted to crawl over Margaret Blennerhassett's bone china and silver, walk over knives and broken glass to possess you in front of every diner there. Yours is the pumping heart that was crafted to fit mine. The voids, the missing bits of us, they'll always call to each other. Please, don't banish us to a life of clandestine groping and reckless longing. I don't care what people think, Theo. I want to marry you, be your husband, call you my wife. Please, send me on this western expedition complete. Say you'll seek a divorce and be free when I return."

Theodosia ducked away from his embrace, her eyes aflame. "We don't even know if you *will* return, Merry." Her nimble fingers groped at his buttons and tugged at his leather belt. "That's why I'm begging you not to leave without letting me feel you one more time." She moved in to claim his lips, but he pushed her away and straightened his clothing.

His face was a hulking wall of granite like the mountains he must have scaled on his expedition. His coldness chilled me. "I can't believe you'd discard the one person who worships you more than any other. Think of what we could accomplish together as the most educated man and woman in America. Sure, we'd suffer a scandal, but we'd weather it together." His face softened. "Please. I'm asking you one last time. Say you'll be my wife. We'll be a force. Our children will be invincible."

I sat a little taller. Was I? Invincible? Did Merry know even then how special his daughter would be?

My mother gasped and covered her face with her hands. When she ripped them away, they were stained with tears. "Do you realize what divorce would mean? My husband would get my boy. I'd never see him again. What I'm proposing—continuing to see you as much as I like because my husband doesn't mind—gives us both what we want."

Merry started to back toward the river, his face a twisted mask of destroyed hope. "Not when I want to wed you. I'll never settle for less,

Theodosia. Never. Your weak husband doesn't deserve you. He can't stimulate your mind or pleasure your body. Remember that the next time you're listening to him describe the points on the last buck he shot right after you pretended to come."

He left her and charged down the path to the river, my mother following behind. I got up and shadowed them until the water yawned wide, riveted by their forgotten chapter of unrecorded history. Merry loved my mother, and she gave up on him.

On the slender beach, my mother threw herself in his way and blocked his route. Tugging his arm, she begged, "Please, Merry. Don't leave things like this. Please. I love you more than any other living thing."

But he clattered onto a dock, ignoring her pleas as he unmoored a keelboat and pushed it into the river. With a lithe leap so like him, his feet settled on the wooden deck.

Her voice, timid and strained, fluttered through a few loose strands of hair. "You'll never understand. It's torture to be born a woman, unable to pursue my own interests, however much my father claims to treat me as a son. I hope someday you'll understand what was at stake."

He turned his sight toward the watery horizon, a point he'd follow to another ocean in the coming years. Murkiness swallowed him and his vessel. He never looked back.

My mother's shoulders hammered through her sobs, but she didn't shriek or beg. Instead, her silk skirts ballooned as she flopped onto the dock and sat there, watching the dark where Merry's boat had just been. I strode onto the planks and floated beside her, wishing she could hear me tell her what I thought of her stupid resolve. Merry loved her. How could she throw his love away?

My mother jumped to her feet and shouted into the darkness. "I owe it to my father. I can't risk damaging our chances of success in his next venture."

As she stumbled from the dock and was consumed by forest, I remained, too churned up to follow her. How did this principled woman, this powerhouse, become a madam, slave to a madman? I was actually proud to call her *mother*. I wanted to be the offspring of such a heroine.

But could who she was in life erase what she subjected me to as a child? Could I forgive her?

As the edges ripped away from the horizon and the running water fled, I still didn't have an answer. I bolted through the void, uncertain I'd work things out before I reappeared in my own time, or in another version of my mother's past. While I didn't know where I was headed, I knew what I needed to understand when I go there.

WILKINSON

I wasn't sure where I was headed when I parked myself at a small airport diner. One possibility was an American backwater, a strip of land I hadn't seen in almost two hundred years. The other was an urban labyrinth of concrete and steel. I took out a coin and flipped it. It clattered on the counter, and George Washington's profile landed face up.

"Might as well gamble a little," I muttered and pocketed the coin. At least, I knew where I was headed.

From my perch at the counter, I swiveled on a red vinyl-topped chrome stool, breathed in the scent of hash browns and bacon, and watched a replay of the President's speech from the evening before. His face was framed in close-up on the television behind the counter.

"Can you turn that up?" I asked the grease-stained cook as he slung another rasher of bacon on the electric griddle. A waitress slopped more coffee into my chipped mug and adjusted the volume on her way to replace the pot. Overcooked sludge stung my throat as the President's camera-ready voice filled the room.

"My purpose was to send a signal that the United States was prepared to replace the animosity between the U.S. and Iran with a new relationship. At the same time, we undertook this initiative, we made clear that Iran must oppose all forms of international terrorism as a condition of progress in our relationship. The most significant step which Iran could take, we indicated, would be to use its influence in Lebanon to secure the release of our hostages held there. Yes, we traded arms for hostages, something I vowed we'd never do."

I sat back on my stool and whistled. The man actually followed my advice. It took a Hollywood actor to look the American people in the eye and tell them the truth. But what did the truth mean for me?

I pulled out a pen and doodled a cipher on a paper napkin. The CIA wasn't scratching the Nicaraguan mission. We were training more refugees than ever, arming them from our cache of dirty weapons, and sending them across the border to be sacrificed. Our strike tomorrow morning was our most ambitious foray yet.

Trece was keeping me updated on our progress. Eventually, the Sandinistas would run through whatever munitions they had. They were already teetering. When they fell, my job would be complete. I'd be done in Nowhere.

Somewhere over Cuba, I decided how to handle my two pussy-bearing problems. If I could get Emmaline to fire upon Theodosia, I'd forget Theo like I had amnesia about everyone else she shot, and maybe that meant she'd cease to exist on any plane. Whatever lay on the other side of the Nowhere divide, I didn't want to spend eternity running into any version of her. I thought I had neutralized Theodosia in my last Nowhere life.

On a frozen January night, I shot her in the head near George Washington's war hangout on the Hudson River. Bullets were cleansing. They plowed through an icy landscape and stripped it bare. I expected the bullet I rammed into Theo's brain to nullify my urge to punish her. After all, I won, right?

Wrong. When she reappeared in New Orleans knocked-up and ready to assassinate me, I couldn't believe the gall of Nowhere. Of all the places she could be assigned, why did it have to be in my playground? For a while, I tried to ignore her, but she made it unthinkable, lurking around my law office and threatening to expose me for who I was.

When I was sworn in as a judge, I used my underworld connections to defile her. They cornered her as I locked up my office late one night. I relished watching them drag her into a dirty side alley and laughed while they each pulled up her skirt and raped her. As instructed, they didn't send her into oblivion before they violated her. No, they made her wait for escape.

But a few hits with the needle made her mine. Oh, her transformation didn't come right away. Over the course of a few weeks, I found the means to drug her repeatedly until she was a true heroin addict. I know from experience that addicts would do anything in exchange for another high, and she was no exception. Whored herself to anyone I identified. Recruited other loose women for her brothel. And promised her only daughter to me.

Her only daughter Emmaline.

In her lucid moments, she still reviled me. Even tried to off me in the early days when she was high. But when she finally learned to accept free smack in exchange for pliability, Theodosia Burr was completely in my thrall, a conquering I found more pleasure in than killing her had given me. I never imagined she possessed the strength of character to go along with my plans all the while marking time for the opportunity to destroy me. She was like that, the bitch. Able to undertake inconceivable depravity if she knew she'd win in the end. When I realized she'd always been working against me, I beheaded her, but as blood pumped from her wounded neck, she vanished into her next Nowhere opportunity.

Now, when I was *this close* to the finish, she cluttered up the fringes and threatened me again.

The rest of them could have Nowhere. I was primed to move the fuck on. Emmaline had to do her parlor trick with the gun one more time. And if she did, maybe she'd commit a sweet form of suicide. Because how could she exist if her mother never did?

I left a few bills next to my empty plate and strolled into watery sunshine. Things in Central America were progressing to critical. I checked in by secure phone during my stop to change private planes and cover my tracks, but nothing required either my directives or physical presence. For a few more hours, I was in the clear.

I leaned against a glass wall and fired up a cigar. I wasn't sure if Emmaline could materialize anywhere, but Theo was married to habit. Stubbing out my cigar under my boot, I left it steaming on the pavement and walked toward my plane's metal stairs. At the top, the pilot noted my intended destination and strapped himself into the front chair.

"How long until we land?" I asked.

"Little over an hour, sir," he replied and steered the metal tube toward the runway. Its nose sniffed the ground like a hound as we taxied en route to Theo and, hopefully by extension, Emmaline.

I took out the quarter and kissed George Washington's profile. "Be lucky for me, Georgie Boy," I hummed and palmed the coin. "You never steered me wrong in life."

When we have nowhere else to go, risk comes easier, right?

EMMALINE

I came to on a bustling street corner. Horns pulsed through the intersection, and buildings lined the street like skyscraper teeth. A man dressed like someone from a Duran Duran video bumped into me. "Hey," he scolded. "Don't step right in front of people when you leave the subway. I've got places to be."

"Sorry," I mumbled and stepped aside.

I fought the natural tendency to be freaked out—*How did I get here? Where am I now?*—and settled into what the landscape shared. Because if recent events taught me anything, it was that my life could be ratcheted back and forth without warning, even lacking Merry's magic book.

I looked up and read the sign at the street corner. *Broadway and 7th Avenue.* Broadway? New York City?

I twirled to fully process the scene. Billboards blared the latest Broadway shows, and neon strobed the latest headlines. I waited long enough to watch the date scroll past: November 14, 1986. Was that the date when Ku transported me from Honduras to Blennerhassett Island?

I weaved between tourists snapping photos and suits scurrying to work, surprised at my agility, not sure where to go. After a couple of blocks, I leaned against a facade, huffing and confused and ravenous. While I rested,

I scanned my arms for bruising from Wilkinson's beating, but the trip to the early 1800s scrubbed me clean. My back didn't throb, and my ribs weren't sore.

Shoving my hands in my pockets, I put my head down and walked along the sidewalk. Movement helped me think. I knew I'd spent part of the previous night learning about my past. My mother dressed down Wilkinson and implored Merry to stay. I heard her deepest hopes wished upon falling stars when she thought no one was there.

My clothes reeked of river water, practical evidence the action actually took place. I didn't dream it.

The journal usually brought me back to the spot I left. Without it, I was in new territory. Meaning how did I wind up here? In New York?

I needed a secluded place to map out everything I'd learned, somewhere I didn't need money, because I had none. I was craving information, and as I walked past the stone lions guarding the entrance of the New York Public Library, I knew this must be where I was supposed to be.

Bounding up the stairs, I walked under the stone archway and pushed through the heavy glass doors. Interior heating caressed my face as I wandered through the lobby and followed the signs to the reading room.

And what a space. I stopped to admire the marching line of arched windows framed by stone pillars and toothy crown molding. As I settled into my chair at a table with a thick wooden top, I leaned back to admire the wooden ceiling decorated with frescoes. The library didn't close until 6pm. At least, I could rest here for free and plot my next moves.

Grabbing a few pieces of scrap paper and a short pencil from a receptacle, I scribbled a heading at the top.

What I've Learned About Nowhere So Far

1. It's an in-between place for souls with unresolved deaths.

I stopped right there, pushed off the chair, grabbed my supplies, and hurried to the reference desk. A cute guy with brown hair smiled behind the barrier. His glasses played up the green flecks in his eyes, and his name tag read *Erwin*. "How can I help you?" Erwin said.

"I'm looking for a couple of books on the founding of America," I said breathlessly.

He leaned an elbow on the counter. "Be more specific. The Native Americans really found what became America. Do you mean them? Or the lead-up to the American Revolution? Or the war itself? Or the years following?"

I bit my lip and wanted to scream. History was a waterfall of details, each droplet another fact. How was I supposed to pick the right drops from the ever-moving torrent? Settling on a narrower topic, I asked, "Do you have something on the time around the Lewis and Clark Expedition?"

He pulled out a paper map and circled an area on the second floor. "Early 1800s America is here." He drew an arrow to a specific bank of shelves. "You'll find several good volumes midway down this aisle. Look on the third shelf. If you don't find what you're looking for, come back." He flashed another fetching smile, and I think I blushed a little. "I'm happy to help."

My feet pounded the stone steps to the second floor. Without running, I found the area Erwin indicated. Scanning the shelves, I pulled down a couple of books: a biography of Meriwether Lewis and a listing of important people from the early 19th century. I sank to the floor and opened the second one first. When I flipped through the index, I found Lewis, Meriwether, p. 86.

My fingers couldn't find page 86 fast enough. I almost ripped his famous side-profile in the upper right-hand corner of the page. Scanning the entry, I gasped near the end.

> Meriwether Lewis died mysteriously on October 11, 1809, seventy miles south of Nashville, Tennessee on the Natchez Trace. Some historians believe he killed himself, but others insist he was murdered. This author presents both positions to be fair to history.

This book confirmed what the journal told me about Merry's death. Plus, Lee Cagney wrecked near there. What was Lee doing near Merry's grave on the day he died?

I tore off a strip of paper, marked Merry's place, and went back to the index. "Burr, Burr, Burr. Only Aaron. No Theodosia. Figures history would be about the men. After all, it's called *his story* for a reason," I fumed and flicked to page 75, the indicated section for Burr, Aaron.

My grandfather's now-familiar eyes locked onto mine, direct, unflinching. I pored over the entry. Killer of Alexander Hamilton. Vice president under Thomas Jefferson. Didn't stand aside to let Jefferson win the presidency. Caused the electoral college to vote 36 times. Jefferson never forgave him. Tried for treason in a plot to overthrow Mexico. His trial caused the supreme court to rule that Americans couldn't be tried twice for the same crime. Exiled. Only child disappeared at sea.

I read those last five words again. *Only child disappeared at sea.*

And that's how she fell into Nowhere.

Pounding my fists into the book, I longed to shout *Is that all my mother deserves, you stupid male historian? Five words? Five words couldn't possibly describe her, you pathetic moron.* Thankfully, I didn't forget I was in a library and kept my mouth shut.

At least, I had my answers to number 1 on my list. I didn't care what put Wilkinson in Nowhere. Going back to my list, I added number 2.

> *2. I'm the Nowhere child of Meriwether Lewis and Theodosia Burr.*

> *3. As a Nowhere child, I can shoot Nowhere inhabitants, and they're eaten headfirst by the air, which is weird and gross and I don't understand it at all. What does it mean?*

> *4. I can also travel to specific scenes from history and witness what really happened. Sometimes of my own will, sometimes not. Why?*

> *5. I believe Wilkinson wants to use me to kill his Nowhere enemies for insults flung at him in life, meaning they'd be chomped on by a voracious, invisible monster, and it'd be my fault. Given what I witnessed on Blennerhassett, I'm sure my mother is one of his primary Nowhere enemies.*

> *6. I think Merry accomplished his Nowhere mission when he delivered me to Lee Cagney, but what about my mother? She*

was still in Nowhere hours ago? Can I find her again?

Did I even want to? After all, I shot at her the last time I saw her. She might not be too keen to see me. But that was before everything I witnessed on Blennerhassett. Maybe if I found her, I could explain.

I closed the book, rested my head on the stacks behind me, and breathed in the scent of a library. A librarian wheeled a squeaky cart along the next aisle, but otherwise, the space was quiet. Nobody else lurked around the American history section.

Glancing side-to-side, I closed my eyes, picked up my notes, tucked them into my waistband, and spoke my heart. "Help me find my mother. Please."

I Am Number 13

EMMALINE

I swirled down a drain and dropped onto a moving train. Illuminated concrete walls scrolled past the windows. I pressed my face to the chilled glass. An exhale frosted the view. Why would my mother be on a subway?

I got up to examine the surfaces of the empty car. Didn't trains usually have route maps or signs to announce the next stop? But every partition was clear and shiny. I slumped into a plastic seat and waited for the train to stop.

The weight of the world pressed on me from all sides. Did my mother spend time here alone? A subway car was like waking up in a moving coffin and realizing I was buried alive. The air would run out before anyone would find me and I'd suffocate. I put my head between my knees and told myself I was at the Parthenon in Nashville or walking along the Natchez Trace or succeeding with Nicaraguan refugees. Anything to change my scenery. The sky flirted with every shade of blue. Spells flowed between the images and frolicked along the grass.

A finger tapped my shoulder and hauled me back to the coffin. I couldn't see the man's expression for the freckles splattered from his hairline to his jaw, but his icy eyes were kind. His navy polyester uniform was decorated with maroon braid, and a cool hat rested on his ginger-fringed head. A white name tag read "Conductor." I shrugged off my fear and attempted a smile.

"Do you have a ticket?" He asked.

"No. Am I supposed to get one?"

"My passengers usually procure them on their way in, but we've got a short ride. I'll make an exception for you."

"I'm looking for my mother, and somehow I found myself here. Meaning I bypassed the ticket machines, I guess."

He sat down beside me and studied his gloved hands. The fingers were dingy white with mottled smudges around the tips. "I'm sure I know your mother."

"You do?"

"Yes. She's one of my charges. I've been wondering whether you'd ever pay me a visit."

"How'd you know about me?"

"When she passed this way almost twenty years ago, she was bloated with child to the point of collapse. Her ankles disappeared, skin stretched almost to breaking. She couldn't stop scratching her stomach. I was afraid she'd deliver before we steamed into New Orleans. I'm not equipped to deal with a live birth."

"This subway goes to New Orleans? I was born there. My birthday's March 24."

"Ah, yes. The day she left my train."

I tried to imagine her hefting her awkward body into the soupy New Orleans air. It hummed with mugginess and reeked of crude oil and fertilizer. Not exactly like the Honduran rain forests, but close, even in March. When I was a toddler, I pretended to swim through the polluted atmosphere. Sometimes, it expanded and bent like I really floated underwater.

I gulped. "What was she like?"

"That day? Her brunette tresses clung to her skull like wet leaves. Misery carved lines in her face, but she bore it with stoic grace. Your mother isn't perfect, but she tries harder than most." He rested his head on the window glass and stared at the empty seats opposite us. "I've not encountered many

Nowhere children during my time. Two or three at most. You're the rarest of the rare."

"There are other offspring like me? How can I find them?"

He took off his cap, scratched his scalp, and replaced it. "That information's above my meager pay grade. Observing people is my gift. Deciphering their connections and understanding their motives is what I do best. That's why I noticed her condition that day, I suppose. Your mother was single and pregnant, significant obstacles for any woman rolling into an unknown city. But she'd also failed an assignment. Once I spoke her name, she never remembered who made her pregnant or whether she loved him. She wouldn't know who gave her you."

"Then why did you say her name? Why not just let her keep her memories?"

"It's against the rules."

My eyes wouldn't remind her of a forgotten encounter with Merry, unless she plumbed the depths of her greatest heartbreak, and how many people went there willingly?

Instead, she watched me, a replica of Merry, and convinced herself I was unrecognizable, foreign, unfathomable. What was she thinking as she stole glances at the cathedral in Jackson Square and bumped through the drunks in the Quarter? Did she even make it that far before I broke her water and streamed onto the ground? Was I her magic, her possibility, her hope? Or was I a mysterious burden it was too late to abort?

"I hated my mother. I mean, not at first. She spoiled me when I was tiny. Her smile lit up my nursery. She led the man I called *Daddy* around on a leash with her bubbly humor. I never realized he wasn't my father, wasn't part of my life from the start. We were the picture of a happy family."

"Yes, Lee Cagney stumbled on her laboring in an alley shortly after she left my train. He rushed her to the hospital and probably saved your lives. Doctors assumed he was your father. When they asked him your mother's name, he made one up and called her *Nadine*. She married him in a show of gratitude for saving her baby, for protecting both of you. I don't think she ever really loved him, though."

"Around the time I entered kindergarten, things started to change. Now I know she was drawing into herself. An unidentified hand ladled on stress. My parents fought all the time. It was like I looked at the staged picture of us in a frame. We were all smiling, but the glass was shattered. It distorted the view. Something happened to her then, didn't it?"

"Theodosia made many unfortunate decisions during her life with you. She blundered into a human mistake, one of thinking she could eradicate pure evil by using enemy tactics to win a war, when besting opponents is the only way to go. Evil is like quicksand. One can't dip in a toe without being consumed by its sinister tentacles. In your mother's case, she became an addict at the hands of James Wilkinson. While I believe addicts must be accountable for their actions, don't blame her for some of the things she forced you to do. In her twisted way, she was teaching you that many men would never respect you, no matter how educated or clever or accomplished you became. Your mother was preparing you to live in a misogynistic world without her. To defend yourself against gropes and leers and unreasonable demands. It was wrong, but she wasn't seeing with clear eyes, either."

"And yet I wound up surrounded by men who loved me."

"Because you took charge of your life, something she instilled in you. And she lost a Nowhere turn for it. Wilkinson tortured and beheaded her."

"So Wilkinson really does have pure evil where his heart should be."

"I can't judge a man I've never met, but I'll tell you this: your mother deserves to know you."

I swallowed. "Do you know where she is?"

"I'm not omniscient. She comes back here for advice sometimes when she gets overwhelmed. At various times, she's told me everything I just told you. If I were you, I'd get off at the next stop, and go out in the city and find her.

"Am I still in New York City?"

"Yes."

I slipped my arms around his thin neck unbidden, and he stiffened but didn't pull away. "Thank you," I whispered. "I hope you don't ever see her again."

His glacial eyes melted along the edges. "Tell her I'm pulling for her, Emmaline."

"How do you know my name?"

He touched my cheek. "She whispers it every time she steps on my train."

Another layer of resistance peeled back. She did?

He tapped my hand. "Your stop's coming up."

I waited for the double doors to swoosh open and stepped onto the platform. The Conductor's face occupied every window as the train pulled away and left me alone in the tunnel. I took gum-spattered stairs to the street.

Above ground, signs read *NYU* and *Washington Square.* I turned left and within a block, I wandered under a massive arch and into a city park. Groups of dark-skinned guys were break dancing on a wide circular area, and I sat on a step along the edge and watched them until twilight. When my stomach clenched with hunger, I got up and stumbled on.

Hours later, I still prowled the streets of New York long after midnight. It might as well've been high noon, though. Bums were passed out on the sidewalk in pools of their own vomit, and those who were awake begged me to spare a few coins for some food. Or booze. Or drugs. Gosh, I was turning into such a judgmental cynic.

Because now I was a street dweller. I forgot when I last ate. My stomach chomped on itself. My pockets were empty.

Late fall air rattled my bones. I put my head down and scampered to the other side of the street. For the first time in my life, I knew what those Nicaraguan refugees endured. Stripped of everything they owned, they fled to a new country with a list of scary unknowns: whether they'd be welcomed; what they'd eat; where they'd lie their heads to rest. I mean, I ran away from my mother when I was a child, but Merry rescued me. I didn't have to fend for myself on the street or in a foreign land, not like those brave people. I wasn't hungry enough to pilfer through trash for food—gross—but with a few more hours of nothing to eat, I wondered where I'd be. Life had a tendency to remind us of the meaninglessness of what we valued.

"Fifty dollars for a blow job, pretty lady. An extra twenty-five if you swallow. I like my whores young and sweet." I jumped back from the curb, where a man's gold front tooth glimmered from the window of a limousine. He held out a cashmere-clad arm and beckoned me. "I've got a whole carload of bankers and lawmakers here, you tasty treat. You'll make a wad for servicing the whole bunch."

When the door inched open, I circled around and ran. Wasted bodies were an obstacle course, but no matter how many times I tripped over an unseen leg or stepped on a hand, I righted myself and kept going. Was that how the men who paid for sex talked to my mother? I couldn't imagine my father or Merry treating a woman like a collection of orifices for them to abuse and discard. Growing up in a brothel was an education, but clearly, I still had a lot to learn about men.

I thundered around a murky corner and stopped. My breath misted in short bursts, and my side ached.

At another turn, I came to a liquor store. A narrow sliver of green sidled up to its back, surrounded by a fence. New York's leaf-logoed park sign hung near the rusty gate. I didn't know where I was on the city map, but I held my breath and inched along the sidewalk, afraid of what or who might be lurking in the park.

At the far end, I glimpsed a thin figure. Her posture was both enviable and memorable. I slipped through the gate and cried, "Mother."

EMMALINE

"How'd you find me?" She didn't turn around, like gazing upon her Nowhere offspring would sear her conscience and make me too real. Her dark mane tumbled down her back. When I was a tiny girl, I wrapped the gossamer threads around my fingers and pulled her laughing face closer to mine. Her straight spine blurred like a watercolor painting.

In hindsight, I understood that she had loved me for a little while. Conflicting emotions hammered my chest. I remembered what it was like to crawl into her lap and enfold myself in her arms. And as soon as the thought of a tender reunion surfaced, I beat it back.

She abused me. Had I not run away, she would've turned her only child into a prostitute for the sake of another heroin hit. Bitter juices scorched the back of my throat. She didn't deserve forgiveness, no matter how many of her real experiences I noted.

For her, our time together never existed. She didn't recall a single work she wrought, a solitary scheme she planned, but her Nowhere-induced amnesia didn't erase *my* memory. After almost a decade, the places she pummeled still ached. I couldn't imagine standing in her presence and having a normal conversation. What was I even supposed to say?

Seeing her as she was in life didn't excuse what she did to me. While it helped me accept the preponderance of who she'd been and what she became, I couldn't flip a switch and suddenly acknowledge her as a badass feminist who stood on equal footing with the men in her life. We only relate to the parts of a person we experience, no matter who they were before we met them or how they improved with age. I mean, I wasn't any weirder than anybody else in that respect.

For years, I told myself what she did to me when I was a child would never define me. I was strong. I could grow up and make a positive difference in the world. Why else was I allowed to escape, to fall into such a hopeful life, to volunteer with refugees, if not to improve the lives I was allowed to touch?

I swallowed and tried to keep my voice steady. "You're my mother, as hard as it may be for both of us to accept. I admit it's tough for me."

Her protracted exhale breezed from her as air from an overfilled balloon. One delicate hand clutched the fence when she turned, enough to throw her face into profile. I studied her small nose, the determined set of her jaw, the remarkable eyes she inherited from her father, my reviled yet gifted grandfather. Still, she didn't look at me. Her eyes were lit by her memories.

"Did you know I grew up right here?" She waved her free hand toward the buildings that formed one side of the park. "This spot was a pond on my father's estate. Richmond Hill. A Georgian mansion used to stand on this plot of land. Hard to fathom now, isn't it?"

I nodded, afraid my voice might break the spell.

She rubbed her eyes, like she was trying to peel back the layers of the landscape, and continued. "When I was a girl, I splashed around in the pond on the few muggy summer days we remained in the city, and in winter, it was my ice skating rink. I loved being outside. I suppose I was something of a tomboy."

She always liked to talk about herself. Every time I crawled into her lap and clamored for a hug and soothing words, she dusted off a personal story and made my devastation about her, like I was supposed to pat her on the head and assure her that everything would be okay. Did she have no concept of what it cost me to stand three feet from her? Why'd she think I even cared about her stupid childhood? After all, she ruined mine.

Hateful words combined like volatile gas and hot lava on my tongue. She deserved them, right? Regardless of her lack of memory, somewhere within her psyche, she was still capable of abusing a child.

She stopped and nibbled her lip, a familiar tic I dragged out ten thousand times a day. My temper froze a little.

"I'm getting this all wrong, aren't I? You're here for me to tell you I'm sorry for whatever's been erased. I can offer you words, but you'll dig in and call them empty and lacking regret."

I put my hands on my hips and stared her down. "You don't know me at all. You have no idea what I expect."

"I'm just trying to think through how I'd see this scene if our roles were reversed."

"Because you're so self-centered, the only way you can ever relate to anyone or anything is by how it impacts your happiness, your goals, and your desires."

She pivoted toward me, her dark orbs two daggers. "And you showed up on an island last night and tried to kill me."

"I didn't know I was going to Blennerhassett, and I didn't know why I was sent there. You were a surprise."

"Wilkinson probably had something to do with it. How can I be sure he didn't send you here to finish the job?"

"I don't even know where Wilkinson is. When I came back from, from—" How did I even explain what I witnessed on Blennerhassett Island? "When I came back from where I went after I shot at you, he wasn't around. And the last time I saw him? He beat the shit out of me."

"You're lying." She scanned my exposed flesh. "Where are your bruises? Wilkinson abused you. What a story. He's probably lurking in the corner liquor store just there, buying a celebratory whiskey and prepping a smelly cigar while you finish me for him. He always worked to corrupt others with his schemes and when they fingered him as the mastermind, he claimed his hands were pristine."

I swallowed. Talking to her was like being trapped on a corkscrew roller coaster. My insides slammed together as fast as I got my mind around a consistent thought. "I don't know why I came looking for you. I guess I hoped we'd fall into each other's arms and fulfill my silly little girl fantasies, but there's not enough witchery in the universe to wipe out what a crummy mother you were."

"You're right. I was a failure as a mother. I have no recollection of my time with you, but you can remind me all you like. You haven't done everything you can for a child, everything conceivable, only to watch them die, feverish in your miserable arms. I even prayed to a God I don't believe exists. I bargained and pleaded for any miracle to save my son."

"What happened to him?"

Her eyes reddened, and her cheeks were streaked with raw tears. "He died of malaria when he was ten. I washed his body and put on his best suit and loaded him into a wooden box and followed it to the mosquito-infested cemetery and threw wads of dirt on my only child. I'll never, ever recover from losing a piece of me, no matter how many lifetimes I'm forced to plod."

I couldn't believe I had a half-brother.

"And even though I know you're buried somewhere in my anima, you're my daughter, my child, I cannot piece together a single thing about my life with you. I'll never be able to love another human being the way I loved my son. It hurts too much to have love pried from your pleading, helpless hands. I can't endure it again, especially not when the very person I created is working with Wilkinson to finish me."

There it was. She admitted it. My mother didn't love me—she never loved me. I sunk onto a wooden park bench and swiped humiliating tears. I mean, I wanted her love not to matter. I told myself over and over I didn't care. As fast as I thought I could finally earn her love by beating Wilkinson, I stomped on those stupid ideas. She said it herself: she was incapable of loving her only daughter.

I leaned on the backrest, exhausted and empty. "I'm not working with Wilkinson. He may've had something to do with my Honduran refugee program, but I never cowed to him, and I never will."

"I still don't believe you."

In a huff, I jumped to my feet, turned my pockets inside-out, and patted my sides to show her I was unarmed. I pulled up my pants legs to reveal bare calves. "I don't have a weapon. I swear I didn't come here to kill you. You're right about Wilkinson, though. He thinks he can use my special gifts as a Nowhere child to eradicate you from the historical record forever. If I shoot you, my bullet will erase you from humanity. It'll be like you never existed. Without you in his path, he'll be closer to whatever stupid thing he wants from this place."

She rotated to face me head-on. "What do you mean, *special gifts? Eradication?*"

"You conceived me during another Nowhere life with a fellow Nowhere soul." I longed to shake her, to will the memory of making a baby with Meriwether Lewis into her blank head, but her stricken expression stopped me. She bit her hand and held her stomach like she might be sick, while I stood by not knowing whether to mock her or try to comfort her.

Her voice throttled like a misfiring engine. "I knew you germinated during another Nowhere life, but I thought you belonged to someone else, a living soul."

"Who? Lee Cagney?"

Her expression was a wash of confusion. "I don't know who. It's like he's been obliterated from memory."

The swirling vortex at the other end of my gun flashed through my mind. I'd caused it two times, but I couldn't conjure anything else. Still, I thought she'd welcome my revelation.

"But I know who my father was." I reached toward her hand. "Meriwether Lewis."

Her face flashed from deer-eyed shock to brief softness along her cheekbones to hardline fury. She ducked away from me and stood defiant a few steps beyond my range, nostrils flaring. "How could you lie to my face? Do you know what he meant to me, how much I loved him?"

"Yes. I mean, I saw you together."

"You saw us? When?"

"I—um." What was I supposed to tell her? She'd never believe I witnessed her and Merry's parting on Blennerhassett. I bit my lip decided to trust her. "Since I'm a Nowhere child, I can travel backward in time."

She sniffed. "That's bonkers. I don't know why you brought Lewis into this. He was the love of my life."

"Yes, I know. It was clear."

"To taunt me that way. I obviously birthed a beast."

The ground tumbled from my feet, and the surrounding architecture spun with the force of my rage. I was a human thunderhead. Unsettled air burbled from my lungs and rumbled through my lips. "You've always been the beast, Mother. You only love what you can control, and when you lose control, you punish. You manipulate. You run through people like trash bags, filling them to the brim with your garbage and sending them off to the landfill to fester and rot. Believe me, I didn't show up here to apologize to you. I don't owe you anything. You should be on your knees begging me to forgive you, whether you mean the words or not. Even an insincere apology would be better than nothing. 'I'm sorry you feel that way, Emmaline. It's too bad your feelings are hurt, Emmaline.' I mean, those are shitty things people say when they don't think they did anything wrong, but at least they're trying. You don't even try. You just twist things around like you always have and make me feel like I'm the jerk. Well, you're the jerk, Mother. You've always been the beast in our relationship, and now I know you always will be."

I fell back, panting and spent. My heartbeat throbbed in my ears and obliterated taxi horns and police whistles and the city's discordant din. When my mother's lips moved, I struggled to make out her words.

"Did Wilkinson somehow rip open your pneuma and pump it full of venom? How do I know this isn't a fairy tale he used to turn you against me?"

"It happened. Every bit of it is etched upon my person. He played a part in carving it there because you let him. And whatever I didn't understand was explained in Merry's journal. It was the magic book that outlined my power and gave me hope."

"How did you have one of his journals?"

"Because he left it behind when he took me to the man I believed was my father. I was his final Nowhere mission. Where he was headed, he didn't need it anymore."

"Where was he going?"

"He accomplished his mission, and I think he became part of Lee Cagney, the man I believed was my dad. Which is exactly as it should've happened, because he was my father all along."

She doubled over and rocked back and forth, hands on knees. I hovered close by, wavering between fleeing and comforting her. Emotions were always schizophrenic with my mother. My hand quaked inches from her shoulder. What would touching her do to me?

EMMALINE

The set of her jaw and softness around her eyes stopped my fingers for a breath too long. I dropped my hands and stared her down. "What now? You go from accusing me of working with Wilkinson to being a beast who wants to kill you to regarding me with motherly love, all in the span of thirty seconds. I don't get it."

She took my hand and cradled it against her chest. My fingers tingled with her touch, and I didn't pull away. She led me to a park bench near the back of the triangular garden and dragged me down beside her. "Finally, something I can comprehend."

"What do you mean?"

"I've always wondered where Nowhere souls go when we're done here. It makes sense that we'd merge with the living." She turned to me, her face child-like. "I don't remember this Lee Cagney, but I think I met him a few months ago."

I leaned toward her. "Oh? Where?"

"Along the Natchez Trace. I went to visit Meriwether's grave, and I came upon a man there. He rushed me like he knew me, babbling about our daughter and telling me not to interfere in her life. I couldn't fathom what he meant. He was so angry, almost deranged. He followed me all the way to my car, and when I peeled away, he jumped in his truck and followed me. I don't know what happened to him afterward, but I managed to outrun him."

"He died that day," I murmured. "Probably while chasing you."

My mother gasped and covered her mouth with graceful fingers. "I didn't mean for him to die."

"I know. It was an accident, but at least I sort of know what he was doing on the Natchez Trace now."

"I hope he was a decent person."

"He was."

"Good. Merry deserved to occupy an honorable vessel." She folded my hand between hers and held it in her lap, and I didn't yank it back. We sat in silence for a few moments. Her lips worked to form words, and after several false starts, she turned to me and said, "We need to talk. If you don't like what you hear, you're welcome to leave. I'll give you enough money to make your way back to wherever you call home."

"Nashville. I live in Tennessee. At least, I used to. I'm not sure where I belong anymore."

"Please. Let me tell you a story."

My mother's voice sputtered from her, like she didn't know where to start. "I want you to know this right from the outset, Emmaline. Your father was the great love of my life. I was already married when we met." She eyed me sideways. "My father's doing. He was desperate for money to feed his political ambitions, and when he suggested Joseph Alston, I found him agreeable enough. I never expected to have true passion with my husband. A woman gives up too much when she allows herself to love a man more than he loves her."

"Why didn't you tell your father you loved Merry? I mean, surely he would've wanted you to be happy."

"I didn't meet Lewis until after I was married. He was preparing for his western expedition. I was plotting with my father and his cohorts. Blennerhassett Island in the Ohio River was our flashpoint, a place where we both spent time on separate projects, sometimes overlapping, sometimes not. Nobody ever knew what we were up to. At least, I don't think they did."

"Still, if you'd chosen him, you could've been with someone who adored you as much as your father did."

She frowned. "How do you know so much about Lewis's feelings for me? It's almost like you were there."

I squeezed her fingers. "I told you I was. I saw you together. When you two made me, you imbued me with the ability to go back and spy on you, as upsetting as that could be. Children don't want to see their parents' passion for each other, even though it's what created them."

Her lips formed a silent, round *O*. With a nod of understanding, she continued, "History doesn't force students to memorize details, does it? My father is memorialized for killing a man in a duel, the sum of his long life reduced to a footnote. If you learned more about him, you'd know that Thomas Jefferson loathed him more than any man alive. And, unfortunately, Meriwether Lewis was Thomas Jefferson's godson, personal secretary, and ardent admirer. Plus, Meriwhether didn't hail from money. While my father encouraged me to have the occasional affair, he frowned upon divorce." Her smile didn't reach her vibrant eyes. "Lewis entered the game with too many marks against him."

"Tell me about the first time you saw him."

"We were on Blennerhassett. My father and I were there to meet with Harman Blennerhassett regarding our idea of starting an independent colony on forgotten lands in western Louisiana. We envisioned ruling a utopia where all creatures, female and male, white and black, immigrant and native, were equal. When James Wilkinson introduced the possibility of annexing part of Mexico, we were certainly keen. Why not expand our holdings and give alternatives to those unsatisfied with blossoming dysfunction in America? If the United States has always been anything, it's been a discordant mess. I believed in our dream more than I thought America would survive." Her story projected the movie of her life as if I could really see it on the dingy wall opposite. I watched it play out like I was in the room, because I had been. At least, for a little while.

She sighed. "Merry spent a few nights on the island en route to his western expedition. Another few here and there in the planning stages. He was intense and singular, aloof and infuriating. On the one hand, here was a contemporary whose education equaled my own. I lapped up his every scientific observation and clung to his meticulous plans for his name-making expedition. Please understand. Once I married, I spent time with women in Southern plantation salons. While I could talk about the latest Parisian fashions and critique a table setting, my brain fired on the knowledge my father ladled into my brain. Merry's intellect feathered across my bare skin like foreplay. I was breathless and heaving, ready to offer him anything he wanted."

I was too absorbed in her picture of Merry to be grossed out by her erotic admission. "What stopped you?"

"His arrogance. The certainty that he'd find what he and his overlord craved: a water route to the Pacific. French trappers spread stories of the terrain. Some even drew maps. I spoke fluent French and had no problem interpreting them. Merry and his band of hopefuls were destined to slam into an impenetrable wall of rock, news he didn't appreciate. The more he pushed, the harder I pushed back. Never had a man so incensed me. I stormed up to my room, red-faced and chest thudding, passions too stirred up to sleep."

I reflected on the man I knew when I was nine. By the time he met me, Merry was ground down to the nub by Nowhere, but I saw snatches of the person my mother described. The way he forced me to wear boy clothes in the woods. How he taunted me with just-caught fish still squirming in the frying pan. And, because he knew better, he carried me all the way home. His certainty led me to Lee Cagney when I never would've found him on my own.

"What'd you do next?" I asked my mother.

"I carried a lamp to the library, intent on reading myself to sleep, and found him there." She ran her pink tongue across her lips. "I'll spare you the rest, but it was glorious. We parted determined to reunite as often as we could before he left for the west."

"Did you?"

"Yes. A handful of reunions on Blennerhassett. After he returned from the expedition, Jefferson forced my father's treason trial in Richmond. Lewis was in the audience on behalf of his master. We'd broken off years prior. I convinced myself we were no longer the same people."

So she was the woman who was with Merry in the courtroom that day! I couldn't believe I'd witnessed them together more than once.

She paused and chewed her lip before going on. "Even though we sat in opposite corners of the room, his very presence electrified me to my core. We pretended to loathe each other. Maybe his show was real at first, but I was his one true love. He eventually succumbed to me. Or I fell into him. Anyway, during those few days in Richmond, I'd never been so alive."

Moonlight painted the sky, but I forgot what time it was. My stomach was full of my mother's story. Still, I had to hear it in her words. "Then why did it end?"

"Merry wasn't content to have me as his lover. He wanted me to marry him. When I refused to leave my husband a final time, he fled Richmond brokenhearted and bitter, and I mourned our parting for the rest of my short life." She closed the space between us and touched my hand. "Don't think I didn't dream of what would've happened if I followed my passion. Maybe our lives wouldn't have played out as Shakespearean tragedies. He wrote me a few months before he died. I saved his letters and wondered whether I could've saved him."

"Do you think he killed himself?"

"No, I never did. But I'm grateful that Nowhere brought us together again, even if I can't summon it from memory. Somehow, we overcame our differences and made you." Her throat worked through a swallow. "I wish I could see him one more time."

"Me too."

I was reeling from my mother's revelations. I was the product of true passion, whoever my mother became. Maybe losing Merry again drove her subconscious to spiral into the woman I knew when I was a child. The spirit always knows where it traveled, even if memory falters.

Like a mendacious beacon, the acrid stench of cigar smoke singed my nostrils. "Theo and Emmaline. I'm so glad I found you together." Wilkinson's hulking frame filled the entrance to the park.

I jumped up and stepped in front of Theodosia. "Wilkinson. How'd you find us?"

He took out a quarter, flipped it with his thumb, and caught it, heads up, in his palm. "Luck. This scrap of land was always Theodosia's favorite place when she was a kid. I knew she'd show her face here eventually, but I never expected to find you both so soon."

In a quick feint, he hooked one arm around my neck. His gut jiggled against my back. I didn't need to see the gun leveled at my head. I felt the muzzle dig into the scalp above my right ear. My jaw was almost sealed shut, but I managed to mumble, "You can't make me do anything to her."

"Oh really? I'll decide how you deploy your Nowhere gifts! After you murder your mother, I have scores of other uses for you. She's been leading a Nowhere contingent that's trying to assassinate me, and you're going to kill them, one by one."

"I won't." My spine groaned when he twisted my neck a bit too far. Fireworks flared behind my eyelids until he loosed his grip and ratcheted my head to face forward, straight into my mother's thunderous eyes.

She crouched like she was ready to pounce. "James Wilkinson, you took everything from me and still aren't satisfied. Your war is with me. Leave her alone, and let's end this thing between us. I don't care what happens to me, but don't harm Emmaline. You and I can settle our differences with honor, gun-for-gun, man-to-man. Isn't that fair?"

Wilkinson shuddered. "That's your biggest problem, Theo. Your bastard father treated you like a man, an equal, even a colleague, but women will always be the inferior sex. You insult my honor to even suggest – what – a duel? That's rich, given your sordid heritage."

"What's pathetic is your spending your Nowhere lives hating me. Do you realize you probably could've been reunited with your precious Ann more than a century ago if you'd only cut loose one perceived slight?"

Wilkinson's bellow probably shattered my right eardrum. "Two. Both you and your blasted father ruined my life! Every dream of wealth garnered through owning a vast swath of Texas and all the resources I'd control, well, you shat all over that, didn't you?"

Her countenance contorted with fury. "I saw what you were, Jimmy, and how you operate. You were using us to get what you wanted, and as soon as you had it, you would've arranged convenient deaths for everyone who threatened your dominion, namely me, my father, and my son."

"Yes, and for the rest of my life, I never came close to such an opportunity. To think I squandered my best chance on the likes of the Burrs. I should've known a man who gave heed to his daughter's emotional advice would fail from the outset."

I strained against his clamp-like hold and yelled, "You've persecuted my mother enough. Take me. Do whatever you want to me. I don't care. But leave Theodosia alone."

"I don't plan to inflict more distress on Theodosia. You're going to execute her right now, or I'll kill you both."

WILKINSON

Theo's eyes rolled back, and I prepared to watch her accursed features be consumed into bones and blood and brain matter, only to immediately forget she ever existed. Nothing would seal my destiny more than obliterating any possibility of ever hearing Theodosia's harpy voice again on any plane. Forcing my pistol into Emmaline's palm, I clenched her fingers around the weapon and pointed it at Theo's head.

"Go ahead, Emmaline," I snarled in her ear. "Use your trigger finger. You have to do it. I can't pull it for you."

When she stiffened against my will, I bit her ear until her salty essence ringed my teeth and she writhed in agony.

A metallic click snapped me to attention. Theodosia brandished her own weapon, a nickel-plated Beretta.

"Let her go, Jimmy."

"I'd be careful if I were you, Theo. If you miss, you'll murder your own child."

I held Emmaline as my shield, ducking my head behind her neck to stay out of the line of fire. The smell of her hair aroused a memory of my Ann. Emmaline sensed my distraction, wrenching free of me. In a singular spiraling motion she grabbed an errant wrought iron picket and swung it my way.

A searing fire bloomed across my gut. I looked down to see Emmaline drive the spike into me. Yowling, I released my grip and staggered backward, and she pivoted and smashed the stake deeper into my abdomen with her foot. I fell next to the paved path and writhed on the ground, blood covering my fingers like it poured from a fountain.

I held my hands up to my face and laughed. "But I'm still here, you bitch. Might have a hard time eating for a while, but your stab doesn't eradicate."

Theodosia Burr straddled me and jabbed her Beretta against my temple. "Maybe not, but a bullet will."

Emmaline put a sure hand on her mother's shoulder. "Let me."

As Emmaline took the gun, the future I'd forsaken scrolled before me. I could've listened to my Gravedigger and helped lead the Contras to victory in Nicaragua. Maybe the President would've given me a commendation to complete my final Nowhere life. And with my chest adorned with swag, I'd strut into whatever came after Nowhere.

In a moment of clarity, I even had a glimpse of what I could've become. A living being was waiting for me to join the myriad souls contained within his shell. That's where successful Nowhere souls wound up, many sharing a body together. They induced sudden career shifts, existential crises, romantic breakups, and life epiphanies every time another of their number came on board.

And just as I felt myself moving toward my destiny, to be forgotten forever, I saw my intended after-Nowhere destination: a brown-skinned immigrant refugee, and female. I recognized one pair of eyes sparkling inside her. My Ann peeled off and wailed, "Jimmy, we could've shared this together for all time, if only you'd stuck to your mission."

What an inglorious final thought.

EMMALINE

I lost my mother that night in New York, but I wasn't sad about it. While I recalled no detail about the person I eradicated that night, I could still see what happened afterward. Theodosia, my mother, started to shimmer before I fully focused on her, and everything clicked into place.

With tear-stained eyes, she whispered, "My Nowhere mission was to protect you. I combed the Honduran rain forest for months, and I watched you from afar. And even though I didn't know you were my daughter, I swelled with pride at your empathy, your vigor, your adventurous spirit." I could barely make out her outline now, and her voice was faraway. I strained to hear the rest. "And I finally succeeded. I'm so grateful for the time we had together. I don't know where I'm going, Emmaline, but I hope to meet you again someday. I love you."

Her final words hung in the air long after she was gone. I turned to the exit, my eyes blinded by tears, and choked to no one, "She was my mother, and she was a badass."

* * * * *

I stepped from the car. In a couple of hours, I was flying back to Honduras to complete my year as a humanitarian. Abroad Together even promoted me to a spot helping refugees gain legal entry into the U.S.A.

I was proud to help countless human beings escape torture, persecution, and even death. In America, they wouldn't ever have to worry about such things, right?

The stone shaft stood sentinel in the pioneer cemetery. It was dark the last time I passed this way. I was nine when I first watched someone bleed out and die on the ground a few feet from me. "And everything ends in a cemetery. Or maybe just before," I spoke under my breath as I approached the massive monument.

Whatever remained of Meriwether Lewis rested under this pile of Victorian stone. I read a ton about him in the weeks since Theodosia—my mother—passed on. Nobody knew for sure how he died, but I'd never accept that he committed suicide. Theodosia knew him better than I, and she didn't believe it, either. Some people claimed the bones, fabric scraps, and buttons emblazoned with his name weren't actually his. Too many soldiers were buried in the area. Any one of them could've been identified as the elusive Lewis. But I knew he hovered there. Maybe some part of Lee Cagney hung around as well.

I folded a two-dollar bill into an origami boat and shoved it between the cracks in stone. It wasn't nearly enough for what he'd given me, but it worked. I wrote my name on it for good measure, in case he ever saw fit to send it back to me.

Wind stirred leafless tree branches and whipped wintry air through the buttons of my coat. "Thanks for being my father," I whispered as I tapped the stone a final time.

I blinked and transported myself to a different clearing in another state. The Ohio River rambled past my feet as I sat on a rickety dock. The sun was rising over the trees across the river, and Meriwether Lewis was alive and standing in front of me. It was the morning after the scene I witnessed on Blennerhassett Island, the one where he left my mother sobbing on a dock, telling his fleeing form she loved him but couldn't abandon her destiny.

Surely, he understood that. When he lay in a frontier Tennessee clearing, gasping his final breaths, he knew what it meant to follow a dream until it killed him. And he accomplished so much more than he realized. America's first scientist. Maker of me.

I bit off words he wouldn't hear and crafted declarations of love he'd never receive. Would it make a difference where he was going? He was glorious as he loaded his keelboat with supplies he bought on credit and continued toward a fated rendezvous with his men. His eyes were alight with the possibility of adventure, discovery, and challenge.

And something else. He'd just untangled himself from my mother's arms. When he wrote about the beauty of the Missouri River, he sprinkled his descriptions with memories of her.

No better magic existed than seeing my father alive one more time. He fanned the flames of hope. Even in the face of adversity, he kept going. He didn't listen to people who bullied him, rejected him, or laughed in his face. Until the bloody end, he always believed in himself. That wholeness was his gift to me.

I murmured, "Thank you. I'm ready to go back to my refugees now."

But before the wind howled, the scrim parted, and I drained into present day, Merry turned and looked directly at me.

"I'll always be with you, Em. You know that, don't you?"

* * * * *

I Am Number 13

ACKNOWLEDGEMENTS

I Am Number 13 took two years to create. As my novel *Hard to Die* was coming out in November 2016, I was diagnosed with an incurable disease that's causing me to go blind. The treatment scrambled my brain. For over a year, I couldn't write.

I'd like to thank my tireless husband, Michael T. Maher, for believing in me, encouraging me, and never abandoning me, even when I was at my lowest. This novel wouldn't exist without you.

And now a word about the historical scenes in the novel.

On Blennerhassett Island, I found a sign. James Wilkinson, Aaron Burr, and Meriwether Lewis all visited the island. Whether they were ever there at the same time is open to conjecture.

While Theodosia Burr Alston isn't listed on that sign, she traveled to Blennerhassett with her father in his scheme's preliminary stages. Her relationship with Meriwether Lewis is historical rumor. We have no evidence they were ever involved in a romance, though they knew one another well enough to exchange letters. However, the scenes on Blennerhassett and elsewhere are drawn from a novelist's imagination.

The Iran Contra Affair occupied the country for the latter part of the 1980s. While we heard a lot from Oliver North about what President Reagan did or did not know about trading arms for hostages and financing a secret war, we didn't get the stories of the people who fled the Sandinista regime. Some joined the Contras and fought to free Nicaragua, but others became humans without a country. I hope they landed in a place of welcome, an adopted home where they and their families could breathe free.

ABOUT THE AUTHOR

Andra Watkins lives in Charleston, South Carolina with her husband, Michael T Maher. She is the first living person to walk the 444-mile Natchez Trace as the pioneers did prior to the rise of steam power in the 1820's. From March 1 to April 3, 2014, she walked fifteen miles a day. Six days a week. One rest day per week. She spent each night in the modern-day equivalent of stands, places much like Grinder's Stand, where Meriwether Lewis died from two gunshot wounds on October 11, 1809. In addition to celebrating the release of *To Live Forever: An Afterlife Journey of Meriwether Lewis,* the walk also inspired her New York Times best selling memoir on the adventure, *Not Without My Father: One Woman's 444-Mile Walk of the Natchez Trace,* published January 2015. *Natchez Trace: Tracks in Time* is a collection of photographs from her 444-mile walk published March 2015.

Hard to Die followed-up *To Live Forever* with an inventive new take on the uncharted fate of Theodosia Burr Alston, the fiery daughter of Alexander Hamilton's murderer Aaron Burr. Breathing fresh air into Theodosia's forgotten life and story, *Hard to Die* was published in November 2016.

I Am Number 13 is the third novel in the Nowhere Series, a speculative blend of riveting suspense, forgotten history, and a dash of paranormal fiction.

I Am Number 13

THE THREE R'S OF 21ST CENTURY READING

- **Read** the book - Authors love to sell books, but they really want buyers to read them. If you've come this far, thank you again for reading. Your investment of time matters to me.

- **Review** the book - Amazon and Goodreads don't tabulate book rankings based on sales alone. Reviews weigh heavily into the algorithms for book rankings. Your review matters. More reviews mean higher rankings, more impressions and ultimately, more readers. Please take five minutes and write a review of this book. If you write the review on Goodreads first, you can copy and paste it into Amazon.

- **Recommend** the book - The people in your life value your opinion. If you enjoyed this book, recommend it to five people. Over lunch or coffee. At the water cooler. On the sidelines. Let people see and hear your enthusiasm for this story. Some of them will thank you for showing them the way to a good book.

This material is protected by copyright. It may not be reproduced in whole or in part, either in print or electronically, without the express written consent of the author. Send all inquiries regarding usage to readme@andrawatkins.com.